D0453132

PRAISE FOR *COLD AS HELL*

'Icelandic crime writing at its finest ... immersive and unnerving'
Shari Lapena

'Another bleak, unpredictable classic' *Metro*

'Intricate, enthralling and very moving – a wonderful crime novel'
William Ryan

'Lilja Sigurðardóttir just gets better and better ... Áróra is a
wonderful character: unique, passionate, unpredictable and very
real' Michael Ridpath

'Three things we love about *Cold as Hell*: Iceland's unrelenting
midnight sun; the gritty Nordic murder mystery; the peculiar and
bewitching characters' Apple Books **Book of the Month**

'Lilja Sigurðardóttir doesn't write cookie-cutter crime novels. She
is aware that "the fundamentals of existence are totally
incomprehensible and chaotic": anything can and does happen ...
Reading *Cold as Hell* sometimes gives you "the bizarre feeling of
having been struck by a hand that had previously been so gentle".
Isn't that what all crime writers should aim for? The good news, my
"cuddle dumplings", is that Áróra will be back' *The Times*

'The writing is intense, taut and spare, the plot lines intriguing and
involving. The complexity of the characters brings a bitter tale of
ordinary lives blighted by crime alive ... A perfect blend of social
critique and jaw-dropping thriller' Crime Fiction Lover

'Her simple, yet not simplistic, writing style renders her work easily
readable ... you should definitely purchase this latest gem and let
yourselves be enchanted by the pen of a renowned young crime
writer' *Tap The Line Magazine*

'A dark, suspenseful thread running through the whole novel ... fast
paced and filled with tension' The Reading Closet

'A beautifully crafted mystery, powered by authentic characters, an atmospheric setting and top-notch storytelling'
Jen Med's Book Reviews

'Short, snappy chapters with an exquisite plot meant I quickly lost myself in this world until the very last page. Seamlessly translated by Quentin Bates, this is a series you all need to be watching for!'
Chapter in My Life

'A dark, suspenseful crime thriller with a bleak setting, *Cold as Hell* belongs on your must-read list. In a similar fashion to Ragnar Jónasson ... Lilja Sigurðardóttir makes you feel as though you're in Iceland while reading the story. I can't wait for the next book in the Áróra Investigation series' Crime Fiction Critic

'*Cold as Hell* continues to see Lilja Sigurðardóttir's development as a writer ... Kudos to the author, her publisher and translator for another memorable and superbly crafted novel!' Fiction from Afar

PRAISE FOR LILJA SIGURÐARDÓTTIR

'Tough, uncompromising and unsettling' Val McDermid

'An emotional suspense rollercoaster on a par with *The Firm*, as desperate, resourceful, profoundly lovable characters scheme against impossible odds' Alexandra Sokoloff

'A smart, ambitious and hugely satisfying thriller. Striking in its originality and written with all the style and poise of an old hand. Lilja is destined for Scandi superstardom' Eva Dolan

'Clear your diary. As soon as you begin reading *Snare*, you won't be able to stop until the final page' Michael Wood

'Crisp, assured and nail-bitingly tense ... an exceptional read, cementing Lilja's place as one of Iceland's most outstanding crime writers' Yrsa Sigurðardóttir

'Tense, edgy and delivering more than a few unexpected twists and turns' *Sunday Times* Crime Club Star Pick

Also by Lilja Sigurðardóttir and available from Orenda Books

The Reykjavík Noir trilogy
Snare
Trap
Cage

Betrayal

ABOUT THE AUTHOR

Icelandic crime-writer Lilja Sigurðardóttir was born in the town of Akranes in 1972 and raised in Mexico, Sweden, Spain and Iceland. An award-winning playwright and screenwriter, Lilja has written eight crime novels, including *Snare*, *Trap* and *Cage*, making up the Reykjavík Noir trilogy, and her standalone thriller *Betrayal*, all of which have hit bestseller lists worldwide. *Snare* was longlisted for the CWA International Dagger, *Cage* won Best Icelandic Crime Novel of the Year and was a *Guardian* Book of the Year, and *Betrayal* was shortlisted for the prestigious Glass Key Award and won Icelandic Crime Novel of the Year. The film rights for the Reykjavík Noir trilogy have been bought by Palomar Pictures in California. She lives in Reykjavík with her partner. You'll find Lilja on Twitter @lilja1972 and on her website liljawriter.com.

ABOUT THE TRANSLATOR

A series of unlikely coincidences allowed Quentin Bates to escape English suburbia as a teenager with the chance of a gap year working in Iceland. For a variety of reasons, the year stretched to become a gap decade, during which time he went native in the north of Iceland, acquiring a new language, a new profession and a family.

He is the author of a series of crime novels set in present-day Iceland. His translations include works by Guðlaugur Arason, Ragnar Jónasson, Einar Kárason and Sólveig Pálsdóttir, as well as Lilja Sigurðardóttir's Reykjavík Noir trilogy, standalone novel *Betrayal* and the Áróra series. Follow Quentin on Twitter @graskeggur.

COLD AS HELL

Lilja Sigurðardóttir

Translated by Quentin Bates

**ORENDA
BOOKS**

Orenda Books
16 Carson Road
West Dulwich
London SE21 8HU
www.orendabooks.co.uk

First published in Icelandic as *Helköld sól* by Forlagið in 2019
First published in English by Orenda Books in 2021
Copyright © Lilja Sigurðardóttir, 2019
English translation copyright © Quentin Bates, 2021

A catalogue record for this book is available from the British Library.
ISBN 978-1-913193-88-1
eISBN 978-1-913193-89-8

The publication of this translation has been made possible through the financial support of

 ICELANDIC LITERATURE CENTER

Typeset in Garamond by typesetter.org.uk

Printed and bound by CPI Group (UK) Ltd, Croydon CR0 4YY

PRONUNCIATION GUIDE

Icelandic has a couple of letters that don't exist in other European languages and which are not always easy to replicate. The letter ð is generally replaced with a d in English, but we have decided to use the Icelandic letter to remain closer to the original names. Its sound is closest to the hard th in English, as found in *thus* and *bathe*.

The letter r is generally rolled hard with the tongue against the roof of the mouth.

In pronouncing Icelandic personal and place names, the emphasis is placed on the first syllable.

Áróra – Ow-roe-ra
Ísafold – Eesa-fold
Björn – Bjoern
Kópavogur – Koe-pa-voegur
Keflavík – Kep-la-vik
Jonni – Yonni
Hákon Hauksson – How-kon Hoyk-son
Grímur – Grie-moor
Hringbraut – Hring-broyt
Lækjargata – Like-ya-gata
Gúgúlú – Gue-gue-lue
Hafnarfjörður – Hap-nar-fjeor-thur
Dagný – Dag-nie
Kristín – Christine
Bústaðavegur – Bue-stath-ar-vayguy
Reykjanesbraut – Rey-kja-nes-broyt
Hverfisgata – Kverfis-gata
Seyðisfjörður – Sey-this-fjeor-thur

Down in the midst of the sharp-toothed lava, he regained his balance and reached for the hand that had slipped from the suitcase. It was as cold as ice. He should have expected it, but the chill and the lifeless feel of the hand came as a shock.

The tears forced their way from the corners of his eyes, and he whispered 'I love you' into the bright summer night, which seemed to have a tranquillity all of its own for the few hours around midnight, as if even the birds drew the line at staying awake all night long. His whispered, loving words were almost a sacrilege against the silence, so he didn't repeat them, even though he would have preferred to shout them out over the lava field, to fill his lungs, and yell with all the power in his body and soul that he loved her. Instead, he crouched and laid his lips cautiously on the hand. He stayed that way for a while, and before he realised it, the warmth of his lips had passed into the back of the hand so that the skin appeared to have come to life. His lips moved over it as he kissed the cold hand again and again, kissing the knuckles, the wrist, the fleshy part of the palm that he had heard somewhere was called the Point of Remembrance, and the fingers, one at a time, until his lips touched something hard: the engagement ring.

He pulled at it, but the finger seemed bloated, and the ring refused to move, half sunk in the swelling that had enveloped the hand. He licked the finger and spat onto the ring, working it back and forth until it finally came off. He dropped it into his pocket and quickly kissed the hand once more, fighting back the desire to unzip the case to see the face one last time. He wanted to know if it had swollen, if it had taken on the same blue tinge as the hand. But at the same time, he had no desire to see what death had done to her beautiful face. Everyone knows that flesh loses its colour once the blood no longer flows, that a grey pallor takes over after a few hours. Death destroys everything.

He wiped away the tears and sniffed hard. Then he carefully

pushed the hand back inside the case and zipped it shut. He climbed out of the fissure and looked down at the dark-red suitcase that lay in it, not right at the bottom, but caught on the jagged lava points. It was still out of sight, though, unless you stood right at the edge of the fissure and looked down.

This moment in the lava field marked a turning point in his life. Sorrow had left him devastated, but at the same time he felt a certainty in his chest that cut deep and pained him like razor-sharp steel. Now everything was different. He wasn't the man he thought he had been. Now he knew he could kill.

WEDNESDAY

1

Disappeared. That was what her mother said on the phone, and Áróra could hear her voice crack in a way that never happened unless there was something serious going on.

'Your sister's disappeared,' she said, and Áróra felt the old emotions return: fear and anger. It hadn't been long ago that those emotions would have dragged her off the sofa, out to the airport and all the way to Iceland. But they wouldn't do that now. Instead they were joined by the feeling that accompanied anything to do with her sister Ísafold, and that was fatigue.

'Mum, she's probably just too busy to answer the phone.'

Áróra knew that protest, or any attempt to wriggle away, was doomed to failure once her mother had her teeth into something, but she tried anyway. She had just switched on the TV to watch a repeat of *Wire in the Blood*, her favourite crime series, and had been looking forward to spending the evening on the sofa.

'She hasn't answered the phone for two weeks now. That's too long to be normal. And Björn doesn't answer either, and I can't figure out from this online Icelandic phone book how to find any of his family.'

Áróra sighed, taking care not to let her mother hear.

'Does her phone just not ring, or is it engaged ... or what?'

'Nobody answers their home phone, and when I call her mobile it goes straight to voicemail.'

'And have you tried leaving a message?' Áróra asked, and heard her mother bristle.

'Of course I've left messages. Time and again, but she doesn't reply to them. It's the same with Facebook, as you must have seen – she hasn't put anything new on there for more than two weeks.'

'You know she blocked me on Facebook, Mum. I don't see anything she posts.'

It didn't matter how often she tried to explain it to her mother, she seemed unable to take on board that there was no contact between the sisters.

Her mother sighed heavily.

'Oh, sweetheart, don't be like that,' she said with the familiar tone of voice that told Áróra she was being difficult, even though everything she had said had been the honest truth. Her mother would never dream of criticising Ísafold for being difficult, for not answering the phone, for not being in touch. After Ísafold had left home, when she was around twenty, it was as if she had become some sort of iconic being, while their mother had continued to treat Áróra like a teenager.

'Do it for me. Go to Iceland. Check up on her.'

'All right,' Áróra agreed, and felt the lump in her throat that appeared every time she had to knuckle down and do something against her will. It was only family that provoked this feeling. In fact, these days it was only her mother who could do this, once Áróra had told Ísafold that enough was enough, and they had ended all communication. Now it was only her mother who made her feel that she was being forced to do things that she didn't want to do. 'I'll try and get hold of Björn or someone tomorrow, Mum.'

'Couldn't you try this evening?' her mother said in a wheedling voice. 'Just to see if everything's all right?'

'Tomorrow, Mum. I'll check it out tomorrow.'

Áróra put the phone down without giving her mother an opportunity to protest. This was a little piece of her sister's martyrdom she could do without right now. She was too tired to deal with her sister's lies, announcing in that imposing voice of hers that everything was just fine. Absolutely, perfectly, completely fine. She would have fallen against a radiator and broken her jaw, which stopped her from speaking on the phone, or taken a tumble on the steps in the block of flats where she lived and broken a finger, so writing anything on Facebook was out of the question. Áróra was also too tired to have Björn sniping at her, telling her that Ísafold was *his* girlfriend, and Áróra shouldn't concern herself with things that were none of her business.

She plucked a bottle of sparkling water from the fridge and took it with her to the living room, where she let herself drop onto the sofa, wrapped herself in a blanket and drank a quarter of the bottle. The programme had already begun, although that didn't matter, as she had seen it several times before, but she found her mind was no longer at ease. Now she had to swat aside uncomfortable thoughts as they came at her, as if her mother's phone call had opened the flood gates that for a while now she had struggled hard to keep shut. Now she couldn't avoid feeling irritation at her mother, anger with Björn and a nagging fear for Ísafold.

THURSDAY

2

'You don't try and strike a bargain after a deal's been done,' Áróra told the car salesman who sat behind his broad desk, leaned back in his chair and made himself comfortable. He was nothing like the man Áróra had met a week before, when he had hunched over the desk, trembling hands fiddling with a row of model cars, practically choking with sobs as he begged her to help him. He said that it wouldn't be long before he would be having to sleep at the showroom; that was if he didn't find out where his wife – with whom he was in the middle of a turbulent divorce process – had stashed the money they had saved over the last twenty years of marriage. It was a very tidy amount. There was a chance that a small portion of it had come from the showroom's overseas commissions, which hadn't all been declared to the taxman. This was why he wasn't keen to get the British authorities involved, but instead had come to Áróra.

She had tracked the cash down, and now, after his initial relief, it seemed that the car salesman had become puffed up with arrogance and wanted to go back on the agreement he had struck with Áróra that would have seen her get a ten percent cut of whatever she found for him.

He snapped a piece of nicotine gum from the blister pack on the table in front of him and popped it into his mouth. His hair had been freshly cut and the jeans he wore with a blazer were a little too tight to be comfortable. She guessed that this was an attempt to turn the clock back. No doubt he had dumped his wife, replacing the person with whom he had built up the company with a newer model. That would explain her bitter enmity.

'That's a ridiculously high percentage for something that took less than a week,' he said, chewing his gum fast and hard, as people do when they've recently stopped smoking.

'That week meant a trip to Switzerland, ten hours of online research and purchasing data, so that week entails significant costs and time on my part. I work fast and I get results,' Áróra said, speaking slowly and clearly to be certain he would understand. 'That's the percentage we agreed on when I said I'd search for your money.'

'That's extortionate,' the car salesman said, folding his arms across his middle. 'I'm not paying that.'

Áróra sighed. This happened more frequently that anyone could imagine. First there would be despair over lost cash, so people agreed to a high percentage, but once the money had been found it seemed that they only then began to realise just how expensive her services were.

'It's ten percent of the overall value, or nothing.'

'Five percent is the absolute limit for this kind of thing.'

'Up to you,' Áróra said and got to her feet. 'Then you can find someone else to track down your money, and good luck with that because I'm as good at hiding cash as I am at finding it.'

The car salesman shot to his feet, cleared his throat and coughed. He appeared to have swallowed his gum.

'What the hell do you mean? You've already put it into my account.'

There was a shadow of the sob she had heard in his voice a week previously.

'I have a twenty-four-hour recall option on all my bank transfers,' Áróra said, taking out her phone, tapping in the banking app code and cancelling the transaction. 'Done,' she said, and walked out of his office.

She dodged between the cars in the showroom, every one polished to a shine, and headed for the door. Through the glass partition of his office, she could see the man tapping at his phone in desperation, undoubtedly checking his bank account, with which he had been so delighted the previous evening.

Áróra was halfway across the parking lot outside when she heard his voice behind her.

'OK, OK, no problem,' he called after her, panting after jogging through the showroom. 'You're right. Of course we'd agreed. My bad.'

Áróra stopped and turned.

'I was doing you a favour by agreeing to pay the whole amount into your account so you could pay my commission through your car business. But now that I'm not able to trust you, I'll make the transfer, but I'm taking my commission out first.'

She held her phone and there was a questioning look on her face. The car salesman nodded and raised his hands in agreement.

Áróra opened the banking app again while the salesman stood there fiddling with his own phone, no doubt wanting to be sure that the cash came through.

'That's it,' Áróra said. 'Now we're all square.' She turned off her phone, dropped it in her pocket and waited a moment, just to see the car salesman's face when he saw the result. She didn't have to wait long.

'No!' he yelped, his voice full of despair and pain. 'We're not all square. That's only half. Less than half...'

'That's right,' Áróra said. 'And it was an educational experience to see just what you're really like. I started to have my doubts about your tales of woe – how your wife had hauled you over the coals during the divorce, had taken the house, and all that stuff you were whining about last week. So I'll return the half that's rightfully your wife's to her Swiss account.'

'You can't do this!' he called, and Áróra turned on her heel and walked away.

'If anything, she deserves more for having to put up with you for twenty years,' she muttered as she got into her car.

She started the engine and drove slowly out of the parking lot, giving a cheerful wave to the car salesman, who stood as if he had been turned to stone. This was one of the real perks of her job: being able to dispense her own justice.

3

The sisters' relationship had been sour right from the start. One of Áróra's earliest memories was the pure loathing in her sister's eyes as she picked up a shoe and flung it at her, hissing from between clenched teeth, 'Lousy kid.'

'Lousy kid' was an expression Áróra had got used to hearing. Her mother called her 'love' or 'darling' and her father used quirky Icelandic terms of affection: 'sweet morsel' or 'cuddle dumpling'. But Ísafold never referred to her as anything other than 'the kid', generally attached to a less than complimentary adjective. That six-year age difference hadn't been good for them.

It all changed when they moved to England, to their mother's home town of Newcastle, when Áróra was eight. Ísafold was fourteen and her raging teenage hormones manifested themselves in a faceful of livid red spots. She was struggling at school, where she was teased, and that was when she began to seek out her little sister's company. After a day of schoolyard humiliation, it seemed to be a relief for her to play Barbie dolls with Áróra, who worshipped her in the illogical manner of younger siblings. Áróra still remembered how thankful she had been for the attention. She even turned down a couple of playdates with friends at school, preferring to spend the time with her big sister and the Barbies.

Thinking back, she couldn't be sure if they had spoken Icelandic or English those first few years in the UK. More than likely they had used some mixture of both languages, as is normal when each parent has their own mother tongue, but it wasn't long after their father died that they switched completely to English. There was something a little silly about speaking Icelandic when there was no clear need to.

In Newcastle they lived in a typical middle-class house, with bedrooms at the top of a steep flight of stairs, a living room and kitchen downstairs, and even a securely fenced garden at the back, where Áróra happily made mud pies all year round. She dug holes for ponds and replanted plants, and whenever her mother complained that she was destroying the garden, her father had always been there to take her side.

'Leave her to it. After all, she's half an Icelander.'

With hindsight, Áróra wasn't sure if he meant that she should be allowed to do it because it was such a change for an Icelandic child to get to play in unfrozen ground all year round, or if it was because there was no point trying to tame her wild Icelandic nature, which had a different rhythm to its English counterpart. There was so much that she now wanted to have asked her father, but when she realised, it was too late.

4

Edinburgh Airport was always a nightmare to get to, so Áróra decided to leave the car at home and take a taxi. It wasn't that far that she could be bothered with trains and buses to save the taxi fare, as her mother would not have hesitated to do, reminding Áróra how badly she managed her finances. Her response was usually that there wasn't much point in having money if you didn't use it to make life easier for yourself.

It was a long time since she had been to Iceland in summer, but she remembered how cool it could be and had packed a few warm clothes in a weekend bag. She'd booked a hotel in the centre of Reykjavík. Its name wasn't familiar, so it had to be a new place. Her mother had suggested staying with some relatives she barely remembered, but she had managed to dissuade her from making arrangements on her behalf. It was an evening flight, but it didn't matter what time of day or night it was – she would arrive in daylight. It was June, with its cold sun that never left the sky.

The sisters had each inherited a mixed bag of genes. By nature Áróra was the more English of the two, but with typical Icelandic looks – a fair complexion and a robust physique. Ísafold's darker looks were more English, with her ivory skin and petite frame, but she had always been instinctively more Icelandic than her sister, as she had spent more of her formative years in Iceland and had been closer to their father.

'One's an elf and one's a troll,' their father had said when they were small, managing somehow to make both appear desirable options. Ísafold was delighted to be an elf child, taking ballet and later gymnastics classes, for which her natural agility was perfect. Áróra was quite happy to be the family troll, taking after her father, whose build brought him work as a doorman and as a competitor at Highland games, so physical strength was often a subject of discussion in their house.

Whether they were in Iceland or England, the sisters found themselves between two cultures, often unsure which way to jump. Generally Ísafold would incline to her father's point of view, while Áróra would side with her mother, whenever comparisons were made between the different cuisines, customs or languages, as if it was a competition.

'Iceland one, England nil,' Ísafold had hissed when their mother had made her feelings plain about Icelandic food, that it was only fit for savages, to which their father retorted that the best thing about food in Britain was breakfast. It always irritated him when his wife hinted that Iceland somehow lagged behind.

It also bugged him that whenever he had a spur-of-the-moment idea for a project or a trip, it never failed to trigger his wife's inner brakes, as she counted the costs and drawbacks. The girls' mother liked to plan things, to be organised in advance, to enjoy the anticipation instead of acting on impulse, as their father and the rest of the Icelandic side of the family were inclined to do.

Right now, as Áróra thought back, sitting in the back of a taxi on its way through Edinburgh, she decided that her father would have liked her to have been more Icelandic, and felt the pangs of loss and helpless regret that always gripped her when she thought of him. In some way, she felt that she had betrayed Iceland, and therefore him as well.

She had allowed Iceland to fade out of her consciousness, in spite of all the summer holidays and Christmases spent there. After her father's death she had spun all sorts of excuses to avoid going there, which had stretched the family ties so much, the invitations to christenings, weddings and family reunions that Icelanders were so fond of became steadily rarer. Ísafold, on the other hand, had revelled in all of that. She had taken every opportunity to go to Iceland, and even made excuses for needing to be there. She had taken her friends there for weekends to show them

Reykjavík's night life, and as soon as she had been old enough, she found herself a summer job there. It hadn't been any kind of a surprise when she hooked herself an Icelandic guy. Somehow, that had been what was always going to happen.

Travelling light, with hand baggage only, Áróra was soon through check-in and the security checks, leaving her almost an hour to kill before boarding. She marched through the departure lounge to the gate, found a seat on a bench and took out her phone. She had already called both Ísafold's mother-in-law and her brother-in-law, Björn's brother Ebbi, leaving voice messages for both of them, plus she had sent text messages to Björn. None of them had picked up, there had been no messages and nobody had called her back.

5

It was three years since Björn had appeared on the scene. It was soon clear that he was different from all of Ísafold's previous boyfriends, none of whom had lasted long – the most enduring of them lasting less than a year. It was as if there had been some quality she had been searching for, and had found in Björn.

Áróra had allowed Ísafold to drag her along to the late-winter gathering of expat Icelanders in London. She had agreed to go against her better judgement, as she avoided the traditional food and found Icelanders less than pleasant once they started to sing. But Ísafold had piled the pressure on her sister, desperate to go and without anyone to go with, until Áróra let herself be persuaded. All she had out of it was an evening's regret, sitting alone at their table, watching Ísafold dancing with Björn.

Björn was a good-looking guy. He was tall and thick-set, and from beneath his rolled-up sleeves complex snake-patterned tattoos peered, twisting along his muscular arms and under his shirt. He was at the party with a couple who lived in London, and he bought them all round after round. Áróra was very drunk by the time she found a taxi to take her back to their hotel, while Ísafold disappeared with Björn.

After that Ísafold had been besotted: Björn this and Björn that – he was all she could talk about. Áróra was delighted for her. Ísafold was overjoyed and in love; it was good to see her so happy. It seemed that the Iceland Ísafold had always pined to be closer to had finally welcomed her. She moved into Björn's flat on Engihjalli in Kópavogur after they had known each other for just a few weeks.

'Now you'll have to find yourself an Icelandic guy as well,' Ísafold had laughed soon after moving to Iceland, and Áróra had jokingly asked if Björn had a hunky friend. It was genuinely a joke. She valued her freedom too much to be tied down.

On the approach to Keflavík Airport, as she looked down at the grey-green moss that even after hundreds of years hadn't managed to cover the jagged lava completely, she couldn't recall exactly when things had turned sour with Björn. It had been quite early on, but not right away – she had visited them in Iceland, slept on the sofa and watched as Ísafold had made valiant attempts to get to grips with the Icelandic Christmas baking tradition. Everything had been fine then. They had laughed together, and she had found Björn fun to be around.

Then things had turned bad. It had begun with a tearful Ísafold calling her in the middle of the night, saying that Björn had hit her. Áróra had gone straight to Iceland, collected her sister and taken her for an interview at the domestic-abuse shelter; for the first time.

6

Áróra usually found Icelandic men brash, and often downright rude compared to British guys, but this one was different. There was nothing flustered about him, unlike those Icelandic men who would approach women hesitatingly but were prepared to shower them with abuse if their interest wasn't reciprocated. This one came across with self-assurance. She sized him up in a moment: he looked fit, slim and good-looking, although there was a youthful look to his face, as the bristles of his beard were pale and sparse. A pressed shirt was tucked neatly into his trousers, and his tie was knotted tightly even though it was evening. She liked a man who took care of his appearance.

'The same again for me,' he said to the barman, handing him his glass. 'And for the lady.'

She smiled and extended a hand. 'Áróra,' she said, triggering a look of surprise on his face.

'You're from Iceland?'

'Half Icelandic,' she smiled. 'Or more likely, half English. I haven't spent much time here these last few years. But I can still manage the language all right.'

'And a sexy accent,' he said, moving a step closer. 'I was sure you were a visitor, either one of the luxury tourists or else a foreigner on a business trip.'

This was her opportunity to disappear, to gently reject his interest in her. But she sat still.

'Thank you,' she said. 'And do you have a name?'

'Hákon,' he said, and they shook hands a second time. He didn't let go right away, and she felt a clear spark of energy between them. She tried to identify the smell of his after-shave, and had to admit to herself that this was one she hadn't encountered before. But it was a good one, fresh with a hint of spice. For a second the thought crossed her mind to invite him up to her room, to try him for size and see how he measured up, to find out if he could get the blood pumping in her veins, but she immediately dismissed the idea. He had to be married.

'Are you married?' she asked, dropping the question without thinking, and he shook his head.

'Separated. Two and a half kids.'

Fuck. She couldn't use that as an excuse. She hadn't gone to the hotel bar to look for prey. It was just that the wretched daylight was keeping her awake. There were blackout curtains in the room, but beams of sunlight still squeezed through the cracks, and after tossing and turning for a while, she had decided that a glass of wine or three might help her cope with this infuriating endless brightness.

7

Different physiques mean different diets and exercise regimes. So elf girls and troll girls don't get the same treatment.

He puts two slices of toast on Ísafold's plate for breakfast and piles mine high with bacon. After breakfast Ísafold goes for a run, and I go with Dad to the gym to lift weights.

Mum has nothing to do with exercise, says she doesn't get involved in that kind of rubbish.

One day Ísafold demands to do weights with us, and I laugh at her and tell her that she won't even manage the beginners' weights. But Dad scowls and takes the weights off her bar, fibbing to her that when I started, it was with a bar with no weights. I start to say something to put the record straight, but he says 'shhh', and takes me to one side.

'Ísafold is your older sister, but you're stronger so you'll have to look after her, so don't put her down,' he says. 'Physical strength is an indicator of inner strength, and you have much more of that than she does.'

Looking in the gym's mirror, I compare the two of us, standing side by side. There are thirty kilos at each end of my bar and nothing on hers, and it's as if I can see myself growing. All of a sudden I'm a head taller than Ísafold, my legs are solid and my arms muscular. At the same time, she seems to shrink, withering away, as if she might shrivel up, as if there's nothing under her pale skin but bone and sinew that she hardly has the energy to keep together.

That evening Ísafold is in tears because she's put on a kilo, while I'm delighted at the extra weight. Muscles are heavy. More muscle means greater strength.

Friday

8

Grímur was startled by the chime of the doorbell of the flat upstairs. Their flat. He got out of bed and tiptoed cautiously to the window, as if he was concerned that whoever was at the door with their finger on the bell might hear him. Not that there was any chance of that. His window, which overlooked the entrance to the block, was high enough up that there was little likelihood his footsteps on the carpeted floor would carry through the insulated walls and double-glazed windows; unlike the noise from the flat upstairs, the noise that came from them.

He was taken by surprise when he looked outside: the woman standing there looked like Ísafold, just a larger, fairer version of her. It took him a moment to realise that this had to be Ísafold's sister, who lived in Britain. He remembered her. From the time she collected her sister from his place. Out in the car park was a car she had left running, with a little red badge from the car-hire company on the windscreen. It was only to be expected. Sooner or later, this had to happen.

Grímur stood still and watched the woman. She rang the bell a second time and shuffled her feet on the steps. Then she peered upward at the building's walls, and he stepped back in alarm from the window, not certain whether their eyes had met for a fraction of a second.

He badly needed the toilet, and although he was determined to wait by the window until she had given up and gone, he couldn't hold it any longer, rushed to the bathroom and noisily emptied his bladder. He washed his hands and splashed his face with cold water to wake himself up properly, and as he looked out of the window again with the towel in his hands, he saw that stupid Arab talking to the woman. Him sticking his nose in was only to be expected. It was as if there was absolutely nothing that was out of bounds to the boy. He wished there was a pane he could open so that he could hear their conversation, but judging by the Arab's body language, he was telling her that he hadn't seen Ísafold. He shook his head and gestured with his hands in every direction, as he always did when he tried to make himself understood in that hopeless mixture of Icelandic and English, while the woman listened and nodded.

When the woman got into her hire car and drove away, Grímur was able to breathe more easily. He choked back the irritation that welled up inside him when he saw the Arab still out there with a broom in his hands, sweeping clean the pavement in front of the entrance. It was true that he couldn't sit still. Olga said she had told him at least a hundred times to stay inside, not to draw attention to himself, but the lad wouldn't be told. That was his problem. Olga had asked Grímur to keep an eye out for him in case he sneaked out, but Grímur had given up on that. He wasn't going to babysit a grown man. The boy would just have to take what was coming to him, just like everyone else.

Grímur could sense the bristles sprouting after their night's growth. He couldn't bear to run a hand over his face to find out just how bad it was. The hair would be growing on his head and his feet, not to mention his chest. And his balls. And then there were those lousy eyebrows.

He hurried to the bathroom and let the water run in the shower. He took a new pack of disposable razors from the cupboard under the sink and extracted four. Normally four was enough. He stripped and stepped into the shower. The water and the heat gradually softened the stubble, making shaving smoother and closer, keeping the growth back until the evening. He squirted a palmful of thick, white foam and rubbed it into his head. He always started with his scalp, then his face – eyebrows first, then beard. Then he would take a new razor and work his way down his body, finishing at his feet. After that he would soap himself all over and go over his body a second time with a fresh razor, to be completely certain that not one single disgusting, bacteria-carrying hair remained.

Sitting at the kitchen table, Grímur tried to calm his nerves, which had left his body as tight as a bowstring. The shower and the shave hadn't been enough to calm him down. In his thoughts, the woman, Ísafold's sister, continued to knock with her knuckles so loudly it was as if she were really at the door. It was only to be expected. It went without saying that sooner or later someone would come looking for Ísafold.

9

There were two people ahead of her in the queue for the information desk on the ground floor of the National Hospital in Fossvogur. Áróra took her place behind the second woman and waited her turn. She had been here twice before, on both occasions with Ísafold. The building's lobby was a busy place, with people coming and going: doctors and nurses, patients in white, sidling out for a smoke, pushing ahead of them stands on wheels with plastic drip bags, as well as people in normal clothes, visiting or collecting elderly relatives, who sat primly in wheelchairs, or stood and shivered behind their walking frames.

The woman in front of her finished asking her questions, and Áróra prepared to step forward, when a young man in a green raincoat stepped in front of her, leaned against the reception desk and said something to the man behind the glass. Anywhere else in the world she would have had a few harsh words for him, but it wasn't worth wasting her energy when faced with this typical Icelandic approach. Men pushed their way to the front of queues and women never gave way in traffic. It was as if joining a queue or giving someone else a chance was an alien concept.

Áróra glared at the man in the green coat as he finished his business and leaned in to the glass, giving the receptionist a smile as she did so.

'I'm here to visit my sister, but I don't know which ward she said she's on,' Áróra said. 'Could you check for me?'

'Sure,' the man replied, and Áróra gave him Ísafold's name, which he tapped into his computer. He peered at the screen. 'I can't see her anywhere,' he said, and shrugged.

'Really?' Áróra said, feigning surprise. 'Could you check again?' He shook his head.

'There's nobody called Ísafold here.'

'Could she be down at Hringbraut?'

'No,' the man said. 'There's just one registry for the whole hospital, it doesn't matter which building someone's in.'

'That's weird,' Áróra said. 'Could she have been discharged sometime today or later yesterday? Could you check back a few days?'

The man tapped something in, squinted at the screen in front of him and shook his head again.

'No,' he said. 'I don't have anyone called Ísafold on record. You'll have to get in touch with her yourself to make sure.'

If only it were that simple, Áróra thought, but thanked the man and went back into the cool summer's day outside. At least she could be sure of one thing: Ísafold wasn't in hospital.

'What are you doing here?'

It was more or less the response she had expected from Björn when she turned up at the phone shop, where he worked some kind of part-time job that wasn't important enough for him to be reachable on the phone. There wasn't a great deal of warmth between her and Björn. The plan was to get this over with as quickly as possible, find out where she could get hold of Ísafold and take this information to their mother, whether it was a new phone number, a new workplace or a new fractured jaw that was the reason they hadn't heard from her. Áróra was looking forward to getting this done, so she could go back to the hotel, dress herself up and go for a meal with the guy she had met in the bar the night before, and maybe spend a night with him before catching the midday flight home.

'It's a long story,' she said. 'Mum asked me to come. She's going crazy because she can't reach Ísafold. So I'm after her new phone number or anything that'll put Mum's mind at rest. Nobody answers the doorbell at your place so I suppose she's at work. Is she still at that boutique in the Kringlan shopping centre?'

'No, she left there a while ago.'

Björn took her elbow and steered her out through the doors and into the street. The sun was high in the sky and it was close to midday, but the contrast between bright sunshine and cool air still took Áróra by surprise every time she stepped outside. She preferred the milder climate in Britain. She could live with Scotland's hard winters, as long as there were some warm days in summer. But the chill of the Icelandic summer was somehow a symbol of hopelessness.

'Where's she working now?'

'How should I know?' Björn asked, taking out an e-cigarette, puffing on it and exhaling a cloud of smoke with a strong straw-berry aroma.

'You live together, so you must know where she works,' Áróra replied, trying to hide her impatience – with little success, judging by Björn's expression.

'We don't live together any more,' he said, dropping the vape into his pocket. 'Ísafold walked out. I reckon she must have gone back to England.'

'What?' Áróra's jaw dropped and she stared.

This wasn't what she had expected. Ísafold was besotted with Björn. In her eyes he was the best, the greatest, the most wonder-ful, and as far as she was concerned, he couldn't say or do anything that fell short of fantastic. That was apart from the hour or so after he had hit her. That was when she wept and wanted to leave. But the feeling rarely lasted longer than the time it took to patch her up. That was the way it had been each of the three times Áróra had hurried to Iceland when Ísafold had called her in tears.

'Yeah,' Björn said, and the familiar look of contempt that she loathed so much appeared on his face. 'And if you were a decent sister to her, you'd have known that.'

He spun on his heel and went back into the phone shop. Áróra stood and stared at a bright-yellow dandelion that had pushed its way up through a crack in the pavement, shivering in the fresh breeze. Something serious must have happened for Ísafold to have decided to go back to England. She had never felt comfortable there, and Iceland had been her home for the last few years. Through most of her adult life she had made repeated attempts to settle in Iceland, taking a job in a fish plant that came with housing, and even spending a year running a farm. Most of these ventures had ended with her returning to Newcastle and immedi-ately starting to organise the next trip to Iceland. Her repeated attempts to put down roots on this cold island had been unsuc-cessful, as if the country just spat her out again – until she met Björn.

Regardless of whether Ísafold was in Britain or Iceland, it wasn't like her to ignore their mother. There had to be something she didn't dare tell her. Maybe she wasn't sure how to break the news that she and Björn had parted. Perhaps she simply didn't want to hear her mother say 'told you so'. Or it could be that Ísafold had something else to hide. Björn might have left her so bruised and battered, she didn't want anyone to see her, knowing that their mother would ask Áróra to go to Iceland and help her out. On top of that, Ísafold knew that Áróra's patience was at an end.

But, as Björn said, Áróra would have known that if they had been closer; if she had been a decent sister.

11

Olga sighed as she got out of the car and saw that not only had the pavement in front of the building been cleared of dandelions, the parking lot had been swept so carefully that there was barely a grain of sand to be seen. The block with its peeling paint wasn't the district's smartest, but the plot around it was without doubt the tidiest. That was down to Omar. He kept on sneaking out into the fresh air, even though she had warned him again and again, asking him to stay inside so as not to draw attention to himself. The police regularly posted photos online of asylum seekers who had gone into hiding after being notified that they would be deported, so there was always the risk that a narrow-minded passerby could recognise him and report him.

'But I want to help you,' he always said. 'Like you help me.'

It made no difference how often she explained to him that he didn't need to work for his board and lodging, that it was a pleasure for her to provide him with a roof over his head and that it was her duty as a human being to shelter a refugee – giving him a haven from the suffering he had endured. All the same, he was determined to help out, to ease her burden.

He did just that. The food bills hadn't increased even though he had become part of the household. He cooked dinner for them from such scant ingredients that she couldn't understand how it could make a full meal. He poured a can of green beans into a pot with a can of coconut milk, a stock cube and three cardamoms, cooking it into a mush they ate with rice two evenings in a row. It had never occurred to her how much doing without fish or meat in every meal would save. He made use of every scrap. Even a tablespoon of leftover food would be kept in a dish in the fridge overnight to appear reheated the next evening.

She turned the key in the lock and a powerful smell of detergent greeted her. One thing he didn't economise on was soap in its various forms. Probably people from hot countries, where there were all sorts of bugs and bacteria, had to be more careful about hygiene than was usual in Iceland.

'The floor's clean,' he called out cheerfully as she closed the door behind her.

'So I see, Omar,' she said. 'You work like a Trojan.'

She was about to ask if he had swept the parking lot, but didn't need to, as the guilty look on his face couldn't be misunderstood.

'I went outside and did a little tidying,' he said. 'There was so much dust everywhere.'

'You know how risky that is, Omar,' she said. 'If one of the neighbours starts to wonder why your name isn't on the door, considering you live here, and puts two and two together...'

'I know, I know,' he said, gesturing as he spoke, as he usually did. 'But there was sunshine outside and so, so good weather. It was so good to feel the sun on my skin.'

She smiled. Sometimes his imperfect command of the language sounded so sweet. It went without saying that it had to be hard for a brown-skinned man to do without sunshine. Brown people had to need more sun than white people, and it seemed obvious now that she thought it through. She sympathised with his discomfort at having to stay inside all the time with an old woman like her. He was bursting with energy, pining for life and activity, while all she could offer him was the TV, knitting and card games.

12

He was really good-looking, Áróra thought. If anything, he was too cute. He was smooth-shaven and smelled of the particular after-shave that she didn't recognise but which made her want to press her face to his neck and breathe deeply. She hadn't been sure if he was going to turn up for their date, and a couple of times had been ready to text him and call it off. But when he stood shyly by the table in the restaurant, she was relieved that she had stuck with it. He seemed so pleased to see her that his eyes shone with happiness, and he even seemed a little nervous when he asked what she would like as an aperitif.

Now that five courses of seafood were behind them and they had reached the coffee and cognac stage, Áróra could feel she was tipsy and told him about her sister and their relationship. Or rather, their lack of a relationship. She told him the tale of how her brother-in-law Björn's mother had practically slammed the door in her face when she had gone there to ask about Ísafold. The old lady had seemed so angry.

'She left him,' she had snarled, as if Áróra bore some responsibility for her sister's treachery. 'It was only to be expected that she'd want to go back to England, but leaving him like that without a single word is just too much. Poor Björn has been a wreck ever since.'

Áróra finished her coffee but pushed the cognac away. 'Sorry. That's not exactly a pleasant subject,' she said apologetically, and Hákon laid his hand on hers.

'True,' he said. 'Of course it's sad not to have a good relationship with your family, but I like listening to you tell the story. I like your accent when you speak.'

'Stop it,' she laughed, slapped his shoulder and somehow they were kissing over the table, which ended with him quickly calling for the bill before they hurried hand-in-hand across to the hotel.

It was around three in the morning when Áróra woke suddenly, as Hákon slipped from the bed and went to the bathroom. It was as bright as day in the room, and there was a loud dawn chorus outside, so it could just as well have been morning.

'Could you bring me some water?' she called, and heard Hákon turn on the tap; a moment later he appeared with a glass of water for her.

'Would you like something else?' he asked. 'I can get whatever you want from room service. Anything you like. They can fix anything.'

'You're a gentleman,' she said, and ran her fingers down his back as he sat on the bed. 'So how do you know they can fix anything you want? Do you stay here often?'

'Well, I pretty much live here. I split up with my wife a couple of years ago ... y'see...'

He didn't finish his sentence, and there was an awkward look on his face. Áróra looked around the room. There was a lot more stuff that was usual in a hotel room. There was a stack of books, a wardrobe full of clothes and all sorts on the desk. This was more stuff than would fit in two suitcases.

'Was it a tough divorce?'

He laughed awkwardly and shook his head.

'No, not at all. Or, yes. But that's not it. I live here, because it's my hotel.'

'It's yours? Your hotel?'

'Um. Yeah,' he said, almost like a question, and looked into Áróra's eyes as if asking what she thought. She hadn't put her thoughts in order before he got to his feet and padded back to the bathroom. She heard the water run again, and then he stood naked in the bathroom doorway as he drank slowly, as if waiting for her to say something. She watched him, surprised that his eyes no longer shone; instead he seemed despondent, and she gradually began to work it out. Her eyes dropped to his feet, where she could see the red rash left by an ankle tag that had clearly only recently been removed.

'Hákon,' she said slowly. 'What's your father's name?'

13

Grímur hadn't been aware of the ideas hatching at the back of his mind, but when he noticed Björn, his neighbour from the flat upstairs, through the window of a restaurant downtown, the plan immediately played out in his thoughts. Björn was sitting there with another woman, and Grímur paused to stand and watch for a moment as they looked deep into each other's eyes, raising their glasses in a toast to each other. The red-gold glow inside the restaurant was warm, welcoming and romantic, while he stood outside in the cold, blue evening light, the sharp northerly wind making him shiver. Three weeks. It hadn't taken him long to find himself a new one. Three fucking weeks. That was all he needed.

Grímur eyed the woman. She was dark-haired, just like Ísafold, but her face was broader, and she looked to be more cheerful. But Ísafold had also been happy to begin with, when she had just moved into the block and Grímur used to run into her in the corridor. After a while the joy had ebbed away, and she couldn't hide the desperation behind the forced smile she used to pretend that everything was fine.

For a moment it occurred to Grímur to go inside, order himself a beer and a snack, and take a seat somewhere near them so he could hear what they were talking about, so he could hear how Björn pitched himself. He'd see how Björn sold the woman the image he wanted to present, reeling her in, making her fall in love. He might even learn a few tactics for his own use, as he'd never had much luck with women. But he dismissed the idea. It would be awkward if Björn were to recognise him, and looking like he did, he was easily recognisable. He could see how people stared, thinking a man with no eyebrows was weird. Anyway, he didn't need to listen to their talk, and he could see that Björn was laying it on thick for the woman, and that she was falling for it. She looked at him with wide eyes, laughing one moment, smiling the next, occasionally running a finger through her hair to push it back from her cheek. Grímur was certain that if he had a clearer view he would see their feet touching beneath the table.

He zipped his jacket up to the neck and walked away. There were only ten minutes before the bus was due. He had finished the walk around the city centre he had decided to take after the film was over. But seeing Björn with a new woman had wrecked any pleasure he might have had from his walk, and now he just wanted to go home and shave all over. Usually he enjoyed seeing the weekend getting under way, late in the evening as the restaurants were closing and the bars and clubs welcomed those who wanted to keep the party going, and you could hear the expectation in the calls and laughter of the people on the streets. But now the moment had been ruined, and the plan sat ready in his mind, so simple but so dangerous. It was a relief to have a plan, a course to follow, but at the same time, as he waited for the green light to come to life on the Lækjargata pedestrian crossing, next to the bus shelter, he was boiling with rage. He saw Björn in his mind's eye, smiling for the dark-haired woman, the dark-red wine swirling in their glasses as they clinked. Not much would have to go wrong for one glass to break and for the wine to spill and flood across the white tablecloth, staining it as dark and red as blood.

14

Hákon Hauksson. The name rang a bell. Áróra recalled that he was some kind of Icelandic millionaire who had done something he shouldn't, but she couldn't remember what. Now she was regretting not having paid more attention to the Icelandic media. The man was a criminal, as the ankle tag demonstrated, but she couldn't remember what crimes he had committed, so she stood up and left. She wasn't going to lie there flat on her back in some rapist's or murderer's bed.

Now she hurried along the hotel corridor towards the lift, her dress quickly pulled on but with bare legs and feet, her bag hanging from her shoulder, and her jacket, tights and bra in a bundle in one hand and her shoes in the other. It was the middle of the night so she hoped she'd be able to get to her own room without being noticed, but that hope was dashed as she stepped into the lift. The man in the lift slurred as he asked which floor she wanted. She told him the second, and he pressed the button, but the lift had hardly started moving before he pressed the stop button and it lurched to a halt between floors.

'Excuse me!' she said sharply, in a tone that was supposed to convey determination, disgust and that she expected his mistake to be rectified. But at the same time she heard how soft her voice sounded. She could hear the sudden, instinctive fear.

'How much?' the man asked in English, although she could tell from his accent that he was a local. His drink-fuddled eyes looked her up and down, and he was unsteady on his feet. He was dressed in jeans and a blazer, with a blue shirt open at the neck, showing where the brown freckles that spotted his face had their origin. He had a broad jaw, a snub nose, and a pair of square glasses that together made him look as if he had been assembled in the shape of a box. A heavy, boxy kind of guy, the kind of guy whose grip she wouldn't be able to twist out of if he were to get hold of her.

Áróra clutched her bundle of clothes to her chest and glanced around as she tried to figure out how she could reach the red button that had to be some kind of alarm, but without getting too close to the man.

'Start the lift, or I'm going to yell,' Áróra hissed. 'Right now!'

The man took a step towards her and began to fiddle with the buckle of his belt, although he was fortunately too drunk to unfasten it quickly.

'I'm so fucking horny,' he spluttered, as Áróra felt a wave of claustrophobia.

She saw red. She lifted one foot so that her knee came up to her belly, and put her weight behind it as she stamped the heel down hard on the man's instep. She was sure she felt something crack beneath her heel, and judging by the whine as the man collapsed to the floor of the lift, he was in real pain. Áróra stepped quickly towards the buttons and set the lift moving again.

'What the fuck is it to do with me how horny you are?' she said as the lift door opened and she jumped out, scuttling along the corridor towards her room. She didn't look around until she was at her door, searching in her handbag for the key, but to her relief, the corridor was empty and the man was nowhere to be seen.

Áróra leaned her back against the door, her breaths coming in short, fast gasps as she waited. She wasn't sure exactly what she was waiting for – the man in the lift to pursue her and try to get into the room, or some kind of reassurance that she was alone and safe.

When her breathing had steadied, she slid the chain into place and pushed one of the two bedside tables against the door. It wouldn't be a great deal of use if someone were determined to get in, but it helped make her feel more secure. Once she had done all this, she felt better, and was thankful that she hadn't hesitated to break the man's instep. To hesitate was to fail. This guy wasn't the type to take notice of a courteous no.

In the bathroom she turned on the water in the shower, and as it began to flow she smiled as she reflected on her panic. Tomorrow she would laugh at herself for having shoved a bedside table against the door. But that was the outcome of violence: consolidating strength. Not that she considered herself a violent person. She would never lash out other than in self-defence, but when it was needed she didn't pull her punches – landing a hard punch in a delicate spot could be the difference between becoming a victim or a survivor.

Under the shower she breathed in the sulphur smell of the water and, to her surprise, this time it didn't get on her nerves. Her father's voice, telling her that 'you get used to the smell after two or three days' came to mind, and although she had come here with the intention of flying back as soon as possible, now she could see herself staying long enough to stop noticing the hot water's rotten-egg scent. At any rate, she'd stay long enough to find out where Ísafold had hidden herself. She towelled herself dry and slipped under the duvet, pulling it over her.

She wasn't sleepy enough to doze off. Every time she felt rational thought giving way to the lightness of sleep, the uncomfortable feeling of not knowing what had become of Ísafold returned to gnaw at her, or she was startled into wakefulness by the boxy face of the man in the lift appearing as clear as day in front of her. This was no good. She got out of bed, switched on the little coffee machine and opened her laptop.

She'd need coffee to wash away the dregs of the alcohol in her system, and the sunshine, illuminating the room even though it was not yet four o'clock, would ensure she wouldn't get back to sleep. She slid one of the disposable aluminium capsules into the coffee machine, wondering if this was environmentally friendly or not. She chose the black one, figuring that this had to be the strongest coffee.

16

Iceland's business newspaper answered her questions about Hákon Hauksson. A rambling feature article told her that he had inherited a chain of pharmacies. His father had been a chemist who had started out with one shop and from there built a business empire, which his son joined straight from school. When Hákon had taken over the business he had been a young man. The company grew rapidly, or so it seemed, and it was registered on the stock market. To begin with the shares rose sharply in value; due to the strict currency restrictions following the financial crash, Icelandic pension funds found themselves limited to investing in Icelandic companies. But the company's share price began to drop after a poor set of annual accounts, and that was when the problems began.

As the share price continued to drop for weeks on end, it seemed Hákon became increasingly desperate. He secured a loan from a German bank and used the cash to invest in overseas companies; boutiques, print shops and advertising agencies all became part of a list of disparate companies he bought into. According to the article, he never intended to run these companies, but simply used them as collateral with which to pull in more loans, using that money to buy shares in his chain of pharmacies in Iceland, thus inflating the share price. But the whole scam collapsed like a house of cards, leaving Hákon with no assets, steeped in debt and facing a prison sentence for market manipulation.

Pushing things beyond their limits, making rash investments and growing too fast was nothing unusual in Icelandic business, and plenty of people had taken desperate measures that weren't always legal. Hákon hadn't been alone in this. But now he owned a hotel, one of Reykjavík's smartest. This was strange. In fact, it was more than just strange.

She googled his name and pulled together all the news articles she could find about him. Then she logged into her Icelandic bank account, which allowed her to use the bank's link to the national registry, where she could locate his ID number. A search through the tax office's company registry was easy. She also opened the European company registry gateway she had set up to save herself time, and with all of these tools at her disposal, she stood up and slid another capsule into the coffee machine. She had a few hours ahead of her to go through the information available online, and she had the feeling that a search through Hákon's companies would reveal all kinds of interesting information.

Business geeks like Hákon habitually had strings of holding companies, and those holding companies owned other holding companies. It was as if making the web of ownership as complex as possible was a competitive sport for these guys, muddying the waters for the authorities and creditors who might want to follow a trail. But this was Áróra's home ground. She could tease the truth from the most tangled web, and she relished it. It wasn't exactly the work itself that she enjoyed – the endless hours in front of a screen, and the hunt for loose ends – but the promise of reaching the finishing line. This was because somewhere at the end of all the twisted strands, when every one had been followed to its conclusion, there would be a crock of gold. There would be a treasure trove in the form of property, diamonds, bonds, or simply cold, hard cash.

She had made a profession of searching out money. To keep life simple for herself, normally she told people she was an accountant. Most people lacked the imagination to appreciate what she actually did, as the world of tax havens and fraud was so alien to them; and generally telling people that she was a financial investigator – a private detective who tracked down missing cash, a financial bloodhound – ended up with tiresomely convoluted explanations. But in her mind she saw it as a treasure hunt. It was a good description, as people still had a preference for hiding their money on Caribbean islands, and just like the pirates of yore, today's thieves had the same obsessive fear that someone would find their cash, so a search would often lead her past obstacles and dangers.

At the end of the search, when she had found the hidden gold and returned it to its rightful owner – generally the tax authorities or a bankruptcy court – she celebrated by taking her fee, her share, in cash and taking it home. There she would spread it out on the bed and roll in money. This was an eccentricity all of her own that she kept strictly to herself, her own little secret. There was nothing like literally wallowing in cash.

Áróra finished the last of her coffee and rubbed her eyes. If her instinct was correct, then Hákon Hauksson had a stash of money hidden away somewhere, and if she could find it, she'd take her cut in Icelandic krónur. Wallowing in krónur would be a new experience.

17

Olga woke to the sound of the boy weeping. She sat up, swung her feet out of bed and sat for a moment as she listened. The sound wasn't coming from his room, so he must have hidden himself away in the bathroom again. With difficulty, she hauled herself to her feet and stood still while the pain in her hip receded. These days she always became so stiff as she slept, she had to be careful not to make sudden movements first thing in the morning. She glanced at the clock and saw that it wasn't exactly morning, even though the daylight that spilled past the curtains told her otherwise. It was only just four o'clock. It was so strange how these nightmares always came between three and four in the morning.

With a hand on the wall for support, she went down the passage towards the bathroom and peered inside. As she had suspected, he lay on the bathmat, wrapped tightly in his duvet and curled into a foetal position, weeping tears so bitter that the sound of them wrung her heart.

'Omar,' she said quietly. 'You're having a nightmare.'

He continued to sob in his sleep so she came closer and touched his shoulder.

'Omar.'

He jerked up in fright, hands in front of his face, and shuffled rapidly away until he could go no further and his back was against the bathtub.

'There's blood,' he whispered, staring in desperation into the distance. 'So much blood.'

'Shh, shh. No,' she said to comfort him. 'There's no blood here. Everything is quiet and fine, Omar. Remember where you are. You're here with me in Engihjalli, in Kópavogur, and there's no war here. Remember? Everything's peaceful and quiet here. Everything's all right.'

'All right,' he echoed, and he seemed to be awake as he looked at her with the special blend of wonder and doubt that seemed to be a part of his disturbed sleep.

'Yes, it's all right,' she said, and extended a hand.

He took it obediently, like a child, and she led him out into the passage and back to his room, where he stretched out, still wrapped in the duvet. She dropped into the desk chair and pushed it closer to the bed so that she could reach out a hand to his head, stroking his hair while he recovered and his sobs subsided. Deep feelings welled up inside her. It had been in this same room that she had so often sat with her son, telling stories and singing songs as he went to sleep. Her Jonni had long stopped coming home to see her by the time he died, so she always felt that this was the place where she had said goodbye to him, sitting in the office chair he had been given as a confirmation present, stroking those pale, fine curls of his.

Omar's hair was coarse and seemed to grow directly outwards from his scalp, and it was so black that it took on a blueish shade when sunlight from the living-room window fell on it. All the same, this coarse black tangle filled her heart with the tenderness that had come to her the day her son was born, and which had been snuffed out with his death two years ago.

Omar had brought her new life. He had woken her from her daze and reignited a desire to live, even if only to help him. She had helped him with shelter and protection. But he had helped her just as much.

18

Ísafold scratches at my window. Somehow she's managed to clamber into the garden at the back of the house, even though she's unsteady on her feet and can hardly speak.

In the afternoon she went to the beach with her friends. Then she called Mum and said she was staying at Abby's place. But when I turn the key in the lock to let her in the back door, I can see she's been out on the town. She's wearing her gear for a night out in Newcastle, a see-through top and a skirt so short it shows her knickers. She's lost her shoes somewhere, she says, just as she pukes on the kitchen floor.

I help her to my bed, as my room's downstairs, because I'm not the one who's afraid of the dark. There's no chance of getting her up the stairs to her own bed without waking Mum and Dad. I tuck the bedclothes around her, and she croaks that she doesn't feel well. I hope she doesn't throw up in my bed.

I really want to leave the pool of vomit so she'll have to clean it up herself in the morning, but I know how furious Mum and Dad will be if they know she's been out drinking. They've told us we can't touch booze until we're seventeen.

It takes half a kitchen roll to clean up the puke, which seems to be practically unadulterated beer, and then I tiptoe upstairs and lie down in Ísafold's bed.

Even though she's my big sister, it's my job to protect her, because I'm stronger than she is.

SATURDAY

19

Áróra wasn't sure if her decision to go downstairs and meet Hákon in the breakfast room was based on a curiosity provoked by her nocturnal investigations, or on a simple desire to see him. She could see that he was tender and sensitive, and she had to admit that the smell of him and the hand that reached across the table to touch hers triggered a whirlwind of feelings inside her. She could well have entertained the idea of crawling back to bed with him after breakfast, pressing herself close to him under the warm duvet and breathing in his aroma. But the results of her research prevented her from making that suggestion.

Sitting alone upstairs in her room with a couple of empty coffee cups at her side, she wanted to laugh out loud once the extent of Hákon's affairs had become clear. The whole thing was almost too weird to be real. It seemed that Hákon owned a company that owned another company, which in turn owned not just one hotel in Iceland, but a string of them; two or three in each part of the country. These were boutique hotels that didn't need stars to attract the right clientele. The price alone saw to that. Áróra couldn't be bothered to figure out how much it had cost to build this business, not forgetting the buildings themselves, which appeared to belong to a property company that seemed to belong to Hákon too, via a few financial twists and turns.

It looked as if Hákon Hauksson, who had been personally declared bankrupt – with debts of a good two billion krónur owed to a German bank, and not far off another billion owed to this and that fund – was sitting on property in Iceland that would easily be enough to cover all those debts. On top of that, if the media reports were anything to go by, this was all common knowledge. The pharmacy chain's bankruptcy proceedings had been concluded, and the assets – or rather, the debts – had been shared out among the creditors. Most of these were Icelandic banks, which had mercilessly pursued people who were behind on their mortgages, but which had been unable or unwilling to use the same tactics on their largest debtors, such as Hákon.

She had read a couple of accounts of the glamorous lifestyles Hákon and other rich kids enjoyed while their business empires were flourishing. One recent article suggested that Hákon appeared to be resuming his former lifestyle, despite the bankruptcy. Áróra could feel the excitement, mixed with an undercurrent of chagrin, that usually settled in her heart when a new assignment got under way. Hákon was a con man. The man was a swindler and a cheat who didn't pay his debts, playing with money that wasn't his.

It looked like she had stumbled across a job completely by chance. Although it had been accidental and there was an uncomfortable personal angle to it, this one just seemed too exciting to resist. She smiled, unable to hide her satisfaction. It wasn't every day that she had the chance to nail an Icelandic criminal. She finished her breakfast and left Hákon with a kiss and the promise of a second date.

She took a deep breath of the summer morning as she went outside. The city centre was coming to life, with tourists ambling between the menus outside the cafés as they looked for breakfast at a reasonable price, while a handful of Icelanders crossed the square. It was easy to identify them: unlike the tourists, they had somewhere to go and walked faster, as if they were already late for work. There was something so peculiarly Icelandic about turning up at the last possible moment, always in a hurry.

When she got to the car park, she stood still for a moment and looked around. This is what she still missed about the Icelandic part of her childhood, the promise of summer mornings. The sun was high in the sky, but the sea breeze hadn't gathered much strength, so the multi-coloured corrugated-iron roofs were drinking in the heat of the bright rays. This could turn out to be a fine day, and she recalled Icelanders' delight when things were looking this fine. There would be barbecues all around town, children would be taking fishing rods down to the harbour, and at kids' football matches parents would haul garden chairs from the boots of cars to sit in the sun, shouting encouragement, instead of huddling inside the car with the heater on.

Áróra remembered all this, and also how as a child she had felt sorry for her Icelandic relatives, who saw so few summer days like this, often asking why they didn't move to somewhere better. But now she recalled being bitten by the anticipation, the joy that infected everyone when there was hope of a little sunshine. Now, standing here and looking out over the city, she felt a little of that anticipation inside. But maybe it wasn't the excitement at the prospect of a warm day ahead that had fired her up, but the thought of Hákon and his hidden treasure.

20

As Áróra pulled up outside Ebbi's garage in the Smiðja district, she saw him on the forecourt, deep under the bonnet of one of the vast 4x4s that were so popular in Reykjavík. He stood up straight as Áróra got out of her car, pulled a rag from the pocket of his boiler suit and wiped his hands. Not that wiping them made much difference, as Ebbi's hands were never anything but black, even when they were clean. He was a coarser version of Björn, with a big nose and a jaw that protruded slightly, while his elder brother had been blessed with a sweet face but without Ebbi's gentle nature. Áróra liked Ebbi.

'Sorry I didn't reply to those messages of yours,' he said. 'I've never figured out how to use voicemail.'

He leaned in to kiss her cheek, taking care not to let the grease or hydraulic oil, or whatever else his overalls were stained with, come anywhere near her clothes. He went into the workshop, fetched coffee in two plastic cups and handed one to her. They perched on a concrete lip that jutted from the workshop wall. Áróra took sunglasses from her pocket and put them on, while Ebbi squinted into the brightness.

'What do you mean, you're looking for her?' he asked. 'Didn't she go to England?'

Áróra shook her head.

'It's not like her not to be in touch with Mum,' she said, and Ebbi quickly glanced sideways at her. She was sure she noticed a trace of concern in his eyes.

'I can't say I'm surprised she had enough of Björn,' he said, looking away and staring at the concrete ground, eyes focused as if he had seen something down there that needed careful inspection.

'It's always seemed to me that she can't get enough. She keeps on going back to him. Even that time he broke her jaw.'

'Yeah. He knows how to entice her back. Then there's always a few good weeks.'

'Pillock,' Áróra said, still searching for a more suitable word in her imperfect Icelandic vocabulary.

'Shitbag,' Ebbi said. 'And he still hasn't improved since he was sentenced. It was like it gave him licence to turn into a complete arsehole.'

This was news to Áróra.

'What sentence?'

'Well, just a slap on the wrist for a bit of dope. You know he's a toker; well, he's been selling pills too.' Áróra was about to ask more about this, but Ebbi continued, so it was clear this was something he didn't want to go into. 'It was obvious last time I saw her that she wasn't happy,' he said. 'And you could see they weren't getting on.'

'Understood,' Áróra said, but she didn't understand. The last she had heard from Ísafold was that things were getting better between them, that Björn was making a real effort, that they would be going to a counsellor. But that had been a year and a half ago, and now it was six months since Ísafold had cut any communication by blocking her on Facebook.

'When did you last see her, Ebbi?'

'About three weeks ago,' he said, and thought for a moment. 'Exactly three weeks ago this weekend, at Mum's place. We were all there for dinner. Ísafold seemed unhappy to me, or maybe under the weather. She lay down on the sofa after dinner and slept for the rest of the evening. Strange for someone who always made a point of helping Mum with the dishes and stuff.'

'And you've no idea where she might be now?' Áróra asked. 'I'm not asking so I can go and make life difficult for her. But I need something to put my mother's mind at rest. She's worried sick with not hearing from her.'

Ebbi shook his head, and again Áróra saw the concern in his eyes.

'No,' he said. 'I haven't a clue. If I knew where she was, I'd tell you.'

Ebbi got to his feet and Áróra did the same.

When she couldn't find Ísafold anywhere else, she had been sure she would be at Ebbi's place, as she had taken refuge from Björn with him in the past. It had seemed so obvious – she would have gone to Ebbi's house and hidden herself away in his spare bedroom while she made up her mind whether to run away to England or go back to Björn. But now Áróra seemed to be out of options.

She had spoken to one of Ísafold's neighbours, who hadn't seen her for three weeks; she had enquired at the hospital; she had tried to talk to Björn, and now she had spoken to Ebbi. Nobody seemed to have any idea what had become of Ísafold.

In the car she called her mother to give her an update.

'Go and talk to your uncle Daníel,' her mother said. 'He's a detective, so he ought to know how to track people down.'

'Hang on. You mean I have a relative who's a cop?' Áróra said in hurt surprise. 'Then why on earth didn't you go straight to him, instead of sending me to Iceland to play at being a private eye?'

'But isn't that what you are – a private detective?'

'Mum, I'm a private financial investigator. I track down money, not people. I don't even know where to start.'

'Well, whatever,' her mother said, her classic move to change the subject. 'I'll give Daníel a call and ask him to help.'

For once, Áróra wasn't inclined to protest. She was all out of ideas concerning Ísafold, and she felt she might soon become as desperate as her mother sounded. Where the hell had Ísafold gone?

21

Her mother had been as good as her word, calling ahead to announce Áróra's arrival. Her finger was poised over the button marked *Daníel Hansson*, ready to press it, when the door swung open.

'Good morning,' he said. His voice was deep and welcoming, and Áróra had the feeling she had heard it before, although the man's serious face was nowhere in her memory. He looked to be well past forty, with a touch of grey in the close-cropped hair that she guessed he clippered short himself. The eyes that met hers were a pale grey but strangely warm.

'Hello,' she said, extending a hand. 'Apologies for the inconvenience.'

'No problem,' he said, ushering her in. 'It's no inconvenience at all. It was good to speak to your mother. I hadn't heard from her for a long time.'

Icelandic style, Áróra took off her shoes in the hall and followed him on stockinged feet into the living room, overwhelmed by the feeling of being a child again, visiting Iceland. She could hear old-fashioned state radio burbling in the kitchen, and there was a smell in the air that she couldn't pin down but which was somehow familiar – some peculiarly Icelandic smell.

'So how are we related?' she asked when Daníel had shown her to a chair. She didn't doubt that her mother had at some time explained the connection, but her interest in her genealogy was limited.

He looked at her with a glitter of amusement in his eyes. 'We aren't related,' he said.

'Oh. Mum referred to you as my uncle, so I assumed you must have been related to my dad.'

The pink flush she could feel flooding her cheeks took her by surprise. For someone who had made a habit of staying in control in the most bizarre situations, there was something about those light-grey eyes that flustered her.

'I used to be married to your aunt, but we divorced more than ten years ago. So it would be more accurate to say that we had links, although a long time ago.'

'Ah. Understood.' Áróra smiled. 'Do you have any children?' she asked, trying to keep the conversation light, chatting as people normally did, but immediately realised that the question seemed to be over-inquisitive. What business of hers was it if this unrelated uncle had children or not? But he responded as if there was nothing more natural than answering a complete stranger's questions about his family circumstances.

'No, we didn't have children,' he said. 'But I have two from a subsequent relationship. They live with their mother in Denmark.'

Áróra nodded and smiled courteously. This was what she found uncomfortable. What could be a perfectly normal conversation in Iceland might be seen as nosey in Britain, and it was frequently difficult to be sure where the thin lines dividing the two lay.

'And you?' he asked. 'Married? Children?'

She shook her head, flustered again.

'No,' she said, not knowing what she could add. She had asked first, so it was to be expected that he would ask about her own circumstances in return, but she felt that he was mentally undressing her, looking her up and down, naked and defenceless. It was difficult to fathom what was happening behind those pale-grey eyes.

'Coffee?' he asked, and turned to go into the kitchen. She remembered the peculiar Icelandic 'ten drops' expression, shorthand for half a cup of coffee, so she used it.

'Maybe ten drops,' she said.

This was one of those expressions that sounded so weird, such an artificial way of speaking. As everyone knew, most Icelanders would gladly knock back a whole mug of coffee, or even the whole pot if it was on offer. She got to her feet and followed him into the kitchen, rather than sit awkwardly on the sofa until he brought her coffee, as if she was some kind of fine lady who demanded to be served.

'Your mother said that you're searching for your sister,' Daníel said as he opened a kitchen cupboard and took out a coffee jar. The kitchen was quite bare, as if he had only just moved in. The kitchen worktop was completely clear, and there was an old-fashioned net curtain in the window that looked to have been there for a long time. He heaped spoonfuls of coffee into a cafe-tière while he waited for the kettle to boil.

'Give me your take on all this. From the beginning,' he said, and Áróra again noticed how mild his voice was. This tone had to be something he used to his advantage when he questioned people. The warmth was reassuring and relaxing.

Áróra sat on a kitchen stool and told the story of how Björn had assaulted Ísafold, and how Áróra had come to Iceland three times to help out, getting her to a doctor or a counsellor, and once staying with her to cook mashed-up meals that her sister could eat despite her wired-up jaw. She told him how, on the fourth occasion, she had refused to run a rescue mission to Iceland, telling her sister to sort out her own problems, or get Björn to help her, as she always went back to him anyway – and she told him how much she regretted this now.

22

Daníel had no memory of having encountered Áróra as a child at any family gathering, and even if he did have some recollection of meeting her, he would hardly have recognised her now. Because Violet had called to let him know that her 'little daughter' was on the way, he had expected to see a very young woman. So he was taken by surprise to open the door to someone who had to be close to thirty. His surprise was also over how stunning she was, a real Icelandic-style beauty. She was powerfully built without being fat, and was almost his height.

During his long police career he had learned that this kind of beauty could be a curse. Young girls who grew up with everyone wanting something from them could either become victims – he had met plenty of those during weekend shifts while he had been in uniform – or else they learned from bitter experience that they needed to bite back, becoming unpleasantly sharp or distant, developing barriers that came across as arrogance.

Áróra looked to be the sharp type. She came across as reserved, and judging by her body language, this was an errand for which she had no enthusiasm. He could understand that. She had been pressured into it by her mother. But by the time she was halfway through a mug of coffee, sitting at his kitchen table, she had relaxed, telling him about her sister and their mother's concerns since she had been out of touch.

'I don't know what's considered a long time to not hear anything, because we're not in touch. But Mum says she usually hears from her every week, and keeps an eye on her on Facebook, but she hasn't heard from her or seen any activity for more than two weeks.'

Daníel looked into her eyes and nodded. He hummed, indicating that he was listening; this had often served him well, encouraging people to open up when being questioned. There was something about a flowing narrative that enabled people to find the words for all kinds of minor details that could be lost if they were asked a series of questions.

'The guy she lives with, Björn, said he thinks she went back to Britain,' Áróra continued. 'But don't you think it's strange that he didn't follow it up – make sure where she'd gone? Of course I can work out for myself what prompted her to leave – either yet another argument, or else he beat her again.'

She fell silent, and Daníel made some mental notes. He would ask for more detail later. He agreed it was strange that Björn had no idea of the whereabouts of the woman he had lived with for three years, and that could indicate that she had fled, and was keeping her whereabouts secret because she was frightened. Where domestic violence was concerned, there was nothing unusual about this kind of story.

'Mum thought that maybe you might be able to help. I'd like to find out more about Björn. He's recently been sentenced for something to do with dope. That's what his brother told me, but he didn't seem keen to discuss it any further,' she said.

Daníel nodded.

'You can check online yourself, to find out what he was sentenced for,' he said. 'The legal archive is open to everyone, and it shouldn't be a problem to find the right case if you know roughly when the court pronounced sentence.'

Áróra nodded, and he breathed a sigh of relief. People frequently expected that he could dig up and pass on information about all kinds of cases under investigation by the police, as if the job came with no duty of confidentiality.

'I'll tell you what I can do,' he said. 'I'll start things rolling by checking if Ísafold has been registered as leaving the country. It would certainly help if you could talk to as many relatives and friends, and maybe neighbours, as possible, to try and work out some kind of timeline, to figure out roughly when she might have been leaving the country, and when she was last seen in Iceland.'

The gratitude was clear on Áróra's face, but Daníel felt a flicker of light at the back of his own eyes, as if he was looking both out and into his own head. He cursed inwardly. He knew that flicker and what it meant, and that he would have no choice but to follow it all the way to its conclusion, regardless of any plans he might have for his time off work. He knew well that this strange flash of light, which only he was aware of, didn't bode well.

23

It was a wrench for Áróra to leave Daníel's flat. There was something about the way he hummed and nodded while he listened that made her want to sit at his kitchen table and spill every secret she had. She felt that she knew him and that he knew her much more intimately than should be possible with such a short acquaintance. His mild voice and the grey eyes that never left her face triggered a warmth inside her that she wanted to sink deep into. It was a warm feeling of contentment that she hadn't known for a long time, and she was almost distraught as Daníel's door closed behind her.

She sat in the car, checked her phone and saw that her mother had called twice while she had been talking to Daníel, so she called her back.

'What does your uncle think?' her mother asked as soon as she picked up the phone.

'It seems he isn't my uncle after all,' Áróra said, and her mother snorted.

'He's an uncle by marriage,' she said, and Áróra decided it wasn't worth an argument, even though she longed to deny any kind of family link with Daníel, as if the pleasant warmth that had developed over the kitchen table would be somehow inappropriate if there were a family connection.

'He says that Ísafold is an independent adult with every right to go where she wants and do as she likes without having to let anyone know.'

'Yes, true. That's right—' her mother began.

Áróra cut her off. 'His guess is that she has decided to leave Björn and is keeping her whereabouts secret because she's frightened of him. He said he's seen this loads of times in the police.'

'Yes, but—'

'And he says that a sudden change in communication patterns is often an indicator that there's something wrong.'

'Communication what?'

'Communication patterns. Meaning that if Ísafold cuts off communication with everyone she knows, such as her own mother, for example, then there's every reason to believe something is very wrong.'

'That's what I've been saying all along!' her mother howled, and Áróra felt a pang of pain at the desperation in her voice. When she finally found Ísafold, there would be nothing pleasant in what she would have to say to her; she would hear in no uncertain terms what she had put their mother through.

'Björn's brother Ebbi said that their relationship has been difficult recently, so it was no surprise that Ísafold had left him,' Áróra said. 'Maybe she's gone away for a break, Spain or somewhere – a place where she has space to think things through.' Áróra heard her mother receive this hypothesis with a reluctant sigh. 'It wouldn't be a surprise if she's on a beach in the sunshine with a drink in one hand, cursing Björn and not even imagining how worried we are about her.'

She said 'we' not only to show she shared her mother's thinking, but also because Ísafold's absence had become a constant irritant, like an unpaid bill or unwashed dishes. And if Ísafold didn't show up sometime soon, it was likely to become a genuine concern – a real fear for Áróra.

'Mum, the next step is that I have to get in touch with everyone in Iceland who knows Ísafold,' she said in measured tones. 'That's relatives and neighbours, to figure out who saw her last and when. Like Daníel said, work out a timeline. He's checking to see if she was registered leaving the country.'

'I'll call her friends here,' her mother said. ' Even if they haven't been in touch, Karen or Abby could have heard from her if she's thinking about coming home.'

Her mother used the word 'home' to refer to Britain, but Áróra knew well that Ísafold was so stubborn, she always meant Iceland when she said 'home'.

24

Daníel had pushed the mower in a circle around the garden a couple of times before he realised that it wasn't picking up grass. The bag was full. He had been caught up in his own thoughts ever since Áróra had left, and now there was freshly cut grass strewn across the lawn. He'd either have to rake it up or else empty the bag and go over the lawn again to pick up the clippings. He took the second option, and the pleasant mutter of the engine was like an accompaniment to his thoughts, as if they needed the stream of bass notes to help them take root in the earth, otherwise they would fly away into the sky and flutter about in his imagination.

There were two aspects of all this that bothered him. To start with, there was Ísafold's disappearance. The family had good reason for concern. It was perfectly true that people could vanish intentionally, in response to an argument with a spouse, or fleeing abuse, and there were teenagers constantly going missing, as he knew well from his years in uniform. But people like Ísafold, with a place to live and a family around them, didn't just vanish – not unless something was very wrong.

He had made all of the usual preliminary calls to A&E, the police station, the women's refuge, the Vogur rehab clinic. Ísafold hadn't been seen at any of these places, and with each call the feeling grew inside him that there was nothing routine going on here, that this was all something strange. This was a feeling he often experienced as he began digging deeper into a case; there would be that little blink of light in his head, the pebble in his shoe, the irritating buzz in his ears that told him he was right to be suspicious. This was an insight that had more than likely always been there but which he had only begun to trust as he got older, and it always preceded something unpleasant.

He emptied the bag, started the mower again and pushed it

once around the garden. It wasn't a large lawn, but making the effort to mow it regularly and make sure it was nourished had resulted in lush green grass that was free of weeds and moss. The people in the upstairs flat had no time for the garden, so it was left to him and Lady Gúgúlú, who lived in the converted garage, but Daníel was the one who spent time looking after it. Lady Gúgúlú had no interest in gardening.

Daníel had built a deck outside his living room, facing south, while the beds packed with lupins closed off the top end of the garden and filtered out most of the sound of traffic on Reykjanesbraut. The remaining noise didn't trouble him. On the eastern side was the garage, while the third side, to the south, was blocked off by a sprawling lava outcrop, leaving the garden sheltered and sunny. Daníel was particularly pleased with how flat the lawn was. There was just one corner up by the rocks that bothered him. That was the patch he couldn't mow. That corner of the garden, with its wispy long grass that waved in the breeze and the expanse of daisies that grinned sarcastically back at him, was a constant irritant.

He couldn't resist one more try. He always tried, even though he knew it was hopeless. He turned around quickly, as fast as the lawn mower would allow, and drove it with all his strength at the unmown patch. The engine was set to full power and as he got closer, he put even more of an effort into it as he approached the long grass, but it wasn't enough. The engine spluttered and died before he had cut so much as one blade of the little triangle's grass.

'You don't stop trying,' said Lady Gúgúlú from where she stood, smoking a cigarette, by the door of the garage conversion. She was halfway through putting on her make-up, her hair held mercilessly back under a headband so that she was ready for her wig. There was a mischievous grin on her face. This was the grin that said she knew better and that Daníel was a fool for even trying. The smirk made Daníel want to run through that lousy patch of weeds even more.

But he knew from bitter experience that it was a waste of time. The petrol mower would always die on him. And the old hand mower would invariably hit a stone that had made an appearance in the grass just at the edge of the patch. The brush cutter would overheat and cut out before its vicious nylon wire had cut so much as one precious blade of grass. Even the kitchen scissors would be as blunt as if they were made of clay. Daníel had tried them all, many times.

'I'm not going to stop trying, because I know elves don't exist.'

'And how can you be sure of that? I don't even know if I exist. What makes you so certain of your own existence that you can doubt that of others?'

'You're quite the philosopher today,' Daníel said. 'Let's just say it's because today's Saturday.'

'You're doing a show?' he asked, pulling the mower back towards himself, away from the unmown patch.

'And how. It's going to be a hell of a show, I can tell you. You're always welcome, darling. Your seat awaits you.'

'Thanks, but I've seen you perform,' Daníel said, and Lady Gúgúlú scowled.

'Honey, that was a year ago. This is a whole new show. This time it's drag and magic, all mixed together. I get sawn in two on stage, and then get inside a box and make myself vanish.'

'Is that so?'

Lady Gúgúlú went back inside, and Daníel thought over her words for a moment. The most likely explanation was that Ísafold had disappeared of her own volition, not least as she had been on the receiving end of the domestic violence her boyfriend handed out. But there was still something about this case that troubled him, the regular flash of light inside his head, the uncomfortable intuition that things weren't right. There was something suspicious about Ísafold's disappearance. At the same time, there was a weird jittery feeling in his belly, as if there was a small, happy animal in there that couldn't contain its excitement.

Then there was the other thing that troubled him: Áróra. Her face was constantly in his mind. His heart beat a little faster every time he thought back to the time she had spent sitting at his kitchen table, and the desperate beast turned somersaults in his belly.

He emptied the contents of the mower's bag into the black compost bin. Then he put the mower away in the shed and took off his boots and trousers there on the decking. It was just as he stepped under the rush of water in the shower that he decided he'd be investigating this case. It didn't matter that he was supposed to be on leave; he needed to find out what had happened to Ísafold. What was less easy to figure out was whether this decision was because of his intuition, the knowledge that something bad had happened to Ísafold, or the fact he longed to meet Áróra again.

25

The masseuse pummelled Áróra's shoulders, releasing the tension that had built up over the last couple of days. She hadn't noticed that her muscles had become so sore – the massage came as part of the body-scrub package the hotel's spa offered, which she had originally booked with Hákon in mind, to make her skin soft and sweet. But now she realised that the massage was exactly what she needed. Her face was pressed into the gap in the bench and when she opened her eyes, she had a view of the floor below. There was nothing like having to lie still for an hour with nothing to look at to clear the mental processes.

Now she was able to look into her own thoughts, which had split into two, as if she had kept them in two separate rooms. In one sat her mother and sister: her mother worn down with worry, while Ísafold was in trouble somewhere. To her surprise, Áróra felt a surge of anger well up inside her. She would release this once she had found Ísafold, because, despite the disquiet that had taken root inside her, common sense told her that Ísafold was probably in someone's spare bedroom, or in a hotel somewhere sunny, licking her wounds after parting from Björn, without having had the sense to let anyone know.

In the other room in her mind was Hákon and the treasure he had buried somewhere. She was always at her best with work ahead of her. She felt a twitch of excitement in her belly at the thought of the chase to come, blended with the dose of chagrin that always came with the start of any job. It came from her need to see that justice was done, ensuring that men like Hákon didn't get away with their misdeeds. Maybe there was some kind of avenging angel inside her.

The masseuse's strong hands kneaded her hips, and Áróra sighed at the combination of pain and relief. The aroma of incense and the relaxing music in the room had an uplifting effect on her, as did the skilled hands that manipulated her body with a warmth and care that she often longed for but rarely allowed herself to enjoy.

Just as the masseuse drew a blanket over her and discreetly retired, and just before Áróra fell asleep on the bench, she decided to look on her trip to Iceland in a new light. She had chosen which thought space she was going to be in. As her drowsiness overwhelmed her, she saw herself walk into the room where Hákon sat and reach out a hand to him, as if she were inviting him to dance. Hákon would be her project: tracing his buried treasure and taking a suitable cut for herself while shaking off the guilt that came from sleeping with him – she hadn't set out to spy on him, after all.

And while she searched for where Hákon had stashed his wealth, she would dig into Ísafold's whereabouts, keeping their mother happy and easing her own conscience.

Of course, the uncertainty of what had become of Ísafold troubled her. It occurred to her that Björn could have gone too far, but she didn't dare pursue that train of thought to its conclusion. She had to take care not to frighten herself. If she let the fear take hold, allowed concerns over Ísafold's safety to pile up and spent too much time searching for her, by the time her sister appeared at their mother's place, coffee brown and dressed like a señorita, astonished at the trouble she had caused, Áróra's fury would be overwhelming.

But that would be nothing compared to the fury Áróra would feel when her sister went dutifully back to Björn, as usual.

26

'Just remember that some men are complete pigs,' Dad says as he teaches me how to defend myself.

Catch hold of a finger and bend it quickly up against the back of the hand until you hear it crack. Power a heel down onto the instep. Bite an ear until you feel your teeth cut through it. Stick fingers into eyes. A knee to the balls. Use all the power you have. Don't hesitate. If you hesitate, you've lost.

All this came good at the festival in the Westman Islands that Ísafold invited me to when I was sixteen. Her mates from Newcastle were flirting with cool guys and singing along on the slopes of the valley that formed a natural amphitheatre around the stage below. After a while I find Ísafold further up the valley, a little way from the path.

She's lying between the tussocks like a sheep flat on its back. She's awake, but so drunk she can't stand up. There's a man kneeling next to her, fumbling with her trousers as he tries to pull them off her.

This is one of the pigs that Dad warned me about, and he comes off badly. I look out for my sister.

The bastard runs off howling, with a hand clapped over one eye, a stream of blood dripping from between his fingers onto the green grass of late summer.

SUNDAY

27

When the woman came to ask about Ísafold, Olga was relieved that Omar had already come back inside after vacuuming the stairs. She had found the key with its wooden tag and its *your week for communal spaces* message hanging on her door handle when she had come back from the bakery. Omar had snatched it from her hands, refusing to even countenance that she might do the vacuuming. She had given in. At least he would burn off some energy vacuuming the stairs and the landings, and she admitted to herself that it was a relief to have someone else do it. Her back was so stiff these days.

The ring on the doorbell had been accompanied by a stab of fear. What if someone had seen him vacuuming the stairs, recognised him from the flyers and online posts the police distributed, showing the faces of illegal immigrants, put two and two together, and called the Directorate of Immigration? What would she do if they had come to fetch him – to take him away from her and send him back to his war-torn homeland of blood and bombs? She practically shoved Omar into his room and shut the door behind him, firmly shushing him a couple of times to make it plain that he should keep quiet, and then she picked up the intercom handset. To her surprise there was a mellow woman's voice on the other end, asking if she could come in and ask a few questions about her sister, Ísafold.

Olga had met Ísafold's sister before, when Áróra had come to collect her after a fight with Björn, but Olga still looked at her, almost mesmerised: she was so like her neighbour. There was no mistaking this was Ísafold's younger sister, but bigger-boned and fairer, and clearly more reserved, shyer than Ísafold. Olga could also make out an accent in her Icelandic.

'Sorry to disturb you,' she said. 'I'm asking around about Ísafold, who lives in the next flat. We haven't heard anything from her for more than two weeks. Have you seen her, or heard where she might be?'

'Isn't she on holiday in Britain?' Olga asked. 'Björn said she was abroad, visiting relatives.'

This had taken the sister by surprise, and she wanted to know exactly when Björn had said this, and precisely how he had worded it. Olga repeated what she had heard Omar repeat Björn saying, but she wasn't going to let Omar get mixed up in this, even though he was more familiar with Ísafold than she was. He often drank tea with her, lecturing her that she ought to find herself a man to marry instead of living in sin with Björn.

'The Middle Ages came calling,' Ísafold had said, giggling as she told Olga what Omar had said, and Olga sighed. Omar was terribly innocent in these matters, and his views were old-fashioned.

There hadn't been much more she had been able to tell the woman, and she was surprised at how concerned she seemed to be.

'Your family hasn't heard anything from her since she left?' Olga had asked, and the woman frowned, saying that their mother hadn't heard from Ísafold since the middle of May.

Olga thought about her Jonni. She knew how children could turn their backs on their mothers, so this didn't necessarily mean much.

As the sister was leaving and Olga was about to close the door on the newly vacuumed stairwell, the woman had turned and asked one more question.

'Do you know where she had been working recently?' she asked. 'Our mother thought she was working in some clothes shop in the Kringlan shopping centre, but Björn said she left that job ages ago.'

This was a surprise to Olga. The family obviously had little idea about Ísafold's life in Iceland.

'She was working as a cleaner at some sheltered housing for

elderly people down in the town,' she replied. 'At least, she was the last I heard.'

She hadn't asked the sister how come she knew so little of Ísafold's circumstances, how come she wasn't aware that Ísafold had left the clothes shop long ago, how come Ísafold hadn't told her mother. Of course, other people's affairs were their business, and it was as well to avoid poking your nose where it wasn't wanted. Olga was grateful that the people living in the block of flats weren't inquisitive about who Omar might be, and why he was living with her.

28

Grímur was about to lock the door of his flat when he was startled by a voice behind him.

'Good morning,' the voice said, and as he turned to face it, he saw its owner was the woman who had rung the bell a couple of days ago: Ísafold's sister.

She was almost her twin, just a younger, larger version. She had to be a head taller than Ísafold and with broader shoulders. She had dark-blonde hair, and eyes that were brown and dreamy. There was a serious look to her, while Ísafold always had some neon tint to her hair, as well as a bunch of rings in each ear and one in her nose. The sister seemed to be more down to earth, tastefully dressed and her hair more carefully styled.

Grímur nodded in reply and tugged at the door handle so the key would turn in the lock. Everything in this block of flats had become a little worn, not least his door, so there was a knack to getting it to open and closed.

'I'm Ísafold's sister. She lives...' the woman said, and hesitated for a second before continuing. 'Or used to live on the second floor, the flat above you.'

'I remember you,' he said, sounding more reserved than necessary. 'That time you came to collect her from my place.'

'That's right. I was wondering if you know her at all?'

Grímur felt his heart beat faster in his chest. Did he know Ísafold? He knew her well. Sometimes he was convinced that he knew her considerably better than her husband had. And he definitely knew her better than this sister of hers did.

'I've seen her on the stairs, and once at a residents' committee meeting. Then there was that time last year, or whenever it was, when you came to collect her. So I know who she is,' he said. 'But that's as far as it goes.'

He wasn't going to let this woman know that Ísafold had often sat at his kitchen table and poured her heart out about Björn, often weeping. This was normally on the mornings after he'd heard the worst noise coming from upstairs.

'Have you seen her recently?' the woman asked.

There was a beseeching tone in her voice, so for a moment Grímur pitied her, and began to understand what Ísafold had meant when she described how infuriatingly meddlesome her sister could be.

'No,' he said. 'It's a while since I last saw her.'

'Do you remember when exactly that was?' the woman asked, and the hint of pity he had felt vanished. She was unpleasantly pushy.

'No,' he said, sounding more abrupt than he intended. He went to the door and opened it, and to make up for his discourteous reply to her question, he held it open for her.

'Thanks,' she muttered, and folded her arms, as if she was expecting to be hit by a blast of cold air the moment she stepped outside. Again he felt a surge of sentiment deep inside, a feeble echo of all the emotions he had felt in Ísafold's presence. And now he wanted to shave, to spend a long time under the hot water to shave off every single hair. Sometimes that was the only thing that would allow him to relax, the feeling of soft skin, free of those narrow threads of disgusting dead protein that sucked all the energy from his body.

'Don't mention it,' he muttered in reply, holding the outer door for her as well.

As soon as they were outside, he walked away. He headed for the shops on the other side of the street without turning to look back at her, even though her body language clearly told him that she wanted to keep talking, to ask him more questions.

But he had no time to stand there and chat about Ísafold. There was always the chance he'd inadvertently let something slip, use a word or a gesture that would let something out, and that would jeopardise the new plan. That absolutely couldn't be allowed to happen. Not now that he had seen through the restaurant window that Björn was working on hooking himself a new woman.

29

It was getting on for three in the afternoon, and Áróra had managed to talk to the woman who lived next to Ísafold in the block of flats in Kópavogur, and had seen another of the neighbours, the bald, weird one. He didn't seem to have known Ísafold particularly well, but at least Áróra had got out of him where she had been working, and that was progress. She should be able to find out from her workplace whether Ísafold had resigned or if she had gone on holiday. She thought of knocking on Björn's door as well, but she had no new questions to ask him, and he would hardly be likely to offer any new answers.

At half past three Áróra was on her way to meet a cousin who had stayed in touch with Ísafold, but with half an hour spare, she decided to park by the shopping centre in Hafnarfjörður and take a stroll around the town. A breeze ruffled the bright-blue sea out by the docks, but close to the shore the water was perfectly still and almost transparent, the boulders that formed the sea wall mirrored in its surface. Past the end of the breakwaters the long Reykjanes peninsula could be seen, stretching out, the conical Mount Keilir jutting up through the mist like an Egyptian pyramid.

Áróra walked along the shore all the way to the small-boat harbour, where fishermen were working on their boats, and on two of the pontoons there were children dangling hooks on lines. She smiled to herself. This would have been just the kind of thing her parents would have argued about. For her father, the freedom children had to do as they pleased would have been a wonderful thing, while her mother would have pointed out that it was incredibly dangerous for children to be playing by the sea unsupervised. Áróra stopped for a moment at the end of the pontoon and watched two boys haul in their line. As a fish appeared on the hook, their cries of delight carried over the quiet harbour. 'Cod!' one of them called out in triumph, lifting a hand for the other to slap in congratulation. Their pride in this achievement was clear, even from a distance. This was something that children in Iceland could experience, the independence and pride that came from doing things for themselves without having to rely on adults for help.

As Áróra thought about it, she realised this was how she had taken the decision to dig into Hákon's affairs. She had thrown caution and doubt aside, and made a start. She had allowed instinct to lead her, without taking into account what anyone else might think. Maybe her nature was more Icelandic than she had imagined.

She walked back into the town and strolled along a shopping street to the coffee shop where her cousin Ellý had suggested they meet. They arrived at the door at the same moment, one from each direction. A smile spread across Ellý's flushed face as she pushed a pram ahead of her.

'Lovely to see you,' she whispered, taking care not to wake the baby in the pram as they hugged.

Áróra peered under the hood to see a tiny head in a crocheted cap peeking from under the duvet.

'We can park him here,' Ellý said, placing the pram by the coffee shop's window and putting on the brake.

Áróra hesitated. This was one of those Icelandic habits that she found hard to deal with.

'You're going to leave him out here? On his own?'

'He's fast asleep,' Ellý said. 'He has his dad's lungs, so there's no chance I won't hear him when he wakes up.'

She picked up her handbag from the basket under the pram and went up the coffee shop's steps.

'We can go for a walk until he wakes up,' Áróra suggested, and Ellý shook her head.

'I'm going to go crazy if I don't get coffee,' she said, pushing open the door. 'I didn't leave the house yesterday, or this morning. So a little time for me is overdue.'

Áróra followed her to the counter, but couldn't stop herself from constantly glancing at the child in his pram outside.

'He's fine,' Ellý said with a laugh as she patted Áróra's shoulder. 'People round here have plenty of children already, so nobody needs more.'

30

When Grímur returned home with his Sunday pastries and opened the main door, he was unpleasantly surprised by a woman almost walking into him as she left the building. It was Björn's new girlfriend. He sucked in his belly and pressed his back against the wall to allow her to squeeze past, sensing the aroma of herbal shampoo and wet hair. The smell called to him, triggering a longing in his heart, and a pain he hadn't experienced since he had first got to know Ísafold. It was a scent of innocence, of spring, of new beginnings. At the same time he longed to yell at the woman, to tell her to save herself, to never again come near this building, to avoid the apartment block like the plague.

His eyes followed her as she strode across the car park, heading for the bus stop opposite. The fact that she was leaving Björn's place at this time on a Sunday meant that she had spent the night there, and as Grímur approached the door of his own flat, he could feel a pressure growing inside his chest. Their relationship developing so rapidly added to the urgency. There was no time to waste to organise everything. He would have to work fast.

He dropped the shopping bag on the kitchen table. He had bought a couple of doughnuts and two pieces of an oat cake known as a 'marital bliss'. Ísafold was fond of it, so he had started buying it some months ago in case she stopped by. More than once she had giggled through the tears that streamed from her black eyes over the irony that her favourite should be called 'marital bliss'. He recalled the turmoil within him that had swelled into a mixture of anger and love, and a desire to liberate her. He longed to set her free from Björn, as well as from herself, from her adoration of a man who didn't deserve her – no more than he deserved this new woman.

This kind of thing had been a burden to him as a young man.

He recalled how the girls had flocked around the idiots at college, the self-obsessed bad boys, convinced they were God's gift, but who treated the girls like dirt. The girls had wanted nothing to do with boys like him, guys who treated them with respect, who never knocked them about or bullied them into doing things in bed, the boys who listened to them when they talked, and asked about their dreams and their feelings, the ones who knew how to truly appreciate them.

Grímur would usually brew a pot of coffee and drink it with the pastry from the bakery, but now a sour frustration, mixed with the pain of love, troubled him so much that he was unable to relax. He needed to shave, even though he had done it before going to the bakery. He undressed and felt an immediate relief as he stepped into the shower. The flow of water always calmed him down, although not as much as the razor did. He soaped his face and felt the burn, his skin still tender from that morning's shave, but running a finger over his eyebrows told him that there was a trace of stubble there.

Eyebrows were the worst; worse than facial hair. It never seemed possible to shave them perfectly, and there was always a hair that was missed and irritated him. He slid the razor over his forehead, back and forth, with the growth of the hair and against, and even though it hurt, it left him calmer.

31

They found themselves seats by the window, so with nothing but the glass between them and the pram, Áróra felt a little more relaxed about Ellý leaving the baby outside.

'I'm so happy to get out of the house,' Ellý said. 'I don't have much reason to go anywhere so I spend far too much time hanging around at home. Anyway, it's great to see you. How long has it been? You haven't come to family reunions or anything since you were a kid. At least, I don't remember, it's been that long.'

She interrupted the flood of chatter to sip her coffee. Ellý clearly had a need to talk to someone other than the baby.

'I don't remember either,' Áróra said, truthfully. It had been a long time since she had been to Iceland for any other purpose than to get her sister out of trouble, and much longer since she had been in touch with relatives here. 'I'm just here to try and track Ísafold down,' she said, then immediately realised how that sounded and hurried to correct herself. 'But it's lovely to see you too. It's been far too long.'

'What mess has Ísafold got herself into?' Ellý asked, lowering her voice. It wasn't quite a whisper, but low enough for sharing a secret.

'I thought *you* might be able to tell *me*,' Áróra said. 'Mum asked me to come over because she hasn't heard from her for more than two weeks. She's so worried, she's freaking out.'

Ellý nodded. 'Yeah, she called me too, asking if I knew anything, and then Daníel called. You remember Daníel? The cop who used to be married to our aunt Didda? We all had crushes on him when we were girls. He took us for a ride on a police bike when I was confirmed, remember? Anyway, he's a detective now, and he called and asked when was the last time I saw Ísafold—'

'And when did you last see her?' Áróra interrupted.

The flow of chatter stopped and Ellý frowned.

'Didn't you hear about that?' she asked, with surprise that was nothing compared to Áróra's.

'Didn't I hear about what?' she replied, and Ellý stared for a moment, shifted in her seat and leaned forward with her elbows on the table.

'I haven't seen Ísafold for ages – a long time before Christmas, anyway. She used to come around all the time when I was due to go into labour. I was having such a hard time with the pelvic girdle pain that I couldn't go anywhere, so I was really grateful to see someone other than my mum, and my boyfriend works all day long. We live at Mum's place, you see. And then the thing with the pills came up, and since then I haven't seen her. I didn't want to say anything about it to Daníel, what with him being in the police, and didn't want to get Ísafold into trouble or anything—'

Áróra raised a hand. 'Hold on, you'll have to rewind the tape. I've no idea what you're talking about. What pills?'

'Well, yeah...' Ellý said slowly. 'So you mean you really haven't heard about this?'

32

Áróra managed to connect her phone to the hire car's hands-free system so she could talk to her mum, taking care to drive on the right at the same time. The conversation with Ellý had left her exhausted, and she couldn't wait to throw herself on the pristine-white hotel bed and nap for a while. It seemed that her thoughts needed to take a rest after hearing the story of Ísafold's life in Iceland. What was clear was that it was very different to how Áróra had imagined it.

'Did you know about this thing with the pills, with Ellý and her mother?' Áróra asked as soon as her mother answered the phone.

'What thing with the pills?'

'That Ísafold had stolen painkillers from Dagný, Ellý's mother – and that she'd then picked up Dagný's prescriptions from the chemist?'

'Yes ... I sort of heard something, but...' her mother said faintly.

'But, what? Why didn't you tell me? I'm running around the city talking to people, and you decide to keep this quiet?'

Her tone was furiously accusatory, but Áróra was angry – and this was so like her mother.

'Well, you know what Dagný's like,' she said. 'You can't quite be sure what's true and what isn't. Ísafold told me that they had been making accusations against her, but she wasn't taking any painkillers, so I reckoned it had to be some kind of a misunderstanding.'

'There was no misunderstanding,' Áróra snapped. 'Dagný has a problem with her hip, so she needs those painkillers. When she went to fetch her prescription she was told it had already been collected. When she asked to see who had signed for it, it turned out it was Ísafold.'

'Isn't there a chance that Dagný asked Ísafold to collect her prescription and then forgot about it? You know she can be a bit—'

'Mum, no,' Áróra said. 'When Dagný called Ísafold to ask for an explanation, she slammed the phone down on her. Then she blocked the whole family on Facebook, and none of them have heard a word from her since.'

'Your dad's family tend to be over-dramatic...'

Áróra withstood the temptation to put the phone down on her mother herself, but she was livid. Her mother had obviously been aware of the situation with the painkillers, but had chosen to keep it to herself and had woven a web of explanations and excuses for Ísafold's behaviour – as she always did.

'I believe them, Mum,' she said slowly and clearly. 'And you should have told me about this.'

She ended the call, hoping that she had been suitably courteous, while also making her dissatisfaction plain. Tomorrow she would call her mother again and make it clear that she had to tell her everything she knew about Ísafold's life in Iceland, without keeping anything back.

33

Omar wolfed down the egg sandwiches Olga had made to have before the rice pudding, and complained yet again about them not being able to keep chickens on the balcony. However many times she explained why they couldn't, he continued to describe how they could close the balcony off with some netting, and then have four hens, or even six. They would pay for themselves in no time – an egg a day from each hen.

'There are rules for blocks of flats,' Olga said yet again. 'No animals allowed.'

'But the guy on the third floor has a dog,' he persisted. 'So why can't we have chickens?'

'Because of the noise, Omar. Hens cluck all the time, and there'd be the smell.'

'But once the neighbours start getting eggs from us, they'd be happy and would forget the noise and the smell.'

She looked at him fondly and smiled, and he looked up and smiled back at her. Sometimes she felt that she was looking into a strange world behind his eyes. His ideas about how they could improve their lives seemed so odd here in Kópavogur, yet were undoubtedly perfectly normal where he had come from. Of course, if she lived in a detached house with enough space, then it would have been a great idea to have a few hens, and she would agree without a qualm. It would give him something to keep him busy while she was at work, and it would help with the food bills.

He stood up and washed his plate. She had also told him many times that he could just stack crockery in the dishwasher, but he seemed to forget every time.

'When did you last see Ísafold from the flat opposite?' she asked.

Standing by the sink, Omar seemed to freeze. He appeared to

be thinking things over. One hand rested on the edge of the sink and the other held the brush. The water continued to flow, and for a long moment the only sound in the kitchen was its patter in the battered metal sink.

'Where is Ísafold?' he asked, without turning around.

'I don't know,' Olga said. 'She seems to have disappeared, and her sister is searching for her.'

'They have taken her. The soldiers,' Omar said in a low voice. 'They take women and keep them chained up so they can rape them.'

Olga was startled. Occasionally he would say strange things that had to be rooted in his memories of war, but normally they only came to him as he lay between sleep and wakefulness, when he cried during the night. Never in bright daylight like this.

Olga stood up and went over to him, laying a hand on his shoulder.

He reacted with such suddenness, she was taken by surprise. He stood in the middle of the kitchen, howling and swinging the brush about him like a sword.

'What?' he shouted over the sound of the water running into the sink. 'What about Ísafold? Why? It's bad. She isn't here. Why do you ask me?'

Olga reached for the tap and turned off the water. Then held out her hands to calm him, struggling to make out from his disjointed rush of words what he was asking for, as he continued to speak in twisted English scattered with Icelandic.

'Shh. Shhh, Omar,' she said in the tone she used to reassure him when he cried in the night. Her voice soothing, she stepped closer to him. 'There. Shh. Shh. It's all right, Omar. Calm down.'

He stopped waving the brush around, and his hands fell to his sides. Drained of energy, he fell silent, and Olga could see from the tension in his face and his eyes that flashed around the kitchen, as if he was watching some invisible battle taking place, that he was still confused and anxious, and becoming angry.

'There, there,' she said, and finally he seemed to return to con-sciousness.

His eyes looked into hers, and she could see a deep well of sorrow in them. These eyes must have seen so much – she could barely imagine what. She could feel her own deep sympathy welling up inside her.

He turned and walked out of the kitchen, and a moment later she heard his door shut behind him. She breathed more easily and collapsed onto a chair. This was the first time she had seen him experience a panic attack when fully awake, and this was the first time that she had been afraid of him.

34

It wasn't far from the coffee shop to Daníel's place on the far side of the brook that flowed through Hafnarfjörður. She had to pass on to him what Ellý had told her. Ísafold stealing drugs from relatives had to be important.

There was no reply when she rang the doorbell, but Áróra could hear the sound of music coming from the garden, so she decided that he had to be outside, making the most of the weather while it lasted, as the local expression put it. As she turned the corner into the garden, she was met by a wall of smoke, billowing from the barbecue on the decking behind Daníel's flat.

'Hello, there,' he called, standing with tongs in his hands and dressed in shorts and a T-shirt.

'Making the most of the weather?' she said with a smile. He laughed and turned a slab of meat on the barbecue.

'There's every reason to,' he said. 'Dinner's early here. Normally people start the barbecue too late in the day, when it's already getting cool. Isn't this what a summer holiday is all about? Meals when you feel like it and sleep whenever you want?'

'Absolutely,' Áróra agreed, taking a seat in one of the garden chairs. The decking was sheltered from the breeze, and she had to admit that it was pretty warm, so she took off her jacket and felt the sun on her bare arms. 'I wanted to tell you something I heard about Ísafold,' she said, accepting the beer he handed her. 'From our cousin Ellý, who I know you've also been in touch with.'

'After dinner,' he said, heaping lamb onto a dish and placing it on the table. 'You will stay, won't you? There's plenty of meat, and we can split the potato between us.'

He disappeared through the glass doors to the flat and re-appeared a moment later with plates, cutlery and a tub of coleslaw, of the kind that Áróra remembered so well from her childhood.

He took a seat opposite her, sliced the potato in two, and as he put half of it on her plate, Áróra realised how hungry she was.

'Be my guest,' he said with a dazzling smile, indicating the mountain of meat.

'Thank you,' Áróra said, taking a slice and thinking to herself that this was a meal of which her father would have approved. 'Troll girls need protein,' he would have said. Daníel put two slices of meat on his plate, cut a piece and put it in his mouth.

'Nice,' he said, heaping a generous helping of coleslaw next to the meat.

Áróra had a sudden feeling of wellbeing. She took a deep breath and sat back in her chair, allowing her back to relax, and then leaned over the table and began to cut into the meat. An aroma of new-mown grass blended with the smell of the food, while the warm sun and Daníel's muscular leg touching hers beneath the table sent a ripple of contentment through her. It was a relief to relax.

'There are just more and more questions I want to ask my sister,' she said.

After dinner, Daníel pointed her to the computer in the living room, and while she went through the register of court judgements, he washed up. She found the Reykjanes District, checked the most recent judgements, and it didn't take long to find what she was looking for: 'The defendant is found guilty of possession and distribution of prescription drugs.'

She clicked on the link and the court documents opened in front of her: *The State vs Björn Hannesson.*

According to the documents, Björn had been given a seven-month suspended sentence for having in his possession two hundred painkillers for which he had no prescription, and his explanation that these were for his own use was not treated as credible. This had to be linked to Ísafold stealing her aunt Dagný's painkiller prescription. If Björn were an addict and needed such a huge amount, then she could well believe that Ísafold would go to great lengths to get them for him. She seemed to be able to accept virtually anything from Björn. This was another piece in the puzzle that would give Áróra a picture of Ísafold's life in Iceland, although it provided no clue as to her whereabouts. Neither did it explain why Björn had told the neighbours that Ísafold had gone on holiday to England but told her that she had walked out on him.

35

Grímur stood naked in front of the bathroom mirror and shivered. His skin was red and raw after shaving for the third time that day, so he had to gently dab himself dry with a towel, and avoid rubbing anywhere. His legs and arms were better, as if they were more resilient than his face, chest and genitals. He set the hair dryer to the hottest setting but one and used it to blow air on to his back and trunk to get rid of the worst of the chill. Once his skin was dry, he began applying ointment, the razor at hand just in case he encountered any stray stubble, some tiny and disgusting stub of hair curling out of his skin as if it were trying to fish for bacteria to draw into his body. It was a feeling rather than any kind of certainty. Grímur knew perfectly well that this obsessive shaving was doing him no good, and he was well aware that the doctor was telling the truth when he had explained that the skin would be much more susceptible to infection when shaved so frequently. But there was no way to explain to anyone the disgust that overcame him at the thought of hair, when he considered what each hair really was – an elongated thread of proteins composed of dead cells that made their way out through a tiny opening in the skin that was full of sweat and fat.

The ointment stung, and his skin felt so delicate that he pulled on a pair of tracksuit bottoms that were padded inside, and a soft, loose T-shirt that hardly brushed against his body. Then he sat at the computer and looked up Björn's new woman on Facebook. She was called Kristín and she was easily found, as she had clicked the Like button on literally anything Björn had posted, whether it was something to do with football, lousy videos of people falling over or pictures of his dinner. She clearly thought Björn was the hottest ticket in town. Another innocent who had fallen for him, he thought; another innocent ready for slaughter.

He saved her profile picture to his computer, printed it out on good-quality paper and inspected it. The woman was a beauty; if anything, more beautiful than Ísafold. Her face was prettier, with a brighter expression. She was clearly younger and plumper. Ísafold had become all skin and bone. He opened the living-room cabinet and began removing the pictures of Ísafold that were clustered on the inside of the right-hand door, moving them carefully, one at a time, over to the left. As soon as Ísafold had been moved, the new woman's picture would take its place at the top of the right-hand door. It was a big door, so there would be space for many pictures of her.

36

Ísafold's right eye has sunk into the swelling. She's in the flat belonging to the neighbour on the floor below, sitting at the kitchen table, and has clearly been there for a long time, judging by the pile of tear-soaked tissues piled up in front of her.

The neighbour is a strange person. He's pale and bald, which makes him look expressionless. He's literally trembling with anxiety. Ísafold is too engrossed in her own misery to realise that the man can hardly wait to push her and her problems out of his door.

A blue bruise is blossoming on Ísafold's left cheekbone. It's dark blue at the centre, encircled by a purple ring, and the shades of colour are reminiscent of oil on water.

However, the bruise on her arm is black, building into a swelling, with the skin so tight that it looks about to split. It looks as if there's a build-up of blood beneath the skin that's waiting to erupt.

'Your arm could be broken,' I say, and she shakes her head, says she absolutely doesn't need to go to A&E. She says she doesn't need anything other than a chance to sleep in peace. I suggest a hotel, as a way of getting the neighbour off the hook, and Ísafold agrees.

On the way to the hotel I call in at the women's refuge so she can get some advice.

Ísafold is too exhausted to protest, but reacts badly to the counsellor's common sense, explaining that it's her own fault. She provoked Björn. She called the black eye and the black and blue bruises upon herself.

MONDAY

37

Áróra took her time, scrubbing her legs with a flannel before soaping them and taking care to shave them without missing anything. She sat on the tiles of the shower floor surrounded by cosmetics and felt a flutter of anticipation in her belly at the thought of the evening to come. She was looking forward to it but did wonder if it was really a good idea, because a date with Hákon wasn't just a date, but also an opportunity to slip a USB drive into his computer.

The USB stick was loaded with software that would give her access to his data, which would allow her to keep track of whatever he did with the computer. The software had been bought from a hacker and had cost almost as much as a car, but it had paid for itself many times over.

She dried herself off after showering and stood at the mirror as she blow-dried her hair, wondering how she would feel after the date with Hákon. She was inclined to think that she should feel devious or treacherous, sleeping with him because she also wanted to get a look at his computer. Would she feel like a prostitute, having a motive for jumping into bed with him other than for the pleasure of it?

Hair dried, she applied oil so it gleamed, trimmed her pubic hair short and rubbed coconut cream all over herself. Her skin looked smooth and taut in the mirror as she looked her muscular physique up and down with approval. Why shouldn't she make use of her looks? Men frequently used the power they had over women, so why shouldn't a woman do the same? In the bedroom she put on underwear and sat on the bed to paint her toenails dark red. It wasn't long since her last pedicure, so that would do. But her hands were another matter. She searched online for a nail bar that didn't require a booking. The one she found cost a fortune, but she reckoned she could afford it. It was in a small shopping centre in Hafnarfjörður. Everything seemed to be in Hafnarfjörður these days, she mused, and her thoughts went to the kitchen table in her uncle Daníel's comfortable flat. Not that he was her uncle.

38

Olga watched as Omar whisked four eggs with salt and pepper, added a generous handful of oatmeal, and whisked some more.

'There's a trick to it,' he said. 'Don't add it to the pan until the oil is properly hot. That way the omelette will be firm and good.'

This had become their weekday morning routine. He cooked eggs in every possible way: scrambled, boiled or he would soak stale bread in egg and fry it in the pan with cinnamon. She had lost weight since he moved in and started cooking every morning, as a solid breakfast meant that by the time lunch came around, she wasn't particularly hungry and was happy with a light snack.

So much had changed since he had come to her, not least that her outlook on so much had changed. The hard, plastic, brown-and-orange kitchen fittings had been an irritant for years, and she had long hoped to replace them with something more modern as soon as she could afford it. Now she no longer cared, as Omar had declared that the kitchen was absolutely fine, and cleaned it assiduously and fixed the cupboard doors, which had a habit of coming loose. Then there was the gratitude. He was so grateful for everything that she had begun to mentally count up all kinds of insignificant items that she was grateful for, and found that this had made her happier in herself.

He split the omelette onto plates and handed one to her, but before he started eating, he looked at her with a thoughtful expression on his face.

'What is it?' she asked through a mouthful of omelette.

'I found a site on the internet where you can get a fake identification number,' he said.

She put down her fork. 'My darling Omar...' she began, but he interrupted.

'I won't use it for anything dangerous. Just so I can go to the gym,' he said. 'I've been collecting cans and bottles, enough for a month's membership, and when I exchange them for the cash then all I'll need is an ID number and a little extra cash so I can go and train at the gym on the other side of the roundabout.'

The look of entreaty in his eyes was so strong that she didn't have the heart to refuse outright, although she knew that every time he went out in public the danger that he would be caught increased. His face appeared regularly in the media, as the police were looking for him. Admittedly, the picture was an old, blurry one, and these days Omar's hair was cut shorter than it had been when the faded passport photo had been taken, but all it would need was one watchful employee at the recycling centre or the gym, and everything would be wrecked. That was on top of the neighbours, who had to be aware of him when his bursts of energy led him to clean the stairs or the area around the block, but Olga hoped they would continue to turn a blind eye.

'An ID number is made up of different factors...'

'I know, I know,' he said. 'My date of birth and four other numbers. But this website fixes those four numbers so they look real, and no computer system will see anything out of order. It was a foreigner who made the website, for people like me.'

'I'll call someone at the movement and check it out,' she said.

Omar smiled with satisfaction and forked up his omelette. It would certainly be good for him to have something to keep him occupied other than cleaning and washing – regular exercise that would burn off some energy. She didn't want to call the No Deportation Movement lawyer, as that would tell him Omar was still with her. The system NDM used was to move those on the wanted list, waiting to be deported, from one place to another, so that as few people as possible knew who was where. That made things more secure.

She knew as well that she would let him have the extra five thousand krónur he would need for a gym membership card. It was so hard for her to refuse him anything.

39

The sheltered-housing centre's lobby was through a yard that opened onto Lindargata and that was clearly used by the elderly residents as a place to enjoy some fresh air. The yellow-painted building provided shelter from three directions, and the yard faced south so the benches and tubs of flowers were bathed in sunshine. Out of the cool breeze, the summer sun was hot on Áróra's back as she strode towards the door, so she took off her jacket and carried it folded over one arm.

It took a while to find the office responsible for social domestic assistance, which Áróra understood from Ísafold's neighbour was where she had been working. The manager was a heavily built woman with a flood of grey-shot curls. She stood up and extended a hand when Áróra knocked at her door.

She shook the woman's hand and introduced herself. 'My name's Áróra. I'm looking for information about someone who works here – Ísafold Jónsdóttir.'

The woman looked at her in silence for a moment, and Áróra had the feeling she was being measured up, as if the woman was figuring out whether her question merited a reply. Áróra perched on the edge of the chair facing the woman and wondered why people had such large desks now that computer screens were so slim.

'Ísafold Jónsdóttir no longer works here,' the woman said, her lips pursed, as if she meant to lock her mouth shut so as not to let anything slip out unintentionally.

'Can you tell me where she is?' Áróra asked, making an effort to sound amiable, not that this made any difference to the woman's obvious suspicion.

'Are you a lawyer?' she asked, squinting at her.

'No,' Áróra said hurriedly. 'I'm her sister. Our mother sent me to look for her as we haven't heard from her for more than two weeks. We don't live in Iceland.'

The woman's expression softened and she leaned back in her chair.

'I see,' she said. 'It's like that is it?'

'That's right,' Áróra said. 'We're trying to work out when she was last seen. I'm curious to know if she took a holiday or if she resigned.'

'Well...' The woman seemed taken by surprise, and squinted, as if the glasses perched halfway up her nose weren't powerful enough to be able to make out Áróra properly. 'Neither,' she said at last. 'She was given notice at the beginning of May and left immediately. This was all done legally, with the required written warnings issued first, so you won't get very far if you're thinking of getting the union involved.'

Áróra held up her hands and shook her head. 'No, nothing like that. As I told you, Ísafold seems to have disappeared.'

'Disappeared?'

'Yes.'

'You mean she's gone away somewhere, or that she's vanished completely?'

Áróra wasn't sure if the woman was slow on the uptake, or if she simply hadn't been listening to what she had said. What was obvious was that the question about Ísafold had taken her unawares.

'She has disappeared completely,' Áróra said. 'My family is becoming seriously concerned.'

'I see,' the woman said, and Áróra waited for her to continue, but she remained silent.

'Can you tell me the reason she was given her notice—?' she asked, and had hardly finished her sentence before the woman interrupted her sharply.

'No,' she said shortly. 'But it was done entirely legally.'

Áróra stood up, and thanked the woman for her help, which

elicited a dry response. The woman turned her attention to her computer screen. Her movements seemed theatrical, as if she was on stage, playing an office girl, and needed to convey what she was doing all the way to the back of the auditorium.

Áróra walked out of the office and across the lobby. Just as the automatic doors swung open, she glanced back to see the woman squinting as she watched her.

40

Áróra had decided against the acrylic nails, opting instead for acrylic nail varnish, which she knew from experience would be more resilient than the usual stuff and would last well into the summer. The chemical smell in the nail bar had given her something of a headache, and she put on sunglasses as soon as she stepped outside the nail bar and into the shopping centre. She was wondering whether to call Daníel, when she realised he was standing in front of her.

'In the police we're always suspicious of people who wear sunglasses indoors,' he said, and Áróra laughed.

'With good reason,' she said, accepting his kiss on the cheek, as she did so touching his upper arm in something that was somewhere halfway between a handshake and a hug. But she held on too long and saw his eyes flicker over her body. Maybe it was unintentional, or some sort of response to her move, which hadn't been supposed to be any kind of a move, and which had happened inadvertently ... or maybe it hadn't. His arm was muscled and she could feel the heat from his skin through the thin shirt. She wouldn't have minded keeping her hand there a little longer.

'I was just thinking about you,' she said with a smile that he returned with a wink.

'Is that so?'

Áróra couldn't help laughing. There was something flirtatious about his tone, and he raised an eyebrow in mock invitation. She was relieved that he was making a joke out of the mild dalliance that had developed between them. She hadn't meant to touch him so firmly or for so long.

'I went to the sheltered-housing centre on Lindargata, where Ísafold seems to have worked, and they said she had left.'

'Hmm,' Daníel said, without opening his mouth.

'I was wondering if you could go there and find out the real reason Ísafold doesn't work there any more,' she said. 'The woman who runs it won't tell me, but I reckon she would be more co-operative if you wave a warrant card in her face. I'm sure there's something weird going on there.'

Daníel smiled again. This time it was an amiable smile, with real warmth, not the intense smile that went with a teasing tone of voice.

'I'll do that,' he said, his tone gentle. 'If you'll have dinner with me tonight.'

'I already have plans for tonight,' she said quickly, relieved that she could be truthful, as her date with Hákon was coming up.

'Tomorrow, then,' Daníel said, and she smiled as she tried to come up with some suitable excuse, but nothing came to mind.

'Sure,' she said. 'Tomorrow.'

She felt herself flush, as if she had suddenly become a teenager, trying her best to read relationship subtexts without understanding exactly what was going on. Was he trying it on with her? Or was he just being a decent older gentleman, who was friendly to his young niece from abroad. Or rather, his not-quite niece.

Áróra didn't calm down enough to inspect her newly painted nails until she was in the car. They were a dark pink, but lighter than her toenails, and the finish was immaculate. She was ready for the evening's date with Hákon, although for some reason she now felt like calling it off.

41

'How often do you usually hear from Ísafold?' Daníel asked, taking care to use the gentle, mild tone that he always fell back on when interviewing relatives.

'At least once or twice a week,' said Violet – Áróra and Ísafold's mother. He could hear the desperation deep in her voice, even though she was clearly doing her best to sound calm.

'You mean by phone?' Daníel asked.

'Yes,' she replied. 'But she puts something on Facebook every day. Well, normally. Now she hasn't posted anything for almost three weeks.'

'I see,' he said patiently, the phone in his left hand, leaving his right free to tap at the keyboard in front of him to find Ísafold's profile. Violet had given him her Facebook login so he could check Ísafold's posts, all of which were visible only to friends.

As she had said, there were no posts for the second half of May and into June. Ísafold hadn't even shared the offers and discounts from boutiques she usually liked to post, nor had she liked any cute videos of children feeding themselves or trying to walk, which seemed to be material that usually attracted Ísafold's attention.

He painstakingly noted down the phone numbers of all the relatives and friends Violet imagined Ísafold could possibly have been in touch with, and ended the call by encouraging her to stay calm and telling her that at the moment there was no reason to be anything other than optimistic. Violet seemed to snatch at this straw of positivity, relieved to hear this from a police officer with many years of experience behind him, as if that tipped the scales of hope in the right direction.

There were two schools of thought among the police when it came to this kind of case; the one he preferred was that it was best to encourage people to be hopeful and stay calm, because relatives who were in shock tended to be practically useless as a source of information. They became overcome with nerves, homing in on all kinds of irrelevant details and placing huge significance on things there was no need to be concerned about. On the other hand, there were some among his colleagues who felt it was best to prepare people for the worst. According to that theory, he should now be telling Violet there was a possibility that something terrible might have happened to Ísafold.

As soon as the conversation with Violet was over, he sat down and systematically went through Ísafold's Facebook posts, going back two years and noting down the names of people in the pictures. Most of them were of her and Björn – having a meal somewhere, or at some nightspot, each holding a glass and surrounded by smiling faces. There were a few pictures of them outside together, sitting on some green grass, and a couple looked to have been taken out in the countryside among spooky lava formations and birch scrub. He guessed these had been taken around the lake at Mývatn.

Áróra could be seen in some of the picture collections from two years before. She looked either to be visiting Iceland – with Christmas lights in the background and a glass of seasonal grog in front of her – or else Ísafold and Björn could be seen visiting her in Edinburgh.

He switched to Áróra's profile, and for a moment he lost himself admiring images of her. She seemed unable to look anything but attractive in any picture. She looked beautiful in every one, in a stately way, as generally she was at least half a head taller than most of the women pictured with her, and often taller than the men as well.

Those dark, enticing eyes seemed to draw the camera's attention, and her heavy lips invited kisses. He imagined holding her in his arms. It had to feel very different from the impression of fragility he had when embracing the delicate bodies of some women. Áróra's frame was robust, strong enough for the most powerful arms, or his weight on top of her.

He coughed, irritated at the direction his thoughts had taken, and stood up. He had allowed himself to be sidetracked into looking at photographs of Áróra instead of continuing as he had intended, building up a picture of Ísafold's life over the last few years.

He opened the glass doors out to the patio and slipped off his socks. As he stepped onto the lawn, he enjoyed the cool feeling of his toes in the thick, soft grass. He walked back and forth a few times. The grass was dark green in the evening light and resembled a covering of felt. Only the untamed patch by the rocks stopped the garden from being perfect.

Daníel walked over to the converted garage and peered in through the window. Lady Gúgúlú was hunched over the sewing machine, concentrating on the glittering, sequinned material she was running through it. He tapped lightly at the window and waved as she looked up.

'Isn't it time for you to come outside for a smoke, my good woman,' Daníel asked when she appeared in the doorway, and saw that she was ahead of him and already had a cigarette packet in her hand.

'It gives me the shivers when someone refers to me as a good woman,' Lady Gúgúlú said as she took out a cigarette and lit up. 'There's something very old about being a good woman.'

'Apologies. No offence intended.'

'*Madame* sounds better. There's a bit of Parisian glamour to being a madame. A good Icelandic woman suggests someone in curlers and the apron she got at a Women's Institute raffle somewhere in the countryside. And she'd be somewhere around seventy.'

'I'll bear that in mind, madame,' Daníel said with a stiff bow, and Lady Gúgúlú inspected him thoughtfully.

'But you can just call me Lady. Considering we're on first-name terms.'

Daníel bowed a second time and mined doffing an imaginary hat.

'Anyway, what are you after?' she asked, blowing out a couple of smoke rings.

'Not sure exactly,' Daníel said. 'Just wanted to see you.'

'Are you lonely?'

'Yes. I think so. It's weird not having anyone to share a coffee break with. That's the only thing I miss now that I'm on holiday, the coffee breaks.'

42

Áróra put on a short black dress, decided to take a chance on bare legs, then put on high-heeled sandals and added a coat. In the hotel's lobby she turned back and fetched a scarf from her room. She would need it when the sun began to set and the evening became cool.

There were food smells everywhere in the city centre. The first diners were taking their places at restaurant tables, and Áróra identified the aromas as she breathed them in: langoustine soup, grilled lamb, fried fish. She picked up snatches of various languages as she walked along the street; a large proportion of those out and about were clearly tourists, in their bright windproofs and comfortable walking boots, looking around as they took in their surroundings.

She had always found Reykjavík ugly, a municipal planning disaster with concrete cubes dropped in among the low-slung timber houses that seemed to shrink as more blocks were built around them. But she had to admit that the surroundings were beautiful. Mount Esja across the bay was always somewhere in the background, changing colour depending on the weather and the cloud cover, so it always looked fresh and never failed to draw the eye.

She took a deep breath and stepped inside the restaurant where they had arranged to meet. It was a trendy place inside a large, old wooden building with two floors. There were people at every table and there was a buzz of conversation that blended with the low murmur of jazz she recognised from her childhood – *Gling-Gló* by Guðmundur Ingólfsson's trio and Björk. This had been one of her father's favourite albums. The waiter took her coat and showed her to the table, where Hákon got to his feet, hugged her and kissed both cheeks.

Now she couldn't understand why she had been so nervous

earlier and had wanted to call off her date with Hákon. How had she forgotten this beautiful smile and toned physique? She'd been in some kind of emotional confusion over the cop-not-uncle she would be going out with tomorrow night. Hákon was good-looking and pleasant, and she would enjoy talking to him and getting him to talk about himself. She was curious to know what account he would give of himself, and how he had managed to get back on his feet in business. It would be worth hearing his side of the story. It would also be interesting to hear how he explained such a rapid turnaround, and to find out how this would tally with the information she would extract from his computer later on. As Áróra considered all this, her hand strayed instinctively to her bag, which contained the flash drive in a little pocket at the front.

43

I'm spooning baby food into Ísafold, feeding her with a teaspoon. The wires that hold her jaw together don't allow her to open her mouth.

Björn is abroad somewhere, and I've come to Iceland to look after her. I keep on asking what happened. Fell against a radiator, she says from between her clenched teeth. I'm so clumsy.

I go to a shop that sells household stuff and buy a blender so I can whizz up fresh vegetables for her. I cook porridge with an egg in it so she gets some protein. I find endless smoothie recipes online. I even get a counsellor from the women's refuge to come round and talk to her.

Ísafold gets angry and refuses to speak to the counsellor, snaps at me not to be so hysterical, tells me Björn's right – that I'm constantly interfering in stuff that's none of my business.

She fell against a radiator. Clumsy cow.

I take my duvet from the sofa and roll it up, and pack my stuff in my case. I stack the cupboard full of jars of baby food – and leave.

I'm more than a little tired of looking after my big sister.

TUESDAY

44

Olga handed Omar the five-thousand krónur note, and his smile of delight brought more warmth to the living room than the morning sun coming through the window. Unusually, he had slept longer than she had, and by the time he appeared, in a singlet and shorts, she had showered and was ready to go to work.

'I will repay this,' he said. 'When I can work, I will repay this.'

Olga shook her head, but he continued.

'When I get to Canada I'll find work and will send you money; or if my appeal is accepted maybe I can work in Iceland.'

He often spoke like this, switching from Canada to Iceland and back, and it was as well that he had a plan B to fall back on if his application for asylum in Iceland was finally refused. Then he could concentrate on Canada. She had seen through her work with the movement how people who had seen Iceland as their destination could break down when they were deported.

'It's fine, Omar,' she said. 'Don't worry about it. Go and get yourself this fake ID number, and then you can get yourself a gym membership. That'll give you something to do. It'll be better than hanging around indoors all day.'

'You called the people and they said it was OK? The people in the movement that helps foreigners? That it's all right to use a fake ID for the gym?'

'Yes,' she lied.

She hadn't called NDM's contact person. She had thought it over from every angle since he had raised the subject the day before, and decided that this was a question of assessing each set of risks. Her conclusion was that it was less of a danger for Omar to register at the gym with a fake ID number than for her to call the movement and let them know that he was still staying with her. That could lead to one of the organisers asking awkward questions and interfering. From there it wouldn't be long before someone would come and take Omar away from her, arguing that it was important for him to be moved around, to go to another household. There had been so much uncertainty in his life that putting him back into that routine wouldn't help him – going back to being shuttled from one family to another every two weeks so the police couldn't track him down and deport him.

Omar wrapped his long brown arms around her.

'Thank you, my mother,' he said in Icelandic.

Her heart skipped a beat, as it always did when he called her 'mother'. She still hadn't found a way to come to terms with no longer being one. Maybe this was the main reason she didn't want anyone to know that Omar was still with her. She wanted to hold on to him, to keep him for herself.

45

Áróra woke next to Hákon with guilt gnawing at her, as if her body had dosed her thoughts with an anguish that made her want to sob. Ísafold was lost somewhere. She could be alone, terrified and in pain. And what was her sister doing – the stronger sister who had promised their father that she would look after her? She was in bed with a stranger, focused on the man's money. That was the truth of the matter.

Lying against Hákon's back, their urges satiated, the smell of him was suddenly strange, even uncomfortable. She slipped from the bed and stretched for her clothes. Her knickers and the skimpy black dress now seemed inadequate clothing, and she felt goose pimples appear on her bare legs as she tiptoed to the desk.

The chair creaked as she sat down, and she froze, sitting completely still and listening for any sign that Hákon had been disturbed by the sound. There was silence for a moment, and then he drew a deep breath and exhaled. This was a long breath, in through his nose, and smartly exhaled through the mouth. It wasn't exactly a snore, but there was a faint rumble deep in his nose with every breath he took. Áróra counted three breaths before she plugged the flash drive into his laptop, and then opened it so that the screen lit up. It instantly demanded a password. Hell. She felt a combination of disappointment and relief. She couldn't do much without a password. So she could use this as an excuse. It couldn't be done, was completely impossible; and that meant she could turn her back on Hákon and his affairs, and concentrate on Ísafold. After all, that was what had brought her to Iceland.

A discreet ping from the computer stopped her just as she was about to extract the flash drive; a dialogue box asking for an email address. So her spy software worked even though the computer was locked behind a password. This investment continued to take her by surprise. She had often used it to access computers, but never for a computer that was locked.

Hákon muttered and shifted in the bed. His face was now turned towards her as she sat in front of his computer, and she held her breath as she waited. There was dead silence in the room, and Áróra could feel her own heartbeat becoming faster as she waited for a signal that Hákon was still sleeping. What would she say if she turned and found him lying there, watching her messing around with his computer? How would she explain that?

She turned her head slowly, taking care not to move her hips, so that the chair would not creak again, and looked over her shoulder. Hákon lay with his eyes closed, and she felt a rush of relief as he took a deep breath and exhaled with a loud snore. Áróra wrote *CU later* on the pad that lay next to the computer and drew a heart under it. She was relieved not to have to look him in the face, not only because she was deceiving him by planting spy software on his computer, but also because thoughts of Ísafold filled her mind, and waking up next to a guy she hardly knew seemed to be so wrong in every way.

She typed her email address in the dialogue box and clicked the start button before taking the flash drive from the computer.

46

Construction work in the city centre prevented Daníel from taking what would have been the straightforward route to the sheltered-housing centre on Lindargata, so he parked further down and walked back along the street. The cranes that stretched skyward between the houses, and loomed over the building like a half-empty promise of something that could be, sparked an inner discomfort. Considering all the hotels that were being built, it seemed clear that a single business model was being milked to death – yet again, and he felt not a little relief that he was no longer a uniformed officer, now that another financial crash was looking likely.

Daníel had the feeling that the large woman in the office of the sheltered-housing centre was the type you'd prefer to have on your side in a tight spot. He saw how she stiffened when he mentioned Ísafold's name, but her face relaxed when he showed her his identification and explained that he was a police officer. He was careful not to mention that he was looking into Ísafold's disappearance, as he had no formal warrant to be doing so now that he was on holiday, although it was certainly true that he was a detective and was helping the family track her down.

His search through Facebook the day before had yielded little information, other than the fact that Ísafold's posts had recently become more infrequent, with noticeably fewer pictures of her with Björn. He wasn't able to see Björn's profile using Violet's access, so he had clearly blocked her. Now his intention was to get to grips with Ísafold's situation, gather the basic information and then take Áróra with him to the station to make a formal statement concerning her sister's disappearance.

'Ísafold Jónsdóttir was given notice in April and left immediately. Notice was legal and all the requisite written warnings had been given first,' the woman said, lifting her chin high so that her head of curls shook.

'Ísafold Jónsdóttir has now vanished without trace,' Daníel said in a low voice, and leaned forward on the woman's desk to look her in the eye, a tactic that always made it harder for people to turn away. When they couldn't look elsewhere, it was harder for them to avoid the truth. The woman sighed and leaned forward herself, towards him.

'We should have gone to the police with this,' she said, 'but we have a duty of care to the people here. My opinion was that it was a bad idea to make the matter public because that would give others like her ideas about how they could operate.'

'People like her? Why was Ísafold sacked?'

'Stealing drugs,' the woman said. 'There are vulnerable individuals living here, and we have to be sure that those who have keys to the apartments are worthy of our trust.'

'So Ísafold was caught stealing drugs from elderly people here?'

'That's right. She worked here as a cleaner, and to tell the truth, she was well liked. She did her job well, was always cheerful and pleasant company for the residents. Then there were complaints that medicines were disappearing. Painkillers. And that rang a few alarm bells.'

Daníel nodded and smiled encouragingly.

'You said she was cheerful and pleasant,' he said. 'Did she come across as likely to be a drug user? Was she punctual?'

'Regular as clockwork,' the woman said. 'So it took me by surprise. Huge surprise. But when we worked out the amounts of painkillers that had disappeared from the apartments she cleaned, it was much more than could have been for personal use. What she stole in a month would have been enough to kill an elephant. Lots of elephants. Most of the elderly people are prescribed painkillers, and many of them also take OxyContin or Contalgin as well, to help them cope with any additional pain, from worn-out joints or serious arthritis.'

'And you're certain that she was the one who was responsible for these thefts?'

'No doubt about it. Absolutely none. She was the only member of staff who went into the apartments where the residents were missing drugs, and CCTV picked her up entering apartments she shouldn't have been cleaning on those days. She did it at lunchtimes, when residents are downstairs in the canteen.'

Daníel stood up and extended a hand in gratitude for the information she had given him.

'We decided to handle the matter as we would any instance of theft,' she said. 'We wanted to avoid it getting out and turning into a media frenzy.'

47

It was past midday when Björn's new girlfriend shut the door behind her and walked across the parking lot to a little grey car. Grímur had watched them come home the previous evening, giggling and happy, Björn with his arm wrapped around her waist, and then he had seen Björn again this morning. Ever since then he had been sitting in the kitchen chair he had placed by the bedroom window, overlooking the outside door and the car park, so that he would see her leave. A couple of times he had quickly gone to the kitchen to make himself some coffee, and then hurried back. He hadn't even given in to the temptation to shave himself, even though the urge to do so had twice been almost overwhelming. He read the news on his phone while he waited, but it turned out to be such a long wait that he had got as far as the gossip columns about people he completely failed to recognise by the time the woman finally appeared. He watched as she got into the car. She fastened her seat belt before starting the engine, and then leaned forward to look in the rear-view mirror and put on lip salve or lipstick, he couldn't tell which. Then she drove out of the parking lot, and he saw her disappear into the swirl of traffic on the roundabout by the DIY place.

He immediately got to his feet, fetched washing up gloves from the kitchen and pulled them on, then put on a hoodie, and put the hood up so that it hung over his forehead. There was no need for this, as there were no CCTV cameras in the building, but somehow he felt it afforded him a little protection and made him slightly less vulnerable. Out in the stairwell he looked around and listened. He heard no movement, so he hurried up the stairs, remarkably nimbly, as if the tension inside gave him an extra dose of energy.

He slipped the key into the lock, and for a moment it refused to turn. It occurred to him that Björn had changed the locks, but with a little massage and rocking it to and fro, the lock clicked open and he was inside.

Ísafold had given him the key. 'Just in case,' she had said. 'In case you hear he's about to finish me off.'

But since then there had been no reason to use it. After that it had been quiet up there – remarkably quiet. But now it was as well that he had a key.

He peered into the hall cupboard, which stood open, and saw only coats that belonged to Björn. He clearly liked to look good, as there were at least three leather jackets hung on the rail, a couple of blazers, a wool coat and one of those silver down anoraks that were advertised on the sides of bus shelters and cost a month's wages. There were no women's coats, and the new girlfriend had come wearing the same coat she had left in.

There was nothing to be seen in the kitchen, so he went to the bathroom. He was surprised to see that everything was new. He hadn't been aware of any builders at work, and the last time he had been upstairs for a coffee with Ísafold, the bathroom had been shabby and old – the linoleum on the floor had come adrift in places and the damp had caused the paint to peel from the walls. Now there were grey tiles on the floor and the walls, and the bathtub had been built into the end of the room, with a rim broad enough to sit on to chat with whoever was in the tub. He sat on the edge and imagined himself looking down at Ísafold in a bubble bath, each of them holding a glass of white wine, the hot steam fragrant, and a breast showing through the foam. Her legs were in his lap and he soaped them with care, applying soft gel and lifting a brand new razor. He quickly got to his feet. He wasn't here to lose himself in daydreams.

In the bathroom cupboards every shelf but one was full of men's cosmetics. That one other was half bare, just a pink toothbrush, a couple of hair bands, a small make-up compact and a perfume spray. He sniffed the perfume cautiously. His thoughts instantly flew southward, as the scent reminded him of tree bark, dry sand, fruits he didn't know the names of and colourful flowers.

In the bedroom the bed was unmade, a stack of Elena Ferrante novels filled one of the two bedside tables, and the hooks on the back of the door were hung with clothes. One held female clothing. He buried his face in the folds and breathed deeply, getting a lungful of the same southern aromas, plus smells of her body and washing powder. The chest of drawers at the end of the bed was empty, apart from a couple of pairs of skimpy lace knickers and a bra in the top drawer. The cups were a B, and as Ísafold was a D-cup, they had to belong to the new woman. He slid open the door of the big wardrobe and saw Björn's clothes on both sides. There was plenty of space around them, as if he had spread them out to make full use of the wardrobe, expanding to fill the gap left where Ísafold's things had been.

Grímur had seen all he needed to. Björn had obviously removed any trace of Ísafold, and the cosmetic stuff in the bathroom, and the books and clothes in the bedroom, showed that the new woman had started to leave things here. She would be moving in before long. He would have to work even faster than he had thought.

48

'I'm meeting an old uncle for dinner,' Áróra said to Hákon, phone to her ear as she waited outside the hotel for Daníel. She had used part of the day to go through background information about Hákon and his companies, and how he had ended up in prison. She hadn't got as far as looking through the contents of his computer via her spyware, simply because she was too nervous about the evening ahead. Hákon wanted to see her again. He'd asked if she wanted to meet for a drink, hesitated and then asked if she thought he was being too pushy.

She laughed. 'Not at all,' she said. 'I'll call you later if I feel like a drink.'

She didn't hear his reply, as at that moment a motorbike pulled up on the hotel's forecourt. She'd switched off her phone and dropped it in her pocket before she realised that Daníel was the bike's rider. He dismounted, and handed her a helmet.

'Hang on. Weren't we going out to dinner?' she asked in surprise. She had expected a restaurant somewhere close by.

'A mystery tour,' he said. 'But don't worry. We're not going far.'

Áróra held back for a moment. She was wearing open sandals and a thin jacket, but fortunately she had put on jeans instead of a skirt or a dress. Reluctantly, she took the helmet.

'I'm not sure if I'm brave enough for this,' she said.

He smiled. 'I drive carefully,' he said, getting back on the bike, closed his visor and patted the seat behind him.

Áróra stood still for a moment, wondering whether to decline, hand back the helmet and walk away. But she knew she would be furious with herself, and, anyway, there was a flutter of excitement in her stomach. She hadn't sat on a motorcycle since she was a child.

A few moments later they were hurtling along Sæbraut as she

tightly held on to him, feeling dizzy at seeing the tourists walking along by the sea, the cars they overtook and Mount Esja in the distance. She closed her eyes, and as she could hear little through the helmet's thick padding, her senses of sight and hearing took a back seat and others became more sensitive. Her skin sensed the closeness of Daníel's strong, leather-clad body pressed against hers, so close that there was a stream of heat between them that she felt took on colours of its own, a glowing, deep pink-red ... and it was as if her sense of time had been paused, because she was startled when the bike came to a standstill.

She was unsteady on her feet as she dismounted and pulled off the helmet.

Daníel laughed. 'Were you frightened?'

She shook her head as she looked around, trying to work out where they were. They seemed to be out of the city now, in a small valley surrounded by steep hills with a lake at the bottom. Some distance away she could see the red roofs of the old Vífilsstaðir TB hospital, so this had to be Vífilsstaðir lake.

'No,' she said. 'That was fun.'

It wasn't what she had wanted to say, the words not strong enough, but she couldn't explain to him just how fantastic this short bike ride had been, how thrilling and how indecently exciting.

'Be my guest,' he said, pointing to a thicket above the road. 'Dinner is served.'

He strode through the undergrowth, and she followed him into a small clearing surrounded by birches, where he spread out a blanket and placed a bag on it.

'Aha,' she said. 'A picnic?'

He sat on the blanket, opened the bag, and she sat beside him. He plucked out cans of mixed malt and orange, and smoked lamb sandwiches wrapped in foil.

'You're going the full traditional?'

'Sure,' he laughed and handed her a sandwich.

They sat and ate in silence. The trees provided shelter, and the sun was still high in the sky. Below them the lake shone like a mirror, the landscape reflected in its surface, and Áróra felt her heart swell inside her, as if it was demanding more space to grow, to hold on to this evening, the sun's brightness and the land around them.

'Another two or three weeks and the slopes here will be completely blue with lupins,' Daníel said.

49

Ísafold agrees with everything that her brother-in-law Ebbi and I tell her, the three of us sitting around Ebbi's kitchen table, with candlelight and a bag of doughnuts.

She's finally ready to leave Björn. She can see for herself that it's not working out. She knows there's a danger that he's going to do her permanent harm. She knows there's a vicious circle that she needs to break out of.

I book flights to Edinburgh for both of us the next day, and a train ticket for her home to our mother in Newcastle. Ebbi goes to Björn's place to fetch her passport and some clothes.

Later that evening her mother-in-law arrives and makes a plea on Björn's behalf. She talks about how distraught he is. She tells her how much he regrets being heavy-handed with her, how much he craves her forgiveness. She finishes by telling Ísafold that she'll have to take care not to provoke him like that.

In the morning when I wake up, Ebbi's sitting at the kitchen table, shaking his head in despair. Ísafold has gone back home to Björn.

WEDNESDAY

50

Daniel pulled up the weeds along the wall of the house by hand, even though a trowel or a scraper would have been useful. But he didn't want to risk the sound of metal against stone waking the neighbours, so he made do with putting on a pair of gardening gloves and relying on his strength to yank out the dandelions and the blades of grass that had taken root where the tarmac of the drive met the building. It was a job that needed to be done, however ridiculous it might seem to be out here weeding in the middle of the bright night. But he couldn't sleep.

He was too annoyed with himself for having kissed her. What the hell had he been thinking? The poor girl was in a state of confusion, they hardly knew each other, and he was much, much too old for her.

All the same, something strange had happened between them. He had told her about his work and his children, and she had told the story of her father and described how she felt like a pendulum, swinging between well-ordered Britain and the wild west, out here in Iceland. Those had been her words, and he had laughed, found her clever, but then she turned serious and said that she often felt that she was somewhere in the middle of the Atlantic, in limbo between two nationalities. That was when he had felt an overwhelming need to pull her close, and as they kissed, the sparks flew between them. He could have told her there and then that he loved her, but the moment was over almost immediately, because she backed away, saying she wasn't looking for love.

Now he was furious with himself, but with no way to let off steam, he felt he might burst with rage. He was unsure how to make good what he had done. Call her and apologise? Or would that be inappropriate? To begin with, she had returned his kiss, placed a hand on his cheek, pressed those delightful lips to his. So was this as much up to her as to him, making no apology necessary?

He reached the corner of the building and the weeds were now gone. His fingers were sore, and he could feel the sweat on his torso, even though his ears had gone numb with cold. He stood up and stretched his back. He took off the gloves and went around the house to the garden. The shed was open, so he dropped the gloves on a shelf, shut the door and slid the bolt into place. As he turned around, he noticed a large dandelion growing from a crevice in the rock. It was in his line of sight, so he wondered how he had missed it. He reached out a hand to pull it up when he heard Lady Gúgúlú's voice behind him.

'You don't really need to pull up every single flower, do you?'

Lady stood in the garage doorway, wearing just a pair of nylon tights. They reached up to her middle, where a pack of cigarettes and a lighter were tucked into the waistband.

'It's a dandelion,' Daníel said. 'I don't want it spreading seeds over the lawn.'

'Imagine how beautiful the lawn would be – green with yellow spots.'

'Weeds aren't pretty,' Daníel said, and Lady shook her head in disgust.

'That's the trouble with you straight types,' she said. 'With your rigid definitions of beauty.'

Daníel shrugged. He would rather avoid a long conversation about a single dandelion right now, and didn't want to allow himself to be accused of destroying nature's beauty. It was too late at night for that. He would try again later. He could spray it with weedkiller sometime when Lady wasn't watching, or even just come outside with the vacuum cleaner and hoover up the seeds once the dandelion had become a puffball. Surely Lady wouldn't object to that.

Now he was going for a shower, then coffee while he waited for the border-control office to open so he could enquire about Ísafold's possible movements. Once he had an answer, he would have a reason to call Áróra, and that would give him a chance to slip an apology into the conversation – something to casually defuse the drama around his ill-conceived move on her. And it would be an opportunity to act as if nothing was amiss – to act as if it didn't matter to him that she had turned him down.

51

Áróra slept fitfully, with dreams that went around in circles, from which she woke with her heart pounding. The circle of dreams began on a motorcycle, an exciting joy alive inside her, and her belly tight against his back, then there were kisses – and in her dreams they went further than they actually had; and then she was back on the motorcycle heading back to the city, the proximity of their bodies now awkward and the speed giving her motion sickness.

Now, standing under the shower and trying to come properly to her senses, it was difficult to separate the dream from reality.

'My emotional side is out of balance,' she had said as she drew away from him. 'While all this with Ísafold is going on I'm not ready for anything romantic.'

'It's the age gap, isn't it?' he asked, his voice low, despondent. She denied that his age had anything to do with it, which was absolutely true, but while her sister was unaccounted for she couldn't bring herself to think about men. That wasn't strictly true, but she decided it wouldn't do to mention Hákon or try to come up with explanations. The closeness between them had evaporated the moment things turned awkward. All the same, she picked up the cans and foil wrappers, and put them in the bag, while he folded the blanket and stowed it away under the bike's seat.

Áróra was hot as she stepped out of the shower, so she patted herself dry and wrapped herself in just a towel. She switched on her computer and took a deep breath before clicking the email link from the spyware that gave her access to Hákon's computer.

It took her a moment to register how fast the spyware worked, and that the screen now in front of her was no longer hers, but Hákon's, her mouse and keyboard operating it remotely. She started by opening a couple of documents with 'hotel' in the file name, but these turned out to be mostly drawings and some kind of construction schedule, so she closed these down one at a time and turned to his online apps.

His email password was clearly stored in the computer, so she opened his email app and scrolled through endless messages concerning plastering, paint colours and purchases of light fittings. It was obvious that the hotels' design and decoration were close to Hákon's heart. From his browser history she saw he had been mainly looking at news, restaurant reviews, and that he had searched for her name. She smiled and felt a warm glow inside that blended with a touch of guilt over spying on him. The browser history also showed that he had visited a Swiss bank's website. She followed the link, but the login page demanded a username and password that apparently were not stored in the computer.

Hell.

To get hold of his passwords she would have to watch him actually type them in, and even that wouldn't necessarily be enough. The best thing would be a video of his fingers on the keyboard. Áróra pondered the options without reaching a conclusion.

She was about to stand up and get dressed when her phone buzzed. She could see it was her mother on the line and picked it up. But before Áróra said a word, she could hear her crying.

'I'm so frightened,' she sobbed, instantly dragging Áróra back to reality – the family reality, the painful reality.

'The more time that passes without hearing from her, the more I'm scared that something terrible has happened to Ísafold.'

52

The understanding expression that Grímur knew so well from the numerous twists and turns of the system was there on the social worker's face. As the man had already been sitting there in the office when Grímur came in, he assumed that the look on his face was a standard-issue expression, used by those who doled out municipal cash.

Grímur sat in the chair facing him across the desk and gazed out of the window at his side, while the social worker peered at the computer screen in front of him. The view from the window took in the Kópavogur church, where a funeral was clearly in progress, the flag at half-mast and a hearse at the door. The curved arches of the building looked more imposing than usual, as a damp grey mist hugged the ground, smothering both colours and shapes so that the reality outside looked washed out, like a pale watercolour. With any luck, it would clear up and the mist would lift, as it was always pleasant to see a little brightness as a funeral came to an end, when the flag was raised again and the soul had flown away to heaven, overjoyed at being freed from Earth's gravity.

'You're disabled due to mental-health problems, aren't you?' the social worker mumbled, peering closer at the screen.

'Yes,' Grímur said. 'That's right.'

'And how's your health now?'

'I'm pretty well balanced right now.'

'And the future?' the social worker asked. 'How do you see the future? Do you have any intention of making use of your aptitude for study to finish the physics course? You were the student with the highest marks at college, and excellent marks at university. You even won a prize for outstanding achievement.'

Grímur smiled patiently. It was obvious that his file stated that he hadn't been far off completing his studies, as every social worker he spoke to touched on this.

'No, I don't think so,' he replied, hoping that a note of regret could be heard in his voice. 'The pressure would be too much. My mother said I read too much at college, and that's what screwed me up.'

The social worker nodded, understanding but disappointed.

'It says here that you run a car?'

The social worker looked up again, eyes enquiring over a pair of reading glasses. Grímur stifled a sigh that he longed to let out with a deep groan. This was an annual event, the meeting with the social worker to renew his request for assistance from the municipality in addition to his disability benefit.

'I have a car, but it's an old banger that's not worth anything,' Grímur explained slowly. 'I hardly use it, except for fetching groceries or if there's heavy snow in the winter. I normally take the bus.'

He couldn't afford to answer too many questions about the car. He had to keep it, as he would need it for his plan.

'Well, I suppose the insurance costs something,' the social worker said thoughtfully.

'Naturally. But the main burden is child maintenance,' Grímur said, sending the conversation in a new direction.

'I see.' The social worker clicked the mouse a few times and squinted at the screen. 'You're paying maintenance for three children?'

'Yes. I have three children.'

'I see. And I assume you contribute to other related expenses – dentistry fees, clothes, hobbies and suchlike?'

'Yes,' Grímur said. 'As much as I can. I'm not able to do that much, being disabled.'

He carefully didn't mention that the mother of his children had declined to accept any money from him, other than the legally required maintenance. The harder the social worker thought his burden was the better.

'That's our largest cohort,' the social worker said. 'Low-income dads paying maintenance.'

Every social worker had the same message, as if it was mandatory for them to inform any prospective recipient of financial assistance that they were just one of a great many in the same position. Maybe it was supposed to be encouraging, but it got on Grímur's nerves. He exhaled slowly through his nose as he tried not to show anything. It wasn't a good idea to show too much emotion, to appear ungrateful or truculent, not when you were relying on the mercy of others.

'You're in social housing, aren't you? A three-room apartment it says here.'

The mouse clicked a couple of times as the social worker filled in the online form.

'Yes, that's right.'

Grímur had no intention of informing the social worker that this three-room apartment was in fact much larger than he needed. Although he had three children, they never came to him, and a small studio flat would have been quite enough. It was none of the social worker's business that he had been banned from seeing his children.

53

The lad behind the counter at the computer shop was friendly and helped her link a small webcam to her laptop and install software so she could record and then scroll through the recordings like a YouTube video on her phone. She told the boy that she wanted to install the camera in a bird box in the garden so she could keep an eye on the fledglings in the nest. This was the smallest camera available in the shop, but it was still awkwardly large. It wouldn't be easily hidden in Hákon's room.

All of the staff in the shop were boys, and it was obvious that she was getting the best service. An older woman stood and waited for far too long while the lad fussed over Áróra, and the others were too busy gawping at her to be of much use. All but the smallest one. He glared at her with the angry contempt that she only ever experienced from short men. There seemed to be something about her height and muscular physique that triggered such a reaction.

Usually she preferred not to take advantage of the effect she had on men, and would maintain a cold attitude to discourage them from focusing their attention on her, giving her priority or being over-friendly. But this time she needed the help, as the software that came with the camera was unpleasantly complicated, and she doubted that she would have found her way through it unassisted.

The camera recorded through a tiny lens. The field of view was similar to that of a door peephole, distorted, but the images were in high resolution. The software allowed her to zoom in to examine a small area of the image, so if she did manage to hide the camera somewhere in Hákon's room, she would be able to enlarge the part of the recording that showed his hands and the keyboard, and she could slow down the replay. That would give her the passwords to the Swiss bank account, and then she would really be making progress in the right direction.

She walked outside into the cold wind that was blowing along Suðurlandsbraut. Her skin tingled almost painfully, and she felt the hairs on her neck rising in her shaggy forebears' instinctive response to the cold. She could well understand why cats seemed to double in size in the cold, becoming balls of fur. Right now she would happily have snuggled into a warm fur coat as she ran from the computer shop over to her hire car. She couldn't understand how people managed to live here in the winter, if this was what the summers were like.

She turned the heater up full blast as she sat in the car and kneaded the chill out of her hands. The dashboard showed it was ten degrees outside. But the chill could have had something to do with her emotional state. It could have been her nerves making her shiver, as both the encounter with Daníel, the heat of his body on the motorcycle still vivid in her thoughts and setting her belly fluttering, and the pain of listening to her mother's tears that morning had thrown her off balance. Now she could only fear that her mother was right, and that something bad had happened to Ísafold – something genuinely bad.

54

Olga took the stairs rather than the lift up to her flat on the second floor, as Omar had suggested. 'A little at a time makes a difference,' he always said. 'Older people need to strengthen their legs.' But she hadn't become aware of any more strength in her legs, even though she had been using the stairs for a few weeks. She felt a pain in her shins with every step and her joints hurt. It wasn't just her hips and her knees, but also her ankle and toe joints that were increasingly painful, especially in her right foot. She had read somewhere that the reason was that she had worn narrow-toed shoes too much, but Omar said it was because she walked with her feet splayed outwards.

She paused on the landing and inspected the worn steps, wondering when the residents' association would have enough money to pay for the stairwell to be freshened up. It could do with a coat of paint and maybe new carpets. But so many of the residents were short of money, the demands for contributions stacked up and the residents' association didn't have the heart to push it as far as getting lawyers involved.

She sighed as she put down her bag in the hall and hung up her coat. She couldn't hear Omar, so he had to be either in his room or else at the gym. He had trained twice yesterday. In the morning he had lifted weights and later in the day he had used one of the running machines, as he had told her proudly, and she could only share his delight in spite of her concerns. For a moment it had occurred to her that she ought to try going to the gym with him. Next year she would be in the same position as him, with her days free and nothing to do. Although she was looking forward to retirement, she knew it could present problems. But she brushed aside any ideas about going to the gym right away, knowing that if she were to mention her thoughts to Omar, he wouldn't leave her in peace until he had dragged her to the gym and made her do all kinds of weird new things. It was tough enough for her to follow his advice and take the stairs. She wasn't going to start hammering away at those machines as well. That would make her joints so much worse.

There was hot coffee in the flask, as there always was when she came home from work, and a couple of biscuits in a bowl on the table. Omar was so good to her, much better than her own son had ever been. In some ways it was as if the fates had sent Omar to her, to make up for Jonni, who had lain transverse across the birth canal, starting his short life by giving her a dose of unbearable pain, and after that had always been somehow fighting against his own existence. Omar was the sticking plaster on her soul, the ointment that soothed her pain, which until recently she had assumed would never fade.

She opened her address book and found the number for NDM's lawyer, who she always called without giving her own name when she enquired about Omar's case. She waited a while for the phone to be answered, and then it was as if the lawyer snatched the phone from his secretary's hand as soon as she answered.

'Just as well you called,' he said, sounding downhearted. 'The appeal was rejected.'

Olga's feeling wasn't of disappointment, as she knew that if Omar were allowed a residence permit, he would be free to go where he chose and to do what he wanted, and would be unlikely to go on living with an old woman like her. She might have been more disappointed if he had been granted residence, as that would signal the end of their time together. But she felt a shiver of dread as the thought crossed her mind that it would be her job to give Omar the news.

'What reasons were given for rejecting the appeal?' she asked.

She would have to tell him why this had happened, give him the reasons again and again why he could not stay in Iceland. She would have to explain to him the rules she did not understand herself. She'd have to use the soothing tone of voice and be ready with a hot-water bottle and a blanket to wrap around him as he huddled shivering on the sofa, as he had the last time his application had been refused.

'That's the thing,' the lawyer said. 'The Directorate of Immigration's investigation turned up another man with the same name and date of birth, registered in a refugee camp in Turkey. Omar Farki, Syrian national. He was found murdered in Istanbul last year. Stabbed, according to the police report.'

'What? That's strange,' Olga said, failing to register what this could mean. 'Couldn't it be a coincidence there's another man with the same name? After all, it's a big world.'

'No,' the lawyer said. 'Omar...' he said, but hesitated '...or whatever his name really is, had the murdered man's papers and used them to travel to Iceland.'

'Oh. I see,' Olga said. She had no idea what else to say. It was all so strange. Omar must have found the documents and decided to use them, considering the other man was already dead. Or maybe his name really might be Omar, and not something else, as the lawyer was implying.

'I know the movement has its own methods, so I'm not asking your name, but I imagine you have been providing him with shelter, considering you're calling to check on his affairs,' the lawyer said, and continued without waiting for her to confirm his suspicion. 'But he isn't the person he claims to be. At any rate, his name isn't Omar Farki, and it's likely he's not from Syria. In fact nothing is known about who he is or where he's from.'

The lawyer fell silent, and Olga heard him draw a long breath before he continued, his voice low.

'I know from experience that the majority of individuals seeking asylum here are good, respectable people who are looking for a better life, so it may sound strange coming from me, but let's say there's a bad apple in every barrel.' He dropped his voice even lower, almost to a whisper. 'So if this so-called Omar is still with you, then take care.'

55

Áróra scanned the hotel room. Hers was smaller than Hákon's, but the design and the fittings were much the same. Her eyes searched for a suitable nook in which she could hide a tiny camera, but the furnishings didn't offer options for many hiding places. There was a bed, two bright-yellow armchairs with a little glass-topped table between them, a TV table that extended at one end into a kind of writing table that was just large enough for a laptop, and next to that was a stool, which was not much more than a cushion mounted on a spring. This had to be one of those back-friendly chairs that were supposed to keep your spine supple by never allowing it to relax.

Hákon's room had a proper desk and an office chair instead of the spring-mounted cushion, but the TV was the same, as were the fitted wardrobes with their mirrored doors. Each room also had its own painting hung over the bed.

Áróra stood on the bed and reached up to slide a finger along the top of the picture frame, but her fingertip found nothing but a thick layer of dust. She felt under the edge of the frame and decided that placing a camera there would be impossible as it was fixed to the wall. Of course, she remembered her father when she was small, fixing the pictures to the walls of their old flat on Grettisgata, a precaution in case an earthquake shook them down. She stepped off the bed, dusted off her fingers and looked around. She shut the wardrobe, and that left nowhere to look but the short passageway leading to the bathroom. There she found just the aircon control panel, a light switch and a folding suitcase stand that she hadn't needed as she had travelled with only hand baggage. All the lights were recessed, so there were no lights or lamps that could hide a camera. Or were there? The ceiling in Hákon's room was fairly low, so could there be a light fitting that she could fix a small camera inside? She closed her eyes and tried to remember what she had seen as she had lain in Hákon's bed, but decided that what she was seeing in her mind was more wish than reality. She seemed to recall that there were two lights – one over the bed and the other overlooking the desk.

Her phone pinged as a message arrived and when she opened it, she saw it was from Hákon.

What are you up to? the message read.

Working, she replied. *A job I need to finish.*

This was the usual version of the truth that she gave him, that she was an accountant working for a small accountancy firm in England, completing tax declarations and annual reports for individuals and small companies.

At work as well, Hákon's reply read. *Dinner tomorrow?*

Maybe Friday's better? she responded. She needed to slow this relationship's development down and buy herself some time, which she would use to dig deeper into Hákon's affairs and to figure out what he was up to. As he said he was at work, that had to mean he would be at his computer – into which she now had a window.

She sat on the stool, switched on her laptop and opened the spyware that would let her into Hákon's computer. She realised that the movements of the cursor across the screen weren't her own mouse at work, but were Hákon's and she had a real-time view of what he was doing. Once again, she thanked her own foresight in having invested in this software.

Hákon appeared to be looking at a bank account, and as far as Áróra could see, it was the Swiss account that was so securely locked away behind its passwords. She took one screenshot after another, saving them to her own computer. Hákon seemed to be going from one account to another, and his movements were so rapid, she couldn't make out if he was making transfers or paying invoices, but she could clearly see that both of the accounts he held at this Swiss bank contained large amounts of money – very large amounts.

Her heart pounded as she opened an Icelandic bank's webpage to get the exchange rate and convert those Swiss francs to sterling or krónur, so she would have a clearer idea of what kind of amounts he was dealing with. She was punching a series of zeroes into the converter when an alert appeared in a blue window in the corner of her screen, and for a second that was all she could focus on.

Her eyes locked onto the message text and the bank accounts became a blurred background. Suddenly, money no longer mattered. Áróra felt that time had been suspended as she clicked on the alert, which took her to Facebook and a picture of Ísafold, a broad grin on her face and wearing a sleeveless yellow dress against a backdrop of a sun-kissed beach. There was a deep-blue sea behind her and a cluster of white houses in the distance.

Italy is wonderful! the text with the picture read, and Áróra stared at the timestamp. Ísafold appeared to have uploaded the picture a moment ago and unblocked her sister so she could see it.

Áróra snatched up her phone and searched through it for her mother's number, but her hands trembled so violently that she dropped the phone, putting her hands to her mouth to stifle the sound that came from deep inside her like a primeval scream. She stood up and paced furiously back and forth, and when she finally felt that she had control of her breathing it was as if a pent-up tension had been released, and tears flooded down her cheeks.

She had been sure that she would be angry with Ísafold, that she would want to yell at her, tell her precisely what she thought of her for causing their mother so much worry and making her sister so anxious. But all she could feel was relief – such a surge of relief that her legs turned to jelly and she dropped to her knees. Ísafold was alive.

56

I've only just got out of the Blue Lagoon, after two hours of lounging with my toes in the white mud, when Ísafold's neighbour calls. I hadn't meant to go into town, just enjoy a quick break at the lagoon during the stopover between the UK and the States.

On the way to her place, this time I don't have a bad feeling, no trepidation over how she's been treated, no anger towards Björn.

I sit in the taxi and take in the sight of Keilir with its slopes blanketed in white, my fingers absently twisting a lock of hair that's stiff with the mineral mud of the lagoon.

The neighbour whispers to me that she thinks Björn's the type who likes to knock women around. She can't hear anything across the hallway but has noticed that sometimes Ísafold wears sunglasses indoors. I look at my sister's split lips and wonder what the difference is between thinking something and knowing.

The neighbour has a visitor who clearly comes from some other background and suggests we work together to hide Ísafold in some distant mountain village until Björn has forgotten about her, and she can find a good man to marry, because living in sin like that isn't good enough.

I have to agree with him that it's a crying shame that anyone would lay a hand on my sister's beautiful face. It's a sin to maltreat that petite, defenceless body of hers.

This time I've no ideas. I drop onto the neighbour's green sofa and cast my eyes over the doilies she's crocheted to cover the worn armrests, and feel nothing but a debilitating despair.

THURSDAY

57

The call from his colleague in border control came ridiculously early in the morning. Daníel had already been up for hours, though. He had even made a couple of barefoot circuits of the garden to enjoy the feel of thick, cool grass under the soles of his feet, as he usually did to get himself in the right frame of mind for the day ahead. He had slept badly two nights in a row and was still unsettled. What the hell had he been thinking, trying to kiss Áróra? He was certain that she thought he was a typical old perv, determined to stave off a middle-age crisis by preying on young women. It wasn't like him at all. Normally he never did anything on the spur of the moment. But she had such a strange effect on him that he had given way to his emotions rather than taking a conscious decision. His thoughts continued to trouble him as he walked around the garden, and it was only the phone ringing that brought them to an end – and that was simply because his mind was then concentrated on someone else – Ísafold.

'We don't register people leaving the country. The automatic gates take a picture of each passenger and register the boarding passes. Ísafold Jónsdóttir does not appear to have taken a flight out of the country during the period you asked to be checked,' his colleague said.

'And facial recognition?' Daníel asked.

'Facial recognition is rubbish. We stopped using it ages ago. It's just as well – the system used to take hours to find a single face, and then it would normally be the wrong one.'

'Hold on, so we can't be completely sure whether or not she left the country?'

'Well, in theory. You can try and sweet-talk customs – get them to go through their recordings from the terminal. But God help you there. The period during which she could have left the country is long. You need a big team working on it, because going through all those recordings would keep them busy for a lot of shifts.'

Daníel thanked him for his help, sat on the edge of the decking and stretched his feet out into the grass. There was no team, and so far there was no formal investigation.

He suddenly felt restless. The growl of traffic on Reykjanesbraut irritated him, practically hurting his ears, and that patch of grass by the rocks that hadn't been mown was just infuriating. Daníel got to his feet, strode over to the patch and, getting on his knees, began pulling up the grass. Since no tools would work there, he'd just have to use his bare hands. He tugged and yanked, but what came up was mostly weeds – dandelions and daisies, and sharp blades of greenery that cut his palms as he snatched at them. He gathered his strength and wrenched hard, then let go, groaning with the pain and cradling his right arm as a jolt of cramp shot through it.

'Hell and damnation,' he swore.

'Ah, the people in the rocks,' Lady said, coming up behind him. 'Are you all right?'

'Yeah. Just a bit of cramp,' Daníel said, massaging his arm with his left hand.

'That should teach you to leave well alone, if everything you've seen before isn't enough. That's a special place, an elf patch.'

'I don't believe in supernatural stuff,' Daníel said sulkily.

'Supernatural depends on how you define nature. There are some who would say that I'm a supernatural being, a supernaturally beautiful being. Joking aside, I imagine police college taught you some superficial stuff about time and space. Well I can tell you here and now that reality isn't what it seems to be. We all live inside the fallacy.'

'Deep stuff for first thing in the morning,' Daníel said, getting to his feet. His arm was still sore, and he gingerly stretched it out.

'It's not about depth, but smallness,' Lady said. 'Inside the smallest particles of existence, inside the atom, there are no rules. It's possible to be in two places at once, and time can run backwards. But I don't suppose that tallies with police logic.'

'Not at all. And it's as well I'm not a detective at the atomic level. Working out a timeline and establishing an alibi would be a problem. And anyway, I have no idea what you're talking about.'

'Physics. Particle physics.'

'Really?'

'Yes. I'm a physicist.'

'What?'

'Yes. Perfectly true.' Lady smiled. 'And that's the same expression my mother had on her face when I told her I was going to use my physics PhD to become a drag queen.'

Daníel pondered. People were still capable of taking him by surprise. He would have guessed that Lady's background would have been in the theatre or music, not science. A disciplined academic background didn't chime with her personality.

Once he had nodded goodbye, he crossed the lawn to the deck. He dried his feet on the doormat he had put inside the French windows, specifically to prevent grass being carried on his bare feet into the living room. In the kitchen he poured himself a cup of coffee from the flask he had made when he woke up during the night, and decided to wait until nine o'clock before calling Áróra to give her the news. It wasn't a call he was looking forward to. For a moment he thought of ways he could get out of speaking with her directly – a Facebook message or an email – but dismissed the idea instantly. While there was an awkwardness between them, she was still the relative of a missing person, and as a police officer he had a duty to treat her as such. It made no difference that he was on holiday; she had approached him in his capacity as a policeman. It also made no difference that his investigation had so far been an informal one. It was time to make Ísafold's disappearance a formal inquiry.

It was as if Áróra had read his mind. As he sat at the computer, the phone rang, and his heart skipped a beat when he saw her name on the screen.

'Ísafold has appeared!' she said as soon as he answered, and he could hear the joy and relief in her voice. 'She's in Italy,' she continued. 'She put a picture on Facebook last night, and as I can see it, she must have made it public. I've sent her a zillion messages already, asking her to call our mother. I checked just now and she hasn't called yet, but at least it's a sign of life.'

'Hmm.'

He opened Facebook and using the login details Violet had given him, went to Ísafold's profile. There she was. The first picture that Ísafold had posted for three weeks. It showed her smiling by the blue sea, with Mediterranean-style buildings in the background, and a few words stating that Italy is just wonderful.

58

Omar was still sleeping when Olga woke up, and while the water boiled, she tried to remember how long it was since she had last made her own morning coffee. He had to be tired after his efforts in the gym; he had fallen asleep before her in front of the television the previous night, and was still asleep.

She still hadn't told him about his residence-permit appeal being rejected. Maybe she wasn't prepared to deal with the sorrow that she knew would engulf her afterwards, the sadness and fear that would meld into a feverish mist. She would have to nurse him like a sick child. But the lawyer's words were also in her mind, and she knew she wouldn't be able to tell him about the failed appeal without bringing that up as well. She would have to ask who he really was, what his name was if it wasn't Omar, and how he had come to be in possession of a dead man's documents.

It made little difference when she brought the subject up. She could give herself time to think things over. He was hiding in her home, and the authorities had no idea where he was. In fact, she was the only person who knew, and it could stay that way for a few more days – or even weeks.

Olga didn't have the energy to boil or fry eggs for breakfast as Omar did, but she placed a mug on the table for him along with a bowl, spoon and a box of Cheerios. It would be waiting for him when he got up, so he could start the day with cereal and keep the eggs for lunchtime. She poured herself coffee, added a little milk and sat at the kitchen table with her laptop open in front of her.

Facebook showed her that her cousin Guðný had returned from honeymoon in Bali, tanned and happy, her brand-new husband sunburned lobster red. There were a few reminders about the reunion for her father's side of the family, later in the summer, for those who wanted to reserve a room rather than sleep in a tent.

She wasn't going to the reunion. The thought of relatives introducing their children and grandchildren was still too painful to contemplate. She had nobody to introduce. All she had was one dead son, and the whole family knew well that he had been nothing but trouble.

She scrolled down the page and stopped at a picture of her neighbour, Ísafold. She was clearly not in England, as her husband had said, but in Italy. It was odd that she was sunning herself by the Mediterranean when he had told her Ísafold had gone to visit family in England. Maybe Ísafold had left Björn, and he didn't actually know where she was. He could have said England to save himself awkward explanations. She could understand that. What Omar had said – that their relationship was doomed – was right. He had been triumphant when he had made that announcement, adding that an unblessed union would never last. She had argued with him, but he had been adamant that Ísafold would be better off finding a man to marry – someone other than Björn.

Ísafold smiled from the screen, looking happy with life. She looked paler than someone who had spent two or three weeks in the sun, but Olga was just relieved to see her. She recalled now just how uncomfortable she had felt when the girl's sister had called to see her. It was always difficult when people disappeared without a word.

She glanced at the clock. It was time to be on her way. The puddings won't wait, she told herself. This was the routine that went back years, always the same. She would put on a hair net, take her seat by the conveyor, tune the radio in her ear defenders to the morning chat show and listen to the debates about the events of the day while she weighed the pudding powder into bags and looked forward to the coffee break, when the four women still working at the factory would laugh and make fun of one another. That was the best way to cope with factory work – as it was to cope with life when things got tough. One hour at a time.

59

Áróra had hoped that Daníel would share her delight that Ísafold had made an appearance, so his dry response left her with a stab of disappointment. Was he hurt that she had fended him off the other evening? She hadn't seen him as the kind of guy who would take offence or make a big deal of it. He had come across as being so sincere and understanding when she told him that she wasn't ready. Of course it had been awkward, and she wouldn't have been here at his place now if she hadn't needed his advice.

'I wanted to ask if you know whether it's possible to trace where a Facebook picture was posted,' she said as she followed him through the hallway and into the living room, where she was again aware of the smell that had triggered a wave of nostalgia the last time she was here; the smell of Iceland. 'We might be able to figure out which hotel she's staying at, so Mum could call and leave a message. She's still worried sick; Ísafold isn't replying to messages and her phone goes straight to voicemail. But it's a relief that we've at least heard something from her.'

Daníel turned and glanced at her, as if he was waiting for her to stop talking. Then he smiled, and immediately looked away. She realised that he wasn't offended. He was embarrassed, even uneasy.

'What is it?' she asked.

'It's that picture,' he said quietly, clearing his throat. 'It's a fake.'

Now he looked at her, eyes a little downcast, as if he was un-willing to raise his gaze to meet hers properly, expecting her to be furious maybe, or perhaps he had some other reason that made him reluctant to catch her eye.

'How?' she asked in confusion. 'How is it a fake?'

She rattled off questions as if someone else were speaking on her behalf; she heard her own voice without feeling her words were her own. Daníel tapped the mouse by the computer so that the screen came to life, and there they were, side by side. There were two versions of Ísafold, the same dress and the same smile, her hair exactly the same, but with two completely different backgrounds. One had been taken in a dim restaurant with dark tables and chairs behind her, colourful tablecloths and candles, while the flash had illuminated Ísafold's pale skin and the yellow dress. In the second picture the rocky shoreline was the background, along with a dark-blue sea and cluster of white houses.

'I saw right away from the outlines that there was something odd about the picture, so it was clear it had been lifted and pasted onto this picture. I didn't have to search all that far through Facebook to find the picture it had been taken from.'

Áróra felt a great weight bear down on her, as if she were sinking into deep water. She only felt able to speak or move painfully slowly, while her mind was working at full speed, digesting what she had seen, trying to work things out and understand them.

'But that means...' she began, but wasn't able to put her thoughts into words. She stared ahead, out of the window, at Daníel's manicured green garden. 'Does that mean...?'

Her voice cracked before she could force out a whole sentence, and she took a deep breath.

'Yes,' he said quietly. His voice was warm and encouraging, completely at odds with what he had to say. 'It means that either she faked this picture herself to lay a false trail, away from where she really is, or else someone else has posted the picture to lead people astray. And now we need to go to the police station.'

The weight that bore down on Áróra now seemed so much greater after the cloud of relief she'd floated on as she had arrived at Daníel's place; it was just a few moments ago, but now seemed an age away. She felt her legs give way and her body dissolved into a howl that swamped everything like an unstoppable wave. He caught her before she fell and held her in his arms, pulling her close to him so that her cheek pressed against his neck, one hand on her head and the other patting her back with a soothing beat. For a moment she felt like a child in his arms – her future and her whole happiness depending on him. As long as he held her tight and patted her back, she felt that the cold reality of what might have happened to Ísafold could not reach her.

Now Ísafold was no longer sour and sharp in her memory, no longer the waspish Ísafold who had called her a lousy kid, blocked her on Facebook and lied that she had fallen against a radiator. She was the fourteen-year-old Ísafold who played with Barbie dolls, smiled at her, taught her to plait her hair and tickled her in bed after dark – her sister Ísafold.

60

Most of the specialist shops Grímur remembered from his childhood had disappeared from the city centre, replaced by tourist shops and restaurants. There had been such a diametric change to the centre during his lifetime that anyone would imagine he was an old man, and not just past forty. He loathed the large shopping malls, but he had no choice but to venture into Kringlan, as it contained the only shop that stocked a range of suitcases wide enough that he might find what he was looking for.

The hiss in his ears began as soon as he stepped inside the mall. There was something about the chatter of the crowds, or the hum of the escalators, or the lights, or maybe a combination of all of these, that magnified his discomfort, and he was always glad when he could step outside again into the fresh air. But now he had a task to undertake, so he would have to grin and bear it. He marched directly to the shop, and was inside, pulling suitcases from the shelves and inspecting them when a shop assistant appeared, asking if she could help. This was a young woman, practically a child, wearing perilously high heels.

'Could I take a look at the largest suitcase you have?' he said, looking at the three he had pulled from the shelves, none of which he felt would be large enough. At least, not when he saw the girl standing next to them.

'Is it the Superlight case you have in mind? A spinner, I suppose?' the girl asked.

He looked back at her, failing to understand. It was a long time since he had last bought a suitcase.

'It needs to be strong,' he said. 'Very strong.'

The assistant smiled understandingly, as if she realised that he wasn't up to date with the latest fashions in luggage.

'The spinners are the ones that have four wheels and they're easily the most convenient. You just push them along next to you, so there's no weight on your shoulders.'

He nodded. That sounded good. The case was going to be pretty heavy.

'If you're really looking for a case that will take some punishment, then you'll probably want a box.'

'Box?'

'Yes. One of the rigid cases made from plastic or reinforced canvas, but not ordinary fabric.'

She fetched two cases to show him. They seemed to be lovely pieces of luggage, but the plastic didn't look like it would withstand a great deal of weight.

'Won't that just break?' he asked.

'That could happen,' she admitted. 'If there's something very heavy in the case, or if someone sits on it.'

Grímur shook his head.

'That's no good. Strength is vital.'

'The largest cases we have are guaranteed up to thirty-five kilos. Of course, they can take more than that, but they aren't guaranteed for anything more, because airlines don't accept anything heavier.'

'It has to take more than that,' Grímur said, and looked around. He was reluctant to order anything specially, as that would create a trail that could be followed. He knew exactly what the suitcase would need to take, and he reckoned that was around eighty kilos. But he couldn't say that to this girl.

'The guarantee doesn't matter,' he added. 'I'm only going to be using it here in Iceland. I need to move equipment and stuff. I'm a roadie.'

The girl looked at him with interest.

'Wow,' she said. 'For which band?'

Grímur hadn't thought out the lie in advance so he turned aside and muttered, 'Loads of bands.'

He went further into the shop and could hear the click of the girl's heels as she followed him. He noticed a row of cases right at the back, behind the counter, and pointed.

'How about those?' he said. 'They look huge.'

'I forgot about those,' the assistant said. 'They're the old US standard type, but they aren't spinners.'

'That'll have to do,' he said. 'Could I look at the grey one?'

The girl shifted some boxes out of the way and brought the case over to him.

'It's a cloth covering,' she said. 'Although it's a very strong nylon fabric. But the case alone is almost four kilos, so we're going to return it. Nobody wants a case this big and heavy these days.'

'I'll take this one,' he said, patting it with one hand and extracting his wallet. The girl stared at him in surprise and looked delighted.

'That's fantastic,' she said. 'That's one we won't have to send back. I can give you a thirty percent discount, but without a guarantee.'

'That's absolutely fine,' Grímur told her. 'And the discount's even better. Thanks for that.'

The girl tapped keys on the till, and Grímur saw the price appear on the card reader in front of him.

'I'm paying cash,' Grímur said, and the girl apologised, starting again and working out the discount, while Grímur sized up both her and the case. As far as he could see, this suitcase was easily large enough for him to fit someone this girl's size inside it.

61

As she hadn't brought with her enough underwear for anything more than a long weekend, Áróra knew it was again time to do some washing. She bundled her knickers into the bathroom sink at the hotel, added a generous squeeze of the complimentary shampoo and kneaded thoroughly until there was a healthy amount of foam. Then she rinsed each pair under the tap again and again to wash away what seemed endless froth.

Daníel had gone with her to make a statement concerning Ísafold's disappearance, and somehow the situation seemed to be more real now that it had become part of an official process, recorded in public documents. The weight had gradually lifted from her shoulders as she had sat in the police station at Daníel's side, but at the same time she had felt a chill as the female police officer sitting opposite them went through her list of questions, and little by little the possible reasons for Ísafold's disappearance became plain.

The officer asked about depression, whether Ísafold had mentioned being low or had thoughts of suicide; she asked about her relationship with Björn, whether Ísafold could have begun a relationship with someone else, whether she had worked anywhere else after being sacked from the sheltered accommodation centre, what drugs she had used, whether she had recently been drinking more than usual, whether she had been involved in a dispute with anyone, whether anyone held a grudge against her.

New aspects of Ísafold's disappearance began to take shape in Áróra's mind as the officer continued her questioning, and it occurred to her that she was hardly the right person to be doing this, as she was unable to answer the questions properly. In reality she had no idea what Ísafold's life had been like recently.

It was just as well that Daníel had been able to join in and explain things, telling the officer that the initial investigation, as he put it, had been done already. He also mentioned Björn – the fact his statements didn't add up, and the domestic violence – and the picture on Facebook; the faked picture. As they left the police station, he offered to call her mother and explain the situation to her. Áróra was so relieved she longed to throw herself into his arms, but withstood the temptation. Then they sat side by side on the steps outside the police station, and she listened to his measured voice as he went through the situation with her mother, urging her to travel to Iceland, describing the situation as 'serious'.

Áróra filled the basin with cold water for a final rinse and swirled her underwear around in it. There was still some foam, but she had had enough. Her fingers were numb with cold, and she felt so tired, she was about to collapse. She knew very well that this was the come-down after the day's emotional switchback, but was still taken by surprise by her own reactions.

She retrieved her knickers from the water, squeezing them in a bundle rather than twisting the water out of them and damaging the lace, and lined them up in a row on the heated towel rack. She would have to buy herself some clothes now that her stay here in Iceland had been extended, and she would have to find a place to stay for herself and her mother, whose flight would be arriving that evening.

62

Áróra could see the worry etched into her mother's face the moment she appeared through the doors at the airport, and immediately her own worries seemed to become lighter. She'd have to be strong and support her mother. The same thing had happened when her father died. Back then she had been the one who provided the strength and support, finding her own solace in the role, as if she had transferred her sorrow to her mother and shouldered the burden of making sure everything was done. As she hugged her, Áróra sensed that her mother would worry enough for both of them about Ísafold. Her body seemed to have shrunk to little more than skin and bone, and Áróra heard a delicate tremor in her voice.

'I'll go straight to Daníel's place,' she said as Áróra took her suitcase.

'What?'

'He offered me his guest room,' her mother said.

'You're staying with him?'

Áróra was astonished. She wasn't aware of much of a connection between Daníel and her mother.

'He's going to support me through all this. He's a lovely man, your uncle.'

'He's not my uncle,' Áróra said, sounding sharper than she meant to. She put her mother's case in the boot of the hire car, and they didn't say a word until they were out of the car park and Keflavík could be seen stretching away down the slope below the road.

'This is familiar,' her mother muttered.

Áróra nodded. 'The airport has really grown since tourism took off. Just wait until you see what Reykjavík looks like.'

'Reykjavík needed to grow a bit,' she replied. 'I never liked the way we always ran into your father's friends and relatives every time we went downtown.'

Áróra had heard the same observation from her mother before. She had never been comfortable in Iceland. She found it too sparsely populated, too personal, and too small in every possible way. Áróra put her foot down once they were past the last of the roundabouts on the road past Keflavík and the straight line of main road lay ahead of them. Her mother sniffed at the smell of the Blue Lagoon, which carried all the way to them, and then stared out over the moss-covered lava that stretched from the shore to their left, all the way up into the Reykjanes Mountains, in the distance to their right. Hanging in the air were the sentences that her mother always dropped when they drove this way when Áróra was small, either with her father at the wheel or sometimes a relative who had come to fetch them. Every comment had been along the lines that this was a tragic and barren place, a cold desert, like the surface of the moon.

If her mother found Iceland a sad place back then, those emotions must be magnified now that she was here to search for her lost daughter.

63

I'm staring at the picture in Ísafold's text message, trying to fathom the emotions I feel deep inside. The last picture she sent before this one was of the cut on her forehead, almost in the roots of her hair, where there were eight neat stitches.

Now she's sending me a picture of her hand, a ring on her finger.

I answer with questions. Are you back at Björn's place? Is that picture what it looks like? She calls right back.

She's happy, and it's all I can do not to snap at her. I don't have it in me to wreck her moment of joy.

My Ice-Bear Björn is changing his ways, she says.

They're going to a counsellor, and they've even booked an appointment. And he's so, so sorry. He came to her on his hands and knees to bring her a ring.

An engagement ring.

FRIDAY

64

Somewhere deep in Áróra's chest a pain burned every time she thought of the tremor in her mother's voice the evening before, when they had arrived at Daníel's place. She appeared to allow herself to be overwhelmed only once she was safe in his little apartment, a mug of hot tea in her hands. Daníel obviously had experience of people in an emotional state. Áróra could clearly see his cautious encouragement, steering her mother's thoughts towards the next stage, towards the details. Maybe it was a particular strategy, preventing the mind taking in the full picture – as the overview of Ísafold's disappearance didn't look positive.

It had been a wrench to leave the flat and walk out into the bright summer night. It was a struggle to leave her mother in the state she was in, her voice quavering and weak, her hands fidgeting constantly with the hem of her blouse; and it was also difficult to turn away from Daníel's comforting voice, his presence that radiated security, like a heater in a cold room. But as soon as Áróra was outside, it was easier to catch her breath, her mother's wellbeing now in Daníel's hands, and Ísafold's wellbeing in her mother's. All the same, she had had to choke back the sob that rose in her throat. That had to be something to do with the way the mourning process worked – the tension relaxing as it was gradually replaced by a sorrow that took over the senses.

She was drinking her third coffee of the morning in her room when the cleaner knocked. She hadn't been down to breakfast, unable to face either Hákon or any food, feeling that she was as drained physically as she was mentally. But when the girl called out 'Room service!' as she opened the door a couple of inches, and was about to close it again when she saw the room was occupied, Áróra came back to her senses.

'It's all right, come in,' she called out to the girl, who looked at her enquiringly and repeated 'room service' in the same ringing tone.

'Please come in,' Áróra said, switching to English. 'I'm going out, so it's all right to clean now.'

She decided that she'd find a café once she had got herself moving. A brisk walk through the city centre would help her wake up. She picked up a scarf and a sweater, but decided to leave the jacket. It wasn't raining outside, even though it was a grey day with thick cloud. The cleaner pulled a vacuum cleaner behind her into the room and was plugging it in when Áróra decided to ask her about her work.

'What's it like, working here?' she asked.

The girl paused, and stared enquiringly, twisting the vacuum cleaner cable between her fingers as if she was trying to wring it out.

'What do you mean?' she asked, her accent from somewhere in Eastern Europe. She appeared frightened now, and Áróra immediately regretted having said anything.

'Just wondering if this is a good place to work, and if the pay is reasonable.'

The girl's hands froze and she dropped the cable to the floor, staring open-mouthed.

'You speak to manager,' she snapped angrily, then plugged in the vacuum cleaner and got to work, running it back and forth across the floor. It was clear that this wasn't up for discussion.

Áróra left the room, and all the way along the corridor and in the lift, she wondered whether the girl's response had been because she was shy, if her poor English had led her to misunderstand, or if her question had hit a sensitive spot.

65

Olga wasn't sure how many times in her long working life she had called in sick, but the fingers of one hand were probably enough to count them all. She had even turned up for work as usual the day after Jonni died. It had been better to keep herself occupied, rather than sit at home, turning over all the things she should have done that might have made his life turn out better. But that Friday morning she felt that the night's insomnia, plus the thought of having to tell Omar about his appeal, had drained all the energy from her. All the same, having called in and climbed back into bed, she wasn't able to get to sleep again. She lay there for an hour, sweating as she thought through all the ways Omar could have obtained this dead man's papers in Istanbul.

Omar had left for the gym but had made coffee for her before going out, so she poured herself a mugful and added cream. With any luck, the coffee would cheer her up. Omar had also fetched the newspaper; it was neatly folded for her on the table, just like in a hotel. Omar was certainly good to her, and she felt a shiver of trepidation, like being ducked in cold water, at the thought of giving him the bad news. She picked up the paper and read the front-page news. Not a lot was happening, as was usual in early summer, so the news items were more than usually positive. A group of middle-aged friends had decided to let their longstand-ing dream come true and had set off on a motorbike trip across America. There were indications that the Breiðafjörður osprey population was rising. This looked to be a record year for tourism.

Olga was startled when the doorbell rang. She got to her feet and limped the first couple of steps as her legs came back to life. She expected it to be Omar, having forgotten to take his key with him, so the sight of an older woman and a tall man holding a police warrant card took her by surprise. Police IDs were nothing new to her. Thanks to Jonni, she had become familiar with them. But the woman didn't appear to be a police officer.

'Yes?' Olga said, one hand instinctively reaching for her head. She hadn't brushed her hair, and now she stood there in her dressing gown, looking a mess. She would never have opened the door looking like this if she hadn't been sure it was Omar. Omar! They had come to take Omar away ... In her mind she searched like lightning through the flat, wondering where she had left her phone, and remembered it was on the kitchen table, probably under the newspaper. She quickly pushed the door closed in the faces of the pair, muttering an apology, that she would only be a moment. She rushed to the kitchen, the pain in her legs forgotten. Sometimes it was remarkable how the mind could be stronger than the body. For a while after Jonni's death she hadn't suffered from arthritis. The razor-sharp pain that afflicted her soul had taken over, and she had felt no other pain.

Her fingers trembled as she tapped in a message to Omar:

Don't come home! Police here. Police!

Then she took a deep breath, went back to the door and opened it.

'I'm sorry. Yes?'

They were still there on the landing, but had stepped back from her door as if they were wondering whether she was going to come back and open it for them or not. Normally people waited by a door with a set expression, facing it and ready with a greeting, but now the man and the woman faced each other, as if they had been whispering. Olga forced a smile and prayed that Omar would see the message as soon he had finished lifting weights, and wouldn't come bursting in while the police were there.

'Hello. I'm Ísafold's mother, the one who lives opposite,' the woman said in slow Icelandic, pointing at Ísafold's and Björn's door on the far side of the landing. Then she switched to English to continue her explanation, and Olga's knees felt weak with relief, and she wanted to laugh. They weren't here to take Omar away.

He was still safe with her, and nothing had changed. The authorities still had no idea where he was.

She said the same to Ísafold's mother as she had already told her sister: that she knew Ísafold well, and they sometimes chatted over tea or coffee. She didn't mention that it was normally Omar who drank tea with Ísafold, as that didn't make any difference. She said Björn had told her that Ísafold was visiting relatives in Britain, so it had been a surprise to see a picture on Facebook of her on holiday in Italy.

Once the conversation was over, she shut the door in what was almost a discourteous rush, as she had to let Omar know that he was safe. He picked up immediately, and she could hear the desperation in his voice.

'Omar, it's all right,' she said. 'It was just Ísafold-next-door's mother looking for her, and the policeman with her is her cousin. I don't know if they're allowed to do that, waving a police ID when it's personal business, but I was just so relieved it was nothing to do with you...'

Her relief evaporated as she heard Omar fighting back a sob.

'Omar—' she began, but he interrupted her, his voice shrill and wild, his gasping breaths roaring down the line like a storm.

'Why do you always ask about Ísafold? Why you ask of her?'

Olga wasn't able to work out if he was confused and frightened, or simply bursting with rage.

66

Daníel wondered about the woman whose door they had knocked at first – Olga. There was no doubt that seeing them had taken her by surprise, and there had been an odd look on her face as she shut the door, and then came back a moment later, and had been perfectly sweet. She must have rushed to flush a stash of grass down the toilet, he decided. He had noticed over the last few years that more and more older people smoked dope, either because it was something they had done in their younger years, or because of the debate about how effective it was for pain relief. It wasn't like in the old days, when hard liquor and snuff were what the older generation preferred. His grandmother had taken snuff, and he remembered how much fun it had been when he was a child to sneak a few grains from her, which would result in a colossal sneeze that they would both laugh over.

There wasn't a lot to be gained from talking to Olga. She said the last time she had seen Ísafold had been more than three weeks ago, not that she was sure exactly when, but she had asked Björn about her and had been told she was away visiting relatives in Britain.

He saw Violet take a deep breath as they knocked at Björn's door. Daníel had felt this wasn't a sensible thing to do. If the conclusion was that Ísafold's disappearance was suspicious, then Björn would naturally be at the top of the list of suspects, so it would be better to leave him be. The police could deal with him – which meant the police who were on duty, not one who was on holiday. But Violet had been adamant that they should approach all the neighbours, including Björn, and that there was nothing unusual in the man's mother-in-law wanting a word with him. Daníel saw his role as providing support for Violet, and holding up his police ID in Björn's face wouldn't do any harm, and might give him something to worry about.

Björn came to the door exactly as Daníel had expected, surly and sulky. His appearance was a long way from the one he conjured up in the Facebook pictures of himself with Ísafold, where his white teeth were pearly white, his dark, dreamy eyes sparkling with fun. The man in person was pale and dishevelled, his face puffy.

'Aren't you going to invite your mother-in-law in?' Violet asked, the peculiarly British disgust clear in her voice.

'Not if you're bringing that with you,' Björn said, and jerked a thumb in Daníel's direction. 'I might have asked you in if you hadn't brought the cop with you, and if you were still my kind-of mother-in-law.'

'What do you mean, Björn?' Violet asked. 'I haven't heard anything about you and Ísafold not being together any longer. The last I heard from her was a few weeks ago, and then she was happy and said that everything was fine between you.'

Björn shrugged.

'Well. It was a surprise to me as well when I came home one day and found she had packed her stuff and left. I haven't heard a word from her since. I reckoned she'd gone home to you in Newcastle. That's what I thought. Where else would she go?'

'Italy, maybe?' Daníel suggested.

Björn stared at him in astonishment.

'What?'

'She posted a picture on Facebook yesterday, saying she's in Italy,' Violet said. 'Does she know anyone in Italy?'

Björn shook his head with vehemence, and for a moment he reminded Daníel of a cornered animal. There was a fury in his eyes, even a hint of fear. The pulsing in his own head was stronger, Daníel could practically feel the beat of it. It was clear that Björn was upset, either taken by surprise or infuriated.

'How the hell should I know?'

'Why did you tell the neighbours that she was on holiday, visiting relatives in Britain, if she's in Italy?' Daníel asked, taking a step closer and placing a hand on the door to prevent Björn from slamming it shut, which was what he seemed keen to do.

'I don't know,' he snapped. 'Maybe because it's not much fun having to tell people that your girlfriend left you, eh? I just guessed that she'd gone back home.' His puffy face had turned red, and the tension in his body made the veins pulsing in his neck stand out. 'And I don't want to see the cops around here,' he said, his voice lower, as if he was struggling to keep control of his temper.

Daníel withdrew his hand and the door banged shut. Daníel would have liked to have asked Björn a few more questions, adding a little more pressure, but this wasn't the time or the place.

'He seems surprised to hear that Ísafold's in Italy,' Violet muttered, and Daníel wondered if she hadn't fully understood when he had explained it to her. Maybe she was living in the hope that the picture wasn't faked and that Ísafold was genuinely in Italy.

'Yes' he said. 'He was surprised to hear that Ísafold *appears* to have posted a picture from Italy,' he said, emphasising the 'appears'.

It was correct that Björn had seemed caught off-guard when Violet mentioned the picture. Maybe he was surprised that Ísafold was posting pictures of herself at all, Daníel thought, and he could feel a weight on his heart, and the flash in his head, his instinct, pulsed faster, like the flashing of a blue light on a squad car in hot pursuit. Maybe Björn was just surprised that Ísafold had shown a sign of life.

67

The chambermaid's reaction that morning had irritated Áróra all day, and her intuition about it was confirmed when Hákon leaned forward over their starter and whispered, just loud enough to be heard over the chatter in the smart downtown restaurant: 'I hear you were asking my staff about their rates of pay. I suppose that's because of the stuff in the papers saying I pay below the minimum wage...'

'What stuff was that?' Áróra asked. This was a surprise, as she had seen no coverage of the topic, despite having spent some time scouring the internet for information about Hákon and his hotel business.

'Well, there was some newshound who got hold of someone's pay slip and published it, without knowing the full story, of course, and as I can't publicly say what the facts are, it looked bad for me.'

Áróra gazed at him. He was agitated and apologetic, and the flush that he was prone to had appeared, as tiny droplets of sweat gathered on his upper lip.

'So what are the facts?' she asked. She was aware how pushy she sounded, so it was unexpected when he appeared to reply candidly.

'Between ourselves, I'll admit that I sometimes pay a small part of people's wages as cash in hand, so they don't have to pay so much tax as it isn't high-paid work. It goes without saying that I know it's against the rules, and I know that as an accountant you don't approve of that kind of thing...'

'Exactly. But I wasn't wondering about that,' Áróra said. 'Your business affairs are no concern of mine. I just wanted to be sure you weren't one of those creeps you hear about in the travel business here who run something that's only just short of slavery, making people work all hours and paying them peanuts, if anything.'

He smiled in relief, obviously taking her explanation at face value.

'I'm not a creep,' he said, raising his glass as she did the same, but hers was empty so they didn't manage to clink glasses before the waiter arrived bearing their main courses. 'I think I can say with pride that my staff are happy to work for me. And everyone benefits when a few krónur escape the tax system.'

Áróra studied his face with interest. There was a childlike simplicity to his argument, and she wondered if he genuinely believed it, or if he had fashioned some slightly shallower version of integrity that allowed him to live with himself.

Hákon ordered more wine for her, and they set to work on their steaks. Out of habit, she pushed the potatoes aside and started on the salad. She made a habit of starting with the green stuff, then the meat or fish, keeping the carbohydrates to last. Keeping slim was a matter of accounting, just the same as finance. And she was smart enough to know that a company can't pay wages on the black unless there's undeclared cash somewhere behind it.

68

Hákon led Áróra towards the restaurant's door; the support was welcome as she was wearing heels and wasn't as steady on her feet as usual. She had lost count of the glasses of wine she had drunk over dinner. There had been white wine with the seafood starter, then red with the lamb main course and finally a dessert wine so sweet that she had no appetite for the dessert itself, in spite of the waiter's long speech in praise of it.

'Hi there, Hákon!'

The greeting cut clearly through the chatter, and Hákon raised a hand and waved. Áróra took a moment to focus properly and figure out where the call had come from. As Hákon steered her to the table where the woman who had called was sitting, along with her friend, she wished she hadn't drunk so much. The friend was younger, stick-thin and at first Áróra thought she was wearing a shirt with intricately patterned sleeves, before she realised that she was wearing a sleeveless top showing heavily tattooed arms. Hákon kissed both women, and before Áróra could protest, he and the women had decided they would join them for one more drink.

'Áróra, this is my business partner Agla, and Elísa, her wife. Elísa and Agla, this is Áróra.'

Agla smiled as she extended a hand.

'Business partner?' was all Áróra could say as she sat in the chair that Hákon had chivalrously brought for her. She hadn't been aware of a business partner. None of the media coverage she had found online had mentioned one – and certainly not this one. No deep insight into the workings of the Icelandic business community was needed to know that Agla Margeirsdóttir was one of the country's best-known financial criminals.

Áróra felt her head swim; it was as though the restaurant was spinning around her. She was struggling to join the dots. Maybe her plan wasn't worth the risk. Hákon's business network seemed to be more complex than she had imagined.

'That's right,' Hákon said. 'Agla came to my rescue when I started building the hotel in Akureyri. She came up with the finance for the construction and for getting the place running, and she's supported me all the way through.'

Hákon asked what she would like to drink, and she requested water, the questions multiplying in her mind.

Why had there been no mention in any of the online coverage that Agla had a share in Hákon's hotel business? Áróra was close to getting the information she needed about his accounts, so it was frustrating not to know exactly what sort of business relationship he had with Agla.

She didn't have to wait long for an opportunity to ask her question and a few others, as, while Hákon was at the bar, Elísa got to her feet, excused herself and headed to the toilet.

'It's too long and complicated a story to go into now,' Agla said. 'But Hákon can explain it all for you.'

'No need for that,' Áróra lied, aware that her question could be seen as suspicious. 'I was just curious.'

The woman raised her glass and smiled to someone in the room. Áróra followed her eye, and saw the smile was intended for Hákon as he stood at the bar with a beer in one hand, which he raised in return. He seemed happy and contented, and Áróra felt a sudden surge of self-disgust at the thought she was betraying him.

'I know who you are,' Agla then said, with eyes that seemed to pierce Áróra to the core.

Áróra felt sick, and the restaurant again began to turn in circles around her. Hákon appeared, and handed her a glass of water, which she drank down in a single draught. It served to ease her nausea, but it returned as Agla leaned close, smiled icily and whispered, 'And I have my own ideas about why you're interested in Hákon.'

69

'Are you all right?' Hákon asked with concern, handing her a serviette. She mopped the perspiration from her face and got to her feet. The restaurant was still spinning around her, and she wasn't sure whether she had been somewhere between a dream and wakefulness a second before, or whether Agla had really told her that she knew who she was and what she wanted from Hákon. How the hell could that have happened? Áróra didn't know Agla at all, apart from what she had read about her in the papers, and was certain she had never met her before.

'Ach. Just a bit drunk,' she said, aware of how her voice slurred. 'Can you take me back to the hotel?'

Hákon kissed both Agla and Elísa goodbye, but Áróra said nothing, certain that she would vomit if she tried to speak. As Hákon supported her on the way to the door, she noticed Agla checking her out with piercing eyes and a faint smile. Hákon's arm was around her waist, keeping her upright, and she slipped her hand into his back pocket to give herself something to keep hold of. They made their way onto the pavement, holding each other tight, and walked straight into her mother and Daníel.

It wasn't easy to tell if it was leaving the warmth of the restaurant for the cool evening air outside, or the razor-sharp dismay in her mother's eyes that brought her to her senses. Her sight cleared, and she pushed Hákon away a little. It was an embarrassing moment, and Áróra longed to explain the whole story for everyone, but her mind wasn't sharp enough to cope with the two worlds she'd inhabited over the past few days crashing together.

'This is Hákon,' she muttered. He responded courteously, offering a hand to her mother and then to Daníel, who ignored it and walked away. As he stepped past Áróra, he leaned close and whispered.

'Looks like you've changed your mind about being ready for romance.'

Áróra clasped Hákon's hand once her mother had set off after Daníel, but, after a few steps, it was all suddenly too much: the evening with all the drinks and Ísafold on her conscience, then Hákon and Daníel at the same time, and she leaned forward to throw up into the gutter.

Fuck Iceland. Tiny, fucking Iceland.

70

He had admitted to himself that Áróra had been on his mind a lot over the last few days, but hadn't realised just how great her effect on him was until he ran into her in the street downtown. It was like a punch in the gut to see her with another man; the pain was physical. She had told him that she had to meet an old friend, so he had taken it on himself to show Violet around the city centre, considering it had been such a long time since her last visit to Iceland. They had a meal together, with ice cream for dessert, and were taking a gentle stroll when a drunk Áróra tumbled out of a restaurant, practically into their arms. As if that wasn't enough, she was hanging on the arm of one of the country's most controversial financial criminals, the one the newspapers had reported as having just been released, and she seemed to be having a whale of a time – with no old friend anywhere to be seen. The guy was holding her tight, and she was giggling as she tottered out onto the steps – until she saw her mother, and then him. Of course, he had no idea if seeing him had been a shock to her, but he guessed she didn't care. She had made it plain that she wasn't interested in him romantically, but he had taken that as meaning she wasn't on the lookout for men in general. That had clearly been a misunderstanding on his part.

'She's out on the town, while her sister...' Violet said, struggling to get the words out. 'While her sister is God knows where.'

They walked silently to the car, but before they got inside, Violet looked like she had put her thoughts in order. He said nothing, unable to say a word. He felt himself burning up with jealousy. He got in the car, started the engine and fiddled with the radio while Violet sat down and put on her seat belt. He should have said something, should have come to Áróra's defence, some-thing along the lines of people approaching this kind of thing in their own way. Some people do it by fending off emotion, immersing themselves in other work, preferably not even thinking about the lost or injured relative, while others meet sorrow head-on and try to get to grips with the situation. But the fire inside stopped him speaking, and anyway, he didn't want to speak. Although he understood perfectly that Áróra would want to go out and have a drink, he was furious that she should be hanging on another man's arm. Especially that man.

'I could really do with a cup of tea right now,' Violet said, and sighed, and he nodded as he turned the car out of the parking lot behind the cathedral. He'd take her home, make some tea, try to talk things over, and then he'd make his excuses and go to bed early. Now he wished that Violet wasn't his house guest, and had to admit to himself that he had invited her to stay in the vague hope that it would bring him closer to Áróra.

Once Violet had gone to bed, Daníel went out in the garden and did star jumps on the soft grass. He was wearing only a pair of jeans, so the fine night mist blended with the sweat that ran down his chest. He switched to squats and did forty before going back to star jumps. He was breathless and his heart pounded, but he still longed for more exercise that would clear the image of the drunk Áróra in another man's arms from his thoughts.

'The view looks good,' said Lady, appearing at her door and lighting a cigarette. She dragged the smoke deep while her eyes lingered on Daníel's bare chest. 'I'm almost tempted to invite you into my garage.'

71

Áróra didn't dare trust that she'd be woken for her night-time mission by the sunshine, which had roused her during the last few nights. She had so much alcohol flowing through her veins, she was sure she'd be knocked out as soon as she lay down and wouldn't wake until well into the morning. She told Hákon that she was going to take a shower and that he should go to sleep, and she would crawl into his bed soon.

She stood for a long time under the shower, turning it alternately hot and cold in the hope that it would sober her up. Her mind was cloudy, and she couldn't understand how her mother and Daníel had appeared suddenly in front of her, bringing the whole Ísafold baggage with them. It demonstrated how her world had been compartmentalised over the last few days, with Hákon and his treasure in one box, and Daníel, her mother and Ísafold's disappearance in another. Now, as these two realities collided, she was left with some very odd feelings.

She wrapped herself in a towel as she stepped out of the shower, sat on the toilet seat and leaned forward to drink cold water straight from the tap. It didn't matter how much she gulped down, she couldn't slake her thirst. Finally she stood up and glared at herself in the mirror. Now it was time to do or die. If this Agla had seen through her, then she would surely warn Hákon. That was what any business partner would do. So this would probably be her last opportunity to install the camera.

She padded into the bedroom and rooted through her bag until she found the camera. It seemed larger and bulkier than it had in the shop, and Áróra reproached herself for having bought a camera in Iceland instead of ordering a smaller one online and waiting a couple of days for it to be delivered. But if she was going to get access to Hákon's login details, then she would have to do it now. She recalled that there was a suspended ceiling light; that was where the camera would have to go. There was no other place for it. It was one of those square lights that belonged in offices, with white and silver bars that criss-crossed the light's housing and the surround.

She held her breath as she crossed the room. But there was no need to tiptoe, as Hákon lay on his front across the bed, fully dressed and fast asleep. Áróra sat on the desk, lifted her feet and got to her knees. Now she'd have to take care to keep her balance.

She supported herself with a hand against the wall and reached for the light overhead. She could just make it, and by stretching up, on the tips of her toes, she managed to clip the camera over the light's surround. The light was directly over the desk where Hákon's computer lay, so if he were to sit there and tap in the password for his bank account, the camera should pick it up. The problem was that the camera was easily visible, but there was nothing she could do about that. Normally people didn't make a habit of looking straight up when they worked at a computer, so she should get away with it – at least for long enough.

Getting down from the table didn't go quite so well, as when she leaned over, she lost her balance and tumbled against a chair and from there to the floor. She winced as she fell, and Hákon mumbled as he lifted himself up onto his elbows, looking around the room in confusion.

'It's all right,' she said. 'Just fell over. Didn't hurt myself. I'm just pissed.'

Hákon lay back, and she sat still on the floor, waiting for him to fall asleep again. Then she would sneak out and go back to her own room. She couldn't face climbing into his bed, all innocence, having just bugged his room.

72

It was Friday evening, and Grímur was at home. He was too agitated to go to the cinema. He wouldn't be able to concentrate on a movie, regardless of how exciting it might be. Instead he was at home in the kitchen, unable to shave himself again as his skin was too tender – it was practically raw having already been shaved twice today, all over. Now he was preparing instant noodles and thinking about what was ahead. The fact that the police were taking an interest in Björn wasn't ideal; it could jeopardise all his plans.

The kettle pinged to let him know that it had boiled, so he opened the noodle pot and poured in the hot water. He would need two or three of these before he would be full, and for a moment he regretted having not gone into town, where he could have treated himself to a hot dog, a Coke and popcorn at the cinema, as he usually did when he had some cash. But in his present state a movie would have been a waste of money. He felt his heart race and his thoughts were working on overdrive.

The thing with plans was that they seemed so straightforward and clear from a distance, but as the time for action approached, minor details took on greater significance. Now they hadn't only taken on greater importance but had become vital factors. The knob of butter melted into his noodles, and he shook salt over them – too much salt. The doctor had told him that his blood pressure meant he would have to cut down, but he had other things on his mind right now. There was more important stuff demanding his attention. He shovelled up a mouthful of noodles – sucking the trailing ends into his mouth so that the butter landed on his cheeks – and chewed. His fingers sought out the chain around his neck, and he tugged at it so that it hurt his neck, until his fingers found the clasp. He opened it, slipped the ring off the chain and placed it on the table in front of him.

The engagement ring. It could play a part in this plan of his – in fact, it would be little short of genius if it were to work out. But he knew he would regret parting with it; he would miss it terribly. Having it against his chest gave him a good feeling inside as the metal absorbed the warmth of his body, nestling against his chest as it hung from its chain. It was like having something of Ísafold close to him, next to his heart. He finished his noodles, stood up and switched the kettle on again, and opened another packet, crumbling the contents into the bowl.

Maybe it was time for another post from Ísafold. After hearing the police arrive, and having listened to the conversation in the corridor outside his door, he was terrified that it would ruin everything if the police were keeping tabs on Björn. He couldn't allow that to happen. There was no way he could let it. He loved Ísafold far too much for that.

73

She's with the neighbour in the block, Mum says. That's good, I reply.

She said you hadn't answered the phone, Mum says.

No, I say. It's four in the morning. I don't answer her calls during the night anymore.

I don't know who I can ask to look after her, Mum says.

I say nothing.

I can't face yet another trip to Iceland to help Ísafold get back on her feet.

Listening to her cry and complain, saying she's leaving Björn. Listening to her repeat all the foul things Björn has said about her family. About me.

Giving her support and encouragement, only to have hopes dashed as she falls for the apologies and the flowers, and goes back to him.

I can't do this any more.

SATURDAY

74

It was six in the morning when Áróra gave up trying to sleep, and dressed ready to go down to breakfast. She had fought against nausea when she lay down in bed, so had sat up, stacked all four pillows behind her and tried to watch TV, but gave up on that, unable to concentrate, instead dozing for a few hours as she re-played the previous evening's disaster again and again in her mind. What was odd was that she didn't feel nearly as guilty for bugging Hákon's room as she did for having possibly hurt Daníel. There had been such a sad look on his face when he saw her with Hákon, she had wanted to do something to make everything better, but no smart solution had come to mind, so she'd just introduced Hákon in a clumsy fashion. 'This is Hákon,' she had said, blind drunk and slurring.

She had no idea how she would be able to face Daníel again, not that she owed him anything. It wasn't as if there had been any-thing between them, and these days women were free to choose their own lovers. And she was as free as could be. All the same, she had the feeling she had trampled on something tender between them, or something that should have been between them. How stupid could you get?

Then there was Agla. Had she really said what Áróra thought she had said? Could she have known who Áróra was, and there-fore had been able to guess why she was tangled up with Hákon?

Áróra squinted into the morning sun that shone in through the window of the hotel's breakfast room, illuminating every speck of dust. This was one of the things her mother had complained about while she had lived in Iceland, that she could never quite dust well enough.

The breakfast room was practically empty. The tourists catching a morning flight home had already left for the airport, and others weren't yet awake. An old man sat in one corner reading a newspaper and slurping coffee, and at the breakfast buffet a plump American couple were discussing the spread of food in loud voices.

'Could you tell me what that is?' the woman asked Áróra, pointing at a dish on the table.

'Herring,' Áróra replied. 'Pickled herring. It's good with eggs.'

The woman laughed and wrinkled her nose. It was clear that she had no intention of trying anything unfamiliar.

'Where are you from?' Áróra asked as she reached for a plate. She didn't particularly want to know more about these people, but decided to be polite since they had spoken to her.

'Austin, Texas,' the woman said, her husband behind her nodding enthusiastically in agreement.

'Is this the first time you've been to Iceland?' Áróra asked amiably as she spooned a generous portion of bacon onto her plate.

'Yes, first time here, and we can't wait to see everything, the hot springs, the waterfalls, the sheep.'

The woman laughed, and Áróra smiled.

'Nice to meet you,' she mumbled and went to sit at a table by the window. She was so hungry that her hands trembled, her body demanding sustenance after the night, and she shovelled the bacon and eggs down so hastily, she made herself nauseous again. She sat still for a while, sipping water from a glass while the hangover guilt again welled up inside her. In some strange way she felt that she was betraying Ísafold – sitting here with a hangover after a night's drinking with a man she was staking out in the hope of making some money, instead of searching for her sister. But where should she be searching?

Áróra felt a burst of illogical anger towards Ísafold in her belly, although she knew herself well enough to recognise that anger was her way of staving off grief. All the same, she felt sick at heart at having this emotion. There was no point in being angry with someone who had vanished.

Hákon strode in at six-thirty, and his appearance snatched away these thoughts. He was smart and well-groomed, not wearing the clothes he had fallen asleep in. She was sure she didn't look as wide awake as he did. Hákon waved cheerfully to her and flashed her a smile, but stopped at the tourists' table, shaking hands and chatting with them for a moment. He patted the man on the back and wished them a good trip home, which sounded odd to Áróra, as she understood from the woman that they had just arrived and were about to set off to explore Iceland.

'Sorry,' Hákon said as he took a seat next to her. 'I had to have a word with them. They're regulars here.'

'Really?' Áróra said.

'Yes,' Hákon said. 'This is their third stay here, at least.'

He reached over for the last piece of bacon on her plate and put it in his mouth, before waving to the waiter and asking for coffee. He leaned over the table and kissed her on the lips.

'I woke up and wondered where you were. There was no reply when I knocked on your door, so I figured that if you weren't there, then you had to be here.'

'I was so hung over I couldn't sleep,' Áróra said, glancing at the American couple, who stood up and waved her goodbye. Why had they claimed to be here for their first visit, if it was obvious that Hákon knew them as regular guests? Why would an ordinary couple on holiday lie like that?

75

Daníel had been awake far into the night, wondering what Áróra was doing with that Hákon, someone everyone knew was a crook. This guy was the kind of criminal for whom he had zero sympathy, the type of bloodsucker who lied and stole from society, skimming off the cream. Around two in the morning he had reached the conclusion that she probably didn't know who Hákon really was. She probably hadn't paid that much attention to the media coverage here in Iceland, so this guy could have told her anything, and they could have only just met, that evening. Maybe it was just a one-off date. But by three he had come to the conclusion that it didn't matter whether or not Áróra was aware of Hákon's criminal background, as it was clear that men were on her radar. Whether for a quick tumble or for something more, it didn't matter, just not with Daníel.

Of course, there was a fifteen-year age gap between them, and that had to be a barrier. Although he wished it wasn't that way, he understood. On top of that, this Hákon was a very different type from him – delicate and lithe, or so he seemed, the type that always looked the part, with a taut, youthful complexion, suits perfectly pressed, fashionably groomed and hair trimmed no less recently than yesterday, a million-króna watch on his wrist. In contrast, Daníel was a head taller, broader across the shoulders, and the bike meant that he normally wore denim or leather, and a haircut meant running a trimmer over his head once in a while.

By seven in the morning he was dozing, somewhere between sleep and wakefulness, mulling over the meaning of Áróra's name, as if it might reflect something of the person who bore it and therefore give him some insight into her. Did the name mean 'dawn', or 'Northern Lights'? Was she day or night? Was she the brightening daylight or the indistinct flashes of electricity in the dark winter sky?

Was it possible to have your heart broken by someone you hardly know and have in fact never been close to, apart from one short motorcycle journey and an awkward kiss in a field of lupins? It was completely illogical, but he felt that her presence had come with a vague promise of something more, and now that promise was gone, and he wanted to weep and at the same time roar. He had a pain in his belly. He hadn't felt this way since he was a teenager. Maybe this was what they called a midlife crisis? He decided to go outside into the garden and talk to Lady. That always cleared his head. Drawing your attention elsewhere for a while so that you became more focused was how some people thought that hypnosis worked.

He was taken by surprise when the door to the converted garage opened as soon as he knocked; for a moment he was sure that an unfamiliar man had answered it.

'Welcome to my humble house,' Lady said, stepping aside to let him in. All Daníel could do was stare.

Instead of nylon tights and a silk dressing gown, today's outfit was faded jeans and a grey T-shirt, and not a trace of make-up to be seen. Instead, there was the shadow of a day's growth of stubble.

'I can see you're surprised. But while femininity is captivating as a competitive sport, there's relief to be had in putting it aside for a while.'

'Wow. You don't seem like your real self...'

'Well, I have many different selves, darling. Just the same as you do. Just like everyone else. Most people only let one of these show.'

'There's a lot of truth in that,' Daníel said, taking a seat in one of the chairs by the table, where a sewing machine stood in the middle of a heap of pieces of cloth, reels of cotton and incomplete drawings of dresses. Lady sat in the other chair, reached to open a small fridge, took out a couple of beers and handed one of the cans to Daníel.

'You don't seem well, my love. Your aura is in tatters.'

Daníel murmured something unintelligible and drank half a

can in one long swallow. He had as much belief in auras as he had in elves. But there was a relief in someone picking up that he wasn't feeling well, that someone paid him enough attention to figure out his inner pain.

'There's a woman on my mind.'

'It had to be something like that,' Lady said. 'There's nothing like love to screw up an aura.'

'I haven't worked out if it's love. I don't know what she wants. She doesn't seem interested, but every time we're near each other, it's like the air between us is electrified. Or maybe it's just my imagination.'

'And you want to analyse and compartmentalise, like you're carrying out a police investigation.'

'I'm not sure about that,' Daniel said, thinking to himself for a moment. 'I'd like to know if she feels the same, if she senses the charge as strongly as I do.'

'You'll feel better when you realise that, in reality, the fundamentals of existence are totally incomprehensible and chaotic, completely crazy,' Lady said. 'And nothing fun or beautiful comes of anything that can be organised.'

'As usual, I haven't the faintest idea what you're talking about,' Daniel said.

'No, you aren't the sharpest chisel in the toolbox,' Lady said, sniffing with disdain, although Daniel saw a friendlier expression than usual on Lady's face. 'What I mean is that you need to loosen your grip and go with the flow. Don't apply pressure or try to influence the way events turn out. Just let things happen.'

76

Áróra's heart beat fast as she reached her room, and this time it was excitement and not a thumping hangover that was the cause. Hákon had said that he needed to do some work, and they had taken the lift together. She got out on the second floor and ran along the corridor to her own room, hurrying inside to switch on her computer. The imaging software showed the view from the webcam, but she couldn't immediately get her bearings as the overhead viewpoint was so different. Little by little, though, the image began to tally with her recollection of Hákon's room. The large black area that occupied half of the picture was the desk, and the dots on it were glasses and other oddments. A large grey circle at the lower end of the image looked like a ball, but had to be the office chair, and some indistinct black shapes beside it had to be clothes on the floor or something that had gone flying when she had tumbled off the table last night. The square that lay at the edge of the deck was the computer; the computer that this was all about.

Her heartbeat gradually returned to normal as she waited for something to happen. She stared at the computer screen, expecting Hákon to appear, so determined not to miss anything that she didn't even dare stand up and make herself the coffee that she had a real need for. Of course, this was ridiculous; the webcam software would record everything and she could replay it if she needed to. But there was something about watching what was happening in another room in real time; it gave her the feeling of becoming a higher being, larger and greater in some way, like an eagle calmly soaring beneath the clouds, but still able to see every tiny movement on the earth below.

Áróra was startled when Hákon finally appeared on the screen. To begin with he appeared as a blurred shape, and when he sat in the chair she could see clearly in the monochrome image how his head became clear against his white-clad shoulders. He worked much faster at the keyboard than she had expected, and in a few moments he had opened the laptop, clicked on something, tapped at the keyboard, again clicked with the mouse and punched something in. At this speed there was no possibility of making out the keyboard strokes. But now she had a recording and could slow down the replay.

She stood up, set the little coffee machine to make her an espresso, then sat at the desk and did as the lad in the computer shop had instructed. By spooling the recording back and stopping the replay at each keystroke, she was able to write down Hákon's password. He clearly took security seriously, as his eight-character password included lower- and upper-case letters, as well as a number. Now that she had what she had been looking for, there was one more thing she needed to check before making her move.

She had sat in the lobby with her phone and checked literally every post on Facebook and read both Icelandic and English online news by the time the American couple finally appeared. They had their luggage with them and were dressed for outdoors, the man in a grey overcoat and the woman in a pink anorak.

'Checkout, please,' the woman called out as she rang the bell, and a young man shot out of the office behind the desk. Áróra pretended to be absorbed in her phone, but carefully followed everything happening at reception. The young man printed out the bill, and in the hope of being able to see the amount, Áróra stood up just as he slid it across the desk towards the couple. She reached for one of the leaflets displayed in a holder by the desk, but there was no way she could make out the figures on the bill at this distance. It was enough to be able to confirm that the bill was a big one, very big. It was ridiculously high, if the wad of two-hundred-euro notes – Arora noted they weren't paying in krónur – the woman slapped on the counter was anything to go by.

Áróra sat back down in the chair by the window and smiled to the American couple as they steered their cases out through the hotel door. She scrolled through to Michael's number. This was the accountant she always went to for help when she needed to get to the bottom of a complex money trail.

'What are you after?' Michael grunted in mock irritation as he answered the phone. Áróra knew that this was his own peculiar sense of humour at work, but she still felt a stab of guilt, because Michael was more than a colleague. He was a friend.

'Michael, I need help,' she said.

'I know that,' he replied. 'You never call unless you need something, so I can't help wondering if you're using me.'

'Of course I'm using you,' she said, and laughed.

This was the banter that had been their usual way of communicating for as long as they had known each other, ever since she had first sought Michael's assistance to figure out a complex business network. Regardless of what she habitually told people, she was no accountant.

'This one's entirely off the record, Michael,' she said. 'Totally confidential. In a few minutes I'm going to email you some documents and a few notes, and I'd really appreciate it if you'd take a look and tell me what conclusion you come to.'

77

The greatest injustice within the Icelandic penal system was that murder usually attracted a sentence of no more than sixteen years. Just sixteen, and normally ten would be served. Ten years passed quickly. This was why he was setting out to do what he had planned.

He wondered whether it had been daring or simply careless on his part to buy the ketamine from Björn. He simply hadn't been able to resist. Somehow it was too neat, taking the circumstances into consideration. It would serve Björn right. He sold it to anyone who asked, through a Facebook page that he called The Sweetshop. Grímur's message had barely been sent when a reply dropped in:

No prob. Plenty of Special K. Where do you want to do the hand-over?

Grímur had suggested the car park outside the kiosk down at Mjódd, and he sat there in his car, watching people going in and out of the shopping centre and wondering why so many of those who shopped there had blue hair. This wasn't just the elderly biddies with walking sticks or frames, and light-blue hairdos, but youngsters sporting electric-blue hair. He watched them all until he saw a young lad get out of a car and glance around as if he was looking for something. Then he got out of his own car and walked straight to the lad, now standing in front of the kiosk, shoulders hunched and his hood over his face.

Grímur extended a hand, money between his fingers, and the boy snatched the wad of notes with lightning speed, simultaneously handing him a package with his other hand as he set off for his car again, and Grímur did the same. No words had been exchanged, and the lad had hardly looked at him, so he doubted that he would be recognised if they were to meet in the stairwell at home. Björn's dealers still showed up occasionally, although more rarely since he had been sentenced. He no longer seemed to keep his dope in his flat, and must have found some other base for the boys, while he stayed at home and handled sales via Facebook.

'Our home is like a bus station,' Ísafold had said, sighing into her coffee, and Grímur had encouraged her to talk to Björn about it, back when he still felt that Björn was a candidate for some kind of redemption. Ísafold had done just that, and Björn had rewarded her with a beating. Her cries and tears cut him to the bone, and the anger, the barely controllable wave of fury directed at Björn, began to take root in his heart. Grímur had called the police, reporting domestic violence and drug dealing in the building, and that had resulted in Björn's sentence. That was just one of the times he had tried to save Ísafold, one of many. But more recently Grímur had learned the hard lesson that there was no saving those who didn't want to be saved.

Grímur waited until he was sitting at the kitchen table at home before opening the package. The phial containing the clear liquid seemed so tiny and harmless, it was hard to believe that this was the key to incapacitating a person. He shook it and held it in the palm of his hand. It would be no problem to hide, up a sleeve or in a pocket, until it was time to spike someone's drink.

78

Olga had thought through every possible way of telling Omar what the movement's lawyer had said, and, as so often in the past, she concluded that honesty was the best option.

'My dear Omar,' she said gently as he spooned a portion of scrambled egg onto a plate and handed it to her. 'We need to talk.'

He smiled, and his eyebrows lifted almost to the middle of his forehead.

'About the chickens?'

She was almost ready to laugh at his innocent expectation, which was in such stark contrast to what they needed to discuss. She thought of the murdered man in Istanbul while he thought of keeping chickens on the balcony. She took the plate and shook her head.

'It can wait until we've eaten,' she said, switching on the radio. The midday news bulletin was about to begin, and just as the last of the headlines was read out, the toaster popped up and Omar handed her one of the two slices. Ever since he arrived, she had wondered how he could handle the hot slices without burning his fingers, and without being in any apparent hurry. He had told her that he was used to cooking over an open fire, so maybe that was the reason. Perhaps he had burned his fingers so often that they had lost all sensation. She felt a sudden urge to touch his fingers, reached for his hand and drew it to her. She ran her thumb over his fingertips and lifted his hand to her cheek.

'Mama,' he whispered gently and smiled. His eyes were so deep, so dark, so gentle, that she felt a sob rise in her throat. She released his hand, returned his smile and forked up some of the scrambled egg as a way to keep the tears from flowing. She wished that she could have had such a moment with her own boy, for Jonni to have looked at her with a sincerity in his eyes, something that might have demonstrated his fondness for her, a little warmth.

They ate in silence during the bulletin, but when Olga had swallowed the last morsel of bread, she cleared her throat and began.

'My dear Omar, your residence application was refused again,' she said, and saw the warmth in his eyes give way to a well of despair beyond description. 'The lawyer said that you came to Iceland using identity papers belonging to a man who was murdered in Istanbul.'

She had expected tears, trembling and a flood of questions. But Omar's reaction was something very different. He picked up his plate, still with a little scrambled egg on it, and hurled it at the wall with all his strength, so that shards rained down around her. She instinctively cowered down, lifting her shoulders and covering her face with her hands. When she looked up, he was gone.

79

Ebbi came across as a far more agreeable character than his brother Björn. He invited them in and welcomed Violet warmly. She had already told Daníel that Ebbi was a mechanic, and that was borne out by the sight of the oil ingrained in his hands as he poured coffee for them both. Ebbi lived in a small terraced house above Bústaðavegur, and a strip of the Fossvogur valley could be seen from his kitchen window, between the apartment block across the street and a flourishing spruce that had been planted in the open space outside a couple of decades ago, and which nobody had expected would grow as well as it had.

'I have to be honest with you, I'm very worried,' Ebbi said, and sighed as he sat at the end of the kitchen table. 'I've spoken to Björn a few times, but he just snarls back at me, so there's no way to get out of him exactly when Ísafold left, even. It's the same with him as it was with her. There's no point trying to talk to people when they're that screwed up.'

'What do you mean, screwed up?' Violet asked sharply, her tone bordering on accusatory.

'Getting high on their own supply?' Ebbi said, framing his statement as a question, as if that would somehow soften the effect of his words. It didn't seem to have the desired effect; Violet's lips pursed, and she folded her arms over her chest.

'Are you suggesting that Ísafold took an active part in Björn's dealing?' Daníel asked, glancing at Violet, who reacted instantly.

'Dealing?' she snapped. 'I was given to understand that his sentence was for possession, and those pills were for his own use. It wasn't a sentence for dealing.'

Daníel took a long breath, deep down into his belly and through his open mouth, so it wouldn't be heard. As was so often the case with relatives, Violet was deeply reluctant to believe anything bad about her own people, standing guard over the reputations of her daughter and her partner, even when the circumstances no longer warranted it.

'It's important to listen to what Ebbi has to say,' he said mildly, laying a gentle hand on Violet's arm. He glanced at Ebbi, nodding to indicate that he should answer the question.

'I don't think she was doing drugs, and I also don't believe that she took a direct part in dealing. Björn has plenty of young kids who deliver prescription drugs all over town, just like they're delivering pizzas,' Ebbi said, shaking his head in disgust. 'All the while, Björn sits safe at home and manages everything through the internet. But I know he used Ísafold to help him get hold of drugs.'

'And how do you know this?' Daníel asked.

'I talked to Ísafold when I met her at my mum's place for Sunday dinner a few weeks ago. She was depressed, so I pushed until I found out what was wrong, and she told me she had been sacked from work for stealing, and...'

Ebbi fell silent, as Violet sobbed and buried her face in her hands.

'And?' Daníel said, pressing him. He had the feeling that Ebbi was about to say something important.

'She said that Björn was angry with her because of it. Because she had lost her job. I imagine that Ísafold's access to the old folks' prescription medicines had been something of a goldmine for Björn.'

Ebbi stood up, tore a sheet from the kitchen roll on the worktop, and handed it to Violet, who carefully blew her nose.

When Daníel took Violet out to the car, he paused before he closed the passenger door.

'Sorry, I forgot to ask Ebbi something,' he said, shutting the door before she could ask what. In two long strides he was at the door. He knocked, and Ebbi, who had only just closed it behind them, opened it immediately. Daníel pushed him back into the hall, closing the front door behind him as he placed his palm on Ebbi's chest and forced him against the wall.

'What aren't you telling us?' Daníel said, staring hard into Ebbi's eyes, while he opened and closed his mouth, like a fish on dry land. 'Spit it out, man,' he hissed, pushing him harder against the wall until he finally spoke.

'I thought it would be too much for her mother. The last time I saw Ísafold, when we had dinner at Mum's place, she had two black eyes. She'd tried to cover it up with make-up, but you couldn't miss it.'

Daníel withdrew his hand from Ebbi's chest and took a step back.

'And?' he asked, returning to his usual mild tone. 'The family had nothing to say about her being treated like that?'

Ebbi shook his head, and his lips twisted into a bitter smile. 'The old lady worships the ground Björn walks on, so she's brilliant at just not seeing all the shit stuff he does. She's even furious with Ísafold for walking out on him. Me, I'm just relieved that she finally did it. I told her that day, and I'd told her a few months before, too, that she would have to leave him. It was getting crazy. He made her steal drugs, and then smacked her about,' he said. His voice cracked and dropped to a whisper. 'I offered to take her to the refuge, and I told her she could stay with me. I could have kept my brother away from her, but she seemed to have this faith that it wouldn't be long before everything would be just fine.'

A single tear escaped from the corner of Ebbi's eye and ran down his cheek, until he jerked his head to shake it off.

80

Now that the time to put his plan into action was approaching, Grímur felt a need to be close to Ísafold, to speak to her. He knew this was stupidly risky, but he had the feeling that he could be close to her by being near her body. He looked around, casting his eyes over the jagged lava before he clambered down into the fissure. He didn't get close to the suitcase, frightened that it would smell. It looked to have sagged in the middle and appeared to have softened, as well as which it had turned darker, so that in the night-time brightness it looked almost black.

The thought returned to him – just sixteen years for murder, and just two-thirds of that would be served.

'I promise not to let you down,' he said out loud. 'I promise I won't let you down. I'm sorry.'

That word, 'sorry', took hold of him, and it was as if his body was swamped with regret, a full bowl of remorse, so that it flooded out of him with the tears he was unable to control, blinding him so that the case blurred into the lava in a grey haze, as if the whole world were dissolving into a river of salt tears.

'Sorry, sorry, sorry.'

While it was too late, it was a relief to say it. He knew perfectly well that she couldn't hear him, but his plea for forgiveness was more for him than for her. He had to forgive himself for not having called the police more often, for not having gone up there a few more times to yell at Björn to pack it in, for not having applied more pressure on Ísafold to get her to walk out, for having allowed things to go on for so long that desperate measures had been called for. He needed to forgive himself for the fact that the woman he loved lay alone, stuffed into a suitcase and dropped into a ravine in a lava field, far away from anything beautiful, her lament the screeches of the wheeling gulls and the roar of jets as they approached Keflavík.

'You won't be alone much longer,' he whispered, wiping his face. 'I hope you can forgive me.'

He hauled himself out of the fissure in the rocks, jogged the little way to his car and sat inside. It was a while before he was able to control his breathing and the tears that threatened again and again to well up in his eyes. Once he was calmer, he reached for the glove compartment, took out the jewellery box containing the ring and opened it. He had bought the box from a jeweller, but now he was assailed by second thoughts. Black with a gilded band; maybe it was too dark. Perhaps a pink bow around it would add some colour, make it more feminine. But, of course, the packaging was unimportant. The ring itself was the main thing. He could allow Björn that the ring was beautiful. He had chosen a wonderful ring, with a ruby as red as fire instead of a diamond, making it different to most of the engagement rings you saw these days. But Björn should never have had the honour of putting it on Ísafold's finger. Björn was a bastard who had never deserved Ísafold. Just as he didn't deserve this new, vivacious and stunning girlfriend.

81

'What have you got yourself tangled up in this time?' Michael asked when he called, shortly before midnight. Áróra was sitting in bed watching TV, having declined Hákon's offer of a takeaway and a trip to the cinema. She had claimed to be too tired and hung over, but the truth was that the guilt was nagging at her. It was becoming a struggle to look him in the eye. On top of that was her gnawing guilt after last night's encounter with her mother, which was preventing her from even calling her. Then there was Daníel, and the look on his face when he had seen her with Hákon. After a couple of hours in bed, numbed by mindless television, she now felt that this whole trip to Iceland had turned into a clusterfuck from which she simply longed to walk away. She could catch a flight back home to Scotland, spend a few days lounging in bed, and put behind her Hákon and everything to do with him, along with Ísafold and all her problems, and never let them cross her mind again. But when Michael called with that tone in his voice, the excitement returned.

'I'm not tangled up in anything,' Áróra said, before correcting herself. 'Or ... Let's just say I'm not sure what I'm tangled up in.'

She sat on the edge of the bed and stretched to reach the light switch. She had done her best to darken the room for a better picture on the TV, but now she needed some brightness to wake her up, so that she would be able to take in everything Michael had to say.

'This guy, the one you sent me the information about, Hákon: he triggers alerts on every system.'

'And what does that mean?' Áróra asked.

'That means nobody will do business with him. He can't get a loan or any kind of finance package from the usual financial companies. It's probably because he's had a hefty debt somewhere and defaulted on it. I can see he's on a list of major debtors with one German bank, another one in Iceland, and a US bank.'

'So how has he managed to own all these hotels?'

'That's where the Swiss accounts come in,' Michael said. 'He clearly has plenty of money, but he doesn't have straightforward access to it, because in formal terms, he's bankrupt. What you said about the tourists paying over-the-top bills? That's a classic way of laundering cash. It could hardly be more obvious.'

'You mean he uses tourists as couriers, bringing the money to Iceland?'

'That's it. Professional tourists. It's well known. A lot of people around the world make a living out of this, couriering money for criminal organisations or individuals. It's a real five-star lifestyle. Presumably he does it this way because he's being watched. More than likely both the Icelandic authorities and the banks he owes money to are keeping a close eye on his business affairs.'

'So he can use the tourists to bring money that nobody is allowed to know is his to Iceland and put it into the hotel's finances?'

'Exactly,' Michael said. 'And doing this means that the hotel returns a profit, maybe even a large profit, so he can invest in the next project, which gives him an opportunity to get on his feet again in business in Iceland.'

'I know he pays the staff some of their earnings cash in hand. He told me that himself.'

'That fits as well. He's using some of the money he can't account for to reduce the hotels' running costs, so that the official profits look healthier. I feel sorry for anyone who buys one of his hotels on the basis of those accounts.'

That was an aspect Áróra hadn't thought of. Maybe it was part of a strategy to make the hotels' finances look healthy. That way he would be able to sell them for a respectable amount, but the buyer would undoubtedly be disappointed once the genuine running costs became apparent. It was a dirty trick, and Áróra immediately felt better about going behind Hákon's back.

'Michael, could I ask you to get in touch with the Icelandic tax authorities and the German bank Hákon owes a pile of money to, and ask if either or both of them have any interest in buying information about Hákon's secret accounts? No names, obviously.'

Michael was silent for a moment, and then cleared his throat. Áróra knew him well enough to recognise that this was an indicator that he was nervous.

'I'll do my best,' he said.

Áróra went to the window and drew back the curtains. Her hangover had cleared, and she was so wide awake after the call that she considered going outside for a walk, or even a run. Now she would have to hope that either the German bank or the Icelandic tax office would take the bait before Agla had her figured out.

82

I can feel the tension inside me, and I can't help but look forward to finding out if Michael can strike a deal with the German bank on my behalf.

I look forward to knowing how much the bank will agree to.

I look forward to knowing if I'll get the money, whether or not I'll have the chance to roll around in a bigger pile of cash than ever.

Then I remember Ísafold.

I shouldn't be looking forward to anything while I don't know how she's feeling. Most of all, I shouldn't be looking forward to making money. That's not only selfish, but contemptible, in a way that only sheer greed can be held in contempt.

I'm not a good sister. I'm not Ísafold's good sister.

SUNDAY

83

'This plate is nicer than the other one,' Omar said firmly, again offering a worn china plate he had bought in a charity shop to make up for the one he had smashed.

Olga sighed and decided to give up trying to explain to him that it wasn't the broken plate that had upset her so much, but his reaction – the fury, the violence that was implicit in hurling something towards her, and the fear it had awakened inside her.

She let her knitting fall into her lap, accepted the plate, and gave him a tired smile.

'Thank you, Omar. That's a really pretty plate.'

'I like it when crockery has flower patterns, not just plain white, or like that stuff from IKEA. And there's gold around the edge, look.'

Most of the gilding had long worn off, as had happened with her old mother's best plates, the ones Olga had taken to the charity shop along with so many of her belongings.

'Thank you, Omar,' she repeated, and he finally sat down. He shifted a few times in the armchair and looked at her intently. She took the knitting from her lap and put it aside.

'I am so sorry, Mamma,' he said. 'I am sad that I broke your plate. I don't understand why I can't stay here in Iceland. I want to work. I want to look after you as if you really were my mother. Because your son is dead, and I can be your son. It's not good to be an old woman and alone.'

Olga felt the emotion begin to choke her, just as it had done yesterday.

'That's what I wish for as well, my dear Omar,' she said. 'But because you came here with false papers, there's nothing more that can be done. The papers belong to a man who was mur-dered...?'

She slid a questioning tone into the last couple of words, to leave him no alternative but to answer her, but without making a direct accusation of her own.

'I knew that the man on the passport was dead,' he said. 'The guy who sold it to me said so. But I didn't know he had been mur-dered. I knew nothing about that.' He shook his head, and Olga looked into his dark eyes. There was no room in those eyes for dis-honesty. There were even tears glistening in his long, black eyelashes, and little pearls dropped to his cheeks as he blinked. 'I swear it, Mamma. I didn't know that the man had been killed.'

He placed the palm of his hand over his heart, so as to add em-phasis to his sincerity.

'I believe you, my dear Omar,' Olga said. 'I believe you.'

She sensed deep inside that this was the truth. She believed him. Sitting in the armchair facing her, he resembled nothing less than an angel, with the morning sun beaming through the window behind him so that he was bathed in its light.

She smiled, and brushed aside all the hesitation and doubt that had plagued her since her conversation with the lawyer. She could-n't believe anything bad about Omar, her wonderful foster son, her gift from the almighty.

84

The moment Björn's mother opened the door, Daníel knew it had been a mistake to bring Violet here. He had expected a quiet chat over coffee and even a pastry, but it was very clear that the old lady had no intention of inviting them in. She glared with hatred in her eyes at Violet, who seemed to stand taller in response, displaying the clearest look of contempt that he had ever witnessed.

'What the hell do you want here?' Björn's mother snarled, and it took Daníel a moment to realise that he would have to translate. It was obvious that they had met before, but there was a bitter chill between them.

'She's asking what we want,' he said quietly in English, and the old lady nodded. It came as a relief when Daníel realised that she wasn't going to understand much English, so he would have to translate both ways. That was just as well, as he saw that he would be able to soften the tone of the conversation.

'Ask her where my daughter is,' Violet said. 'Ask if she knows where she might have taken refuge from that vicious son of hers.'

'We're looking for Ísafold,' Daníel said, and the old lady snorted.

'Then you're definitely looking in the wrong country,' she said with a scowl. 'She walked out on my poor Björn and went back home. And only just engaged. So you can see what her promises are worth,' she said, with vehemence, spitting out the last few words.

'She says Ísafold went back to England,' he told Violet.

'She hasn't showed up there, and there's nothing to show that she went back,' Violet said, continuing before Daníel could translate. 'Maybe she's hiding somewhere that Björn can't find her and beat her, yet again.'

'What did she say about Björn? I heard she said something about Björn,' the old lady said, an accusing finger levelled at Violet.

'Were you aware that Björn was violent with Ísafold?' Daníel asked, and the woman's face fell. She took a step back and coughed awkwardly.

'Ísafold can blame herself for that,' she said. 'She used to provoke Björn until he didn't know which way to turn. And she didn't always talk nicely to him.'

This was an attitude that Daníel had encountered before. It was exactly what he had heard from families where domestic violence occurred.

'They had a tense relationship,' he said, and the old woman nodded. 'All the same, that doesn't justify domestic violence,' he added and the woman snorted and shook her head.

'It's not my problem that your daughter doesn't want to be in touch with you,' she said, staring at Violet.

'She has no idea where Ísafold is,' Daníel translated.

The two women glared at each other for a long moment, and the mutual loathing was almost palpable. He sighed with relief when Björn's mother shut the door, and he and Violet turned to make their way down the steps. There was nothing to be gained here. There would be police officers on duty who would take statements from Björn's family in the next few days.

85

The night's rain had washed away the grey cloud that had shrouded the city, and now the sun shone, warming the glass shell around the escalator at the airport so that the atmosphere inside was like a greenhouse. Áróra sat on a bench facing the steps and wondered whether to call her mother or not. She had expected her mother to call first, and the fact that she hadn't was a surprise. She had been anticipating the call the day before, the morning after their chance meeting in town, for her mother to go into detail concerning the error of her ways. She had her answers prepared. She was ready to explain that she had met Hákon there in the restaurant, and he had offered to accompany her back to the hotel, as she was tipsy. She knew perfectly well that her mother would figure out the lie, but also knew that sometimes she would gratefully accept a lie if the truth was too disquieting. But even though Áróra had her lies to hand, she still hadn't plucked up courage to take the initiative and call her mother.

She watched the escalator as it carried a steady flow of people up to the departure lounge. Most of them looked to be tourists heading home after spending time in Iceland, with just a scattering of Icelanders among them. Áróra couldn't put her finger on what it was that enabled her to unerringly pick them out. Perhaps it was something in the expressions, or the delight with which they moved, the anticipation on people's faces as they prepared to leave the country. Nobody understood more clearly than Áróra why Icelanders were always excited about going abroad. It didn't matter where people were going, they could be fairly certain that their destination would be cheaper, and with better weather.

She hadn't been waiting long when Michael's text message pinged, letting her know that his flight had landed, so she stood up and went over to arrivals. This wasn't such a pleasant place to wait, as between the throng of bemused tourists, the calls from guides holding signs, and all the taxi drivers, she felt that she was in the way, wherever she stood. Time and again someone shoved their way in front of her, so that she finally stood by the column directly in front of the doorway that emitted a stream of people, like a river in springtime flood.

The summer tourist season was clearly in full flow. In a few days it would be the summer solstice, with the sun barely kissing the horizon at midnight before rising again, and photographers and tourists from around the world would be waiting on beaches and docks to snap pictures of it.

Michael glanced around nervously as soon as he appeared in the arrivals hall, and Áróra had to wave and call out until he located her in the crowd.

'We'll have to be quick,' he said. 'I'm catching the return flight and meeting the German bank's collections director when I land at Heathrow, and we'll deal with an agreement then. They wanted to make this quick.'

Áróra took Michael's arm and steered him through the crowd to the pavement outside the terminal.

'Shit, it's cold,' he said, pulling on the jacket that had been folded over his arm.

'This is Icelandic summer weather,' Áróra said, shivering.

'I swear, here and now, in the presence of witnesses, that I'll never complain about Scottish weather again.'

Áróra laughed, and pointed to the car. An unusual stroke of luck had allowed her to park close to the terminal building. They got inside, and Michael opened his briefcase on his knees. A sheaf of tightly printed papers pinned together lay there.

'These are the documents I emailed to you,' he said. 'This is where you sign to give me authority to negotiate on your behalf. And this is where you agree to the payment schedule. And this is where you sign to agree my fee. As you can see, it's a big one, but you screwed up my weekend, and this is all happening so fast that my head's in a whirl.'

Áróra signed where he directed, and Michael returned the paperwork to his briefcase. They got out of the car, and she led the way back inside the terminal. As Michael stepped onto the escalator that would whisk him back upstairs, she quickly planted a kiss on his cheek.

'Michael,' she called after him. 'I'll be in touch soon. I'll take you out to dinner.'

He turned around and looked at her.

'I know you won't,' he called down to her, so loudly that his voice echoed against the glass. 'I know you're only using me,' he added, sounding sorrowful.

Áróra laughed, but felt a touch of embarrassment as the curious eyes of travellers turned towards her.

86

Grímur checked that Björn and the girlfriend, Kristín, were at the table with menus in their hands before he walked away and headed for the hot-dog stand. He asked for two with all the trimmings, and sat on one of the two wooden benches next to a couple of Japanese tourists, washing the hot dogs down with a carton of chocolate milk. The milk cut the bitterness of the onions that he felt were an essential element of a proper hot dog, regardless of any subsequent bad breath.

His usual Friday-night hot dogs, eaten this time on a Sunday, triggered childhood memories, and his mother's voice and her hoarse laughter as she tickled him echoed in his mind. They had always been so happy to treat themselves to a hot dog, at this very same hot-dog stand, before going to see a film on their monthly day out. Normally the cinema of choice was Gamla Bío, or Nýja Bío, as they didn't need to catch a bus and could walk there from the hot-dog stand, and Grímur was in no doubt that these days out had been the best days of each month for them both.

The sudden thought of what his mother would say about his plans cast a shadow over his happy memories, and he quickly stood up; too quickly, as the Japanese couple with their half-eaten hot dogs were startled. He apologised for alarming them and hurried away.

He knew how brusque he could be when he was immersed in his thoughts and emotions, and he understood that people could be frightened of him when he was at his most nervous, but right now it was irritating, as he wanted to blend into the crowd. Tonight he *had* to blend in. That was why he was wearing his wig. It was nylon, as he would have been revolted by genuine hair, and was shiny and looked slightly unreal. But he allowed the wig to sit tilted forward over his forehead, hiding his lack of eyebrows, which people seemed to see as the weirdest thing about him. He needed to maintain his appearance through to the evening, and he would have to keep his focus and not become absent-minded. He had to, because now it was a question of life or death.

The city centre was quieter than it was on Friday evenings, without the usual pre-weekend excitement. He dipped into his pocket and felt for the ring box. It was ready, with a deep-pink silk ribbon tied around it. He told the waiter who approached him at the door that he didn't need a table; he was just going to have a drink at the bar. He chose a seat that gave him a view of the table where Björn was doing his best to charm his new girlfriend. The place wasn't full, but was busy enough for the waiters to hurry back and forth, and there was a buzz of conversation. He half turned away from them, not so much that he couldn't keep a watchful eye on them, but enough, with the wig on his head, for him to remain unrecognised.

Grímur ordered a treble rum and coke, and sipped it slowly. His drink was sweet and strong, and he would happily have knocked it back quickly and ordered another. He would need all his courage tonight, but he also knew that more than one drink like this would jeopardise everything. He needed to be fit to drive and in full control of all his strength if this was all going to work out. And for Ísafold's sake, now that she lay abandoned and bundled into a crack in the rocks, it had to work out.

Grímur's heart lurched when Björn finally got to his feet and made his way to the toilet. He waited until the door had closed behind him, stood up and went straight to the table where Kristín sat, even more beautiful than before, if such a thing was possible. Her hair was pulled back, displaying her high forehead, and her eyes were highlighted wonderfully with silver eye shadow.

'Delivery for you,' Grímur said, handing her the case containing the ring.

'What is it?' she asked, her smile giving way to a look of surprise. For a moment, he pitied her. She certainly deserved to experience this moment, to be given a ring by a man she loved. But before his heart softened too much, Grímur reminded himself that he was saving her from Björn. This was going to hurt, but it would be so much better in the long run.

'No idea,' he said drily. 'I'm just the delivery boy.'

He turned and walked away, threading his way between the tables, taking the most direct route to the door and the outside world beyond. He took a few more steps, almost as far as the corner, and then turned and ambled back. He put a deerstalker on top of the wig, lifted the hood of his coat over both and strolled past the restaurant's big window, peering inside as he made his way slowly past. His view of their table in the middle of the room was partly obscured by those closer to the window, but by leaning and peering, he was able to make out Björn's expression as it went from astonishment to confusion, and then to the emotion that was always his final resort, fury. Grímur stayed by the edge of the window and tried to imagine what words were flooding from Björn's face, twisted in anger, as he gestured furiously with his hands, apparently shouting at both the waiters and Kristín, who sat with the box that had contained the ring in her hands. The ring itself was clamped between Björn's fingers, as he held it first in front of the waiter's face, and then Kristín's, as she burst into tears. Grímur would have preferred to have shielded her from this emotional switchback from surprise to delight, to confusion and finally to terror. He was able to see all of these feelings in her eyes as Björn snatched the ring box from her and rushed out of the restaurant, the veins in his neck pulsing and his face such a bright red that he seemed ready to explode.

'That's nothing,' Grímur whispered to the glass that separated him from her tear-streaked face. 'Compared to what I've saved you from.'

This was exactly how it had been supposed to play out. He felt a deep sympathy for the woman, but dramatic measures had been needed to push them apart. Because tonight the time was ripe.

87

'The city police are searching for Ísafold Jónsdóttir, aged thirty-four, who has not been seen since May. Her disappearance was reported to the city police on Thursday. Ísafold is one metre, sixty-three centimetres in height, of slim build and she has dark-brown hair and brown eyes. Anyone who can provide information on her whereabouts is asked to contact the police on 444 1000 or via the City Police Facebook page.'

A picture of Ísafold appeared on the screen as the report was read out. It was a close-up photo, quite grainy, as if it had been enlarged from a small picture, but it portrayed Ísafold's features well. The police contact number was at the bottom of the screen in large red letters. Áróra rewound and replayed the report. Then she did the same again. Ísafold's disappearance had become very real now that the police had put out an appeal for information. A chill ran down Áróra's back, and she wanted to cry, but the tears refused to come. She watched the appeal again and again in a daze, wondering why on Earth she had not flown to Iceland the last time Ísafold had asked her for help. Why hadn't she come here when her mother had asked her to go and help her sister? Now, as the appeal from the police played out on the screen, her fatigue and despair seemed so little in comparison to what could have happened to Ísafold. Her chagrin over Ísafold repeatedly returning to Björn now seemed so uncharitable.

If she had been tough, taken a flight to Iceland and done what she could to support her sister, then Ísafold wouldn't have blocked her on Facebook, wouldn't have stopped calling, would have carried on sending her YouTube clips of puppies and kittens. She hadn't realised until now that by not responding when Ísafold had been looking for help, she had been confirming the image that

Björn had been creating of her in Ísafold's mind – that she wasn't a good sister, that she had no fondness for her, that she couldn't care less about her. Not responding then had nullified all the occasions when she had. It made no difference that she had flown in from another country many times to support Ísafold and help her out. It didn't matter that she had comforted and assisted her since Ísafold had been a teenager, because deep down Ísafold had held on to her childhood resentment and the feeling that Áróra was just a 'lousy kid'. All the little acorns that Björn had sown to poison Ísafold's thoughts had fallen on fertile ground.

88

The early hours of Monday was the ideal time: few people went out in the city on Sunday evening, and the night that followed was so quiet and still, the drowsy houses could almost be heard snoring. He waited until three in the morning before lugging the suitcase out to the car. The final few revellers had already made their way home from bars and cinemas, and the dawn chorus hadn't yet woken Monday's early birds.

These few hours after midnight were also the darkest, and although it wasn't dark enough to hide his movements, the shadows cast by the low midnight sun were so impenetrable that anyone who saw him struggling to lift the suitcase into the boot of the car wouldn't easily be able to discern what was mirage and what was reality.

The case was much, much heavier than he had thought it would be, and the effort fatigued him more than he expected. But it wasn't only the exertion, it was also the emotional overload that was drawing all the energy from him. He had been terrified when he realised he wouldn't be able to lift the suitcase into the boot, but had quickly regained control and decided to try and get it onto the back seat instead. That worked better, as he could get inside the car, brace his legs and haul it in.

He was dripping with sweat by the time he got behind the wheel. It was getting on for five o'clock. He talked to himself without a break for half of the drive along Reykjanesbraut, giving free rein to his feelings. The terror inside him had found its voice, as it had the last time he had been ill, reminding him that someone must have seen him and now he'd be arrested and locked up in a dark, narrow cell where he wouldn't be able to shave whenever he needed to. He retorted – in his own voice, which was on the verge of cracking – that people bustling about with suitcases was such a common sight in Iceland these days that nobody would have taken any notice. The terror snapped back at him: the suitcase had clearly been far too heavy for him; anyone seeing him try, and fail, to get it into the boot of the car would be left in no doubt that it contained a body. His own voice was more controlled as he argued back that a heavy suitcase didn't automatically suggest the contents were a corpse. He gradually calmed down, and the sharp nagging of the terror deflated like a punctured balloon, so that the steady mutter of his retorts and arguments soon managed to drown it out.

He wasn't far short of the Grindavík turnoff when he noticed blue lights in the mirror. He slowed down and edged the car almost onto the hard shoulder to let them pass, but the lights continued to flash behind him, and he realised that this wasn't an ambulance in a hurry; it was the police stopping him.

I knew it! the terror inside him shrieked, and he began to hyperventilate, feeling the oxygen flowing through him and poisoning his thoughts. He stopped the car. If he didn't slow his breathing, there was every chance he would pass out. But that wasn't his main concern right now. He hadn't changed his trousers; neither had he checked to see whether they had been spattered with blood. And the giant suitcase couldn't be missed, bulging and looking ready to burst. His breathing came even faster as he saw in the rear-view mirror that a police officer had got out of the patrol car and was walking towards him.

Now the cops are coming to get you, murderer, the terror inside squealed, and this time he had no retort.

89

His thoughts were a whirl of indecision as he sat in the back of the patrol car and the policeman told him that the breathalyser showed he had been drinking.

'I have a flight to catch,' he said, trying to protest, knowing it was hopeless. 'I have to get to the airport.'

'And where are you off to?' asked the policewoman who sat in the driving seat. Her tone was amicable, as if she was making an effort to be cheerful, even friendly. Maybe they could see that Grímur was frightened.

'London,' he said without thinking. He hadn't prepared any kind of story that would justify this weird trip with an outsized suitcase, so he just said the first thing that came into his mind.

'Are there London flights this early?' the policeman asked, and Grímur quickly replied that he wanted to be in good time, that he had a horror of being late, that he was terrified of missing his flight.

'You can come down to the station with me for a blood test, and he'll drop your car off at the terminal,' the policewoman said, nodding in her colleague's direction. 'You're right on the blood-alcohol limit. So we can't allow you to drive.'

'No,' he said. 'We can leave the car here. I'll fetch it when I get back from London.'

The policeman had opened his door and already had one foot on the ground outside.

'It's not a problem. But there's no question of leaving your car here by the road while you're in London,' he said, extending a hand. 'Let's have the key. I promise I won't damage it.'

'He has a truck licence,' the policewoman joked. 'He'll park it in the long-term car park and you'll catch your flight. Just take care that you're stone-cold sober when you collect it. Not even one drink.'

Grímur's inner terror screamed at him that it was all over, that he was on the way to a dark cell with a bolt on the door. He handed the policeman the key, cursing last night's rum and coke, and his desperation gradually smothered all other sounds, including that of the policewoman's voice as she indicated and pulled out onto Reykjanesbraut, cruising past Grímur's car just as the policeman opened the door and sat behind the wheel.

He'll see the case on the seat, full to bursting, and it's game over, the terror howled. *Game over. You're going to prison, murderer. Handcuffs, a straitjacket and locked up in a dark cell where you'll choke on your own hair.*

90

Now I regret everything.

I regret making Ísafold's favourite Barbie doll do the splits and breaking it.

I regret sneaking into her make-up and ruining her new eye-liner by experimenting with it.

I regret the times I called her short-arse once I had grown taller than her.

I regret losing the scarf that was a gift from her first boyfriend.

I regret the time we had a row, and I called her a whore.

I regret not calling her.

I regret not getting the first flight to Iceland the last time she needed help.

MONDAY

91

It was around seven in the morning when Grímur stopped the car in the lay-by not far from the fissure in the lava. The low sun, which had been in his eyes, forcing him to drive at a snail's pace to keep the car on the narrow dirt road, had now vanished behind a heavy mist, rendering the green moss cloaking the lava almost colourless. He could barely understand how he had made it through the night's adventures. He was still numb with terror, but also proud of himself, that he had been able to hold it together well enough to chat about this and that with the police officers and the nurse who had come to take the blood sample, managing to come across as more or less normal. At least, he had been normal enough for them to release him once they'd parked his car in the long-term car park at the airport, handing him the key with a few wise words about not driving after even a single drink. The policeman who had driven his car to the airport appeared not to have paid enough attention to the suitcase to notice that it bulged oddly.

The terror that had screeched inside him ever since he had set off in the middle of the night and the loud howls of desperation that had taken over when the police had pulled him over had now both fallen silent, replaced by a deep, dark sadness that chimed with his soul. The sadness spoke to him with his own voice.

He got out of the car and looked around. There was open ground all around him and no traffic as far as the eye could see. The lava field looked to be perfectly flat, but it deceived the eye, which failed to see the fissure slashed into the hard surface. Some of these jagged ravines stretched so deep and so far that they reached the sea. There was more to this place than what was on the surface. You needed to look closely to make out what lay beneath.

He set off over the uneven lava, and found the place where it opened into the fissure where the red suitcase lay, caught fast between two outcrops, far below. He wasn't going down there now. That would take too much time, and he didn't have any energy to waste. He was exhausted, and the last hurdle was still ahead of him.

'So, this is it,' he whispered into the fissure, then walked back to the car, where he opened the back door. It was easier than he thought to haul the case out, but he noticed with horror that there was a patch of blood on the seat. He froze for a moment, and the terror deep inside him gave a low moan. He brushed his concerns aside. This was a detail he could pay attention to later in the day. Now there were more urgent things to attend to.

He set off, dragging the suitcase behind him, cursing every step, as each rewarded him with only a few centimetres of progress. The gravel underfoot was coarse and the canvas caught on every jagged edge. But in the lava field itself the going was easier, as the case slid along more smoothly over the hard surface of the rock. He had hauled it a metre or more when he noticed that the case left a trail of blood that was clearly visible, so he had to use precious energy to turn the case over. Then he sat for a while on the cold rock at its side and rested, the sadness echoing a steady tone inside his head, and the dark bloodstain on the suitcase a clear symbol that his life would never be the same again.

He finally got to his feet and dragged the case further, more by force of will than muscle power, and managed with an extraordinary effort to shove it over the edge so that it tumbled into the fissure, making dull thuds as it collided with the walls. He was too weak to stand, so he lay on his belly at the edge of the ravine and peered down. The grey case hadn't fallen alongside the red one that contained Ísafold's remains, but had dropped on top of it, so that only the grey case could be seen. For a moment Grímur wondered whether to climb down and push the grey case aside so that it would slide further down, but decided against it. It was better left as it was. Grey was less visible from a distance than red, in the unlikely event that anyone were to come this way and peer into this gap in the lava. And anyway, Ísafold was long gone, so she would hardly mind. Her soul, with its feelings and joy, and the beauty that was inside her, had forsaken this deep, dark hole long ago.

'I'm so sorry,' he whispered to her, all the same, before he got to his feet and made his way back to the car. Ísafold's soul would be somewhere free and beautiful, maybe here above the lava field, or higher up, above the clouds, where the sun always shone. Wherever she was, he felt it was right to ask her forgiveness for dishonouring like this the last resting place of her earthly remains.

He sat in the car, took the engagement ring from his pocket, unhooked the chain around his neck and threaded the ring onto it. He hadn't been able to withstand the temptation to take the ring from Björn's pocket, before smashing his kneecaps so that he would fit in the suitcase. On his way to eternity, Björn had no use for this ring. On the other hand, Grímur would treasure the feeling of keeping the jewel Ísafold had worn close to his heart.

92

Áróra steered the trolley the waiter had brought to the room and placed it like a coffee table between the two chairs. It was arrayed with a coffee pot, a milk jug, a sugar bowl, two cups and a bowl of pastries, along with a little vase containing a single tulip, everything beautifully arranged on a white cloth. She had dressed early that morning, and since then had nervously paced the room, rehearsing what she would say to the representative of the German bank who was on the way to deliver her fee.

Her nerves were making her fingers tremble, and she could feel the sweat collecting under her armpits when the knock on the door finally came. She was always like this on the home straight. The stress would always take hold of her, and she wouldn't believe that things were going to work out until she finally spread the cash on a bed and rolled in it. That would be the moment when she knew that the money was actually hers.

For whatever reason, she had assumed that the bank's representative would be a man, so she was taken completely by surprise when she opened the door to see a woman outside, holding a briefcase and a vast bouquet of flowers – a woman she recognised.

'Congratulations,' Agla said as she walked into the room. 'And a pleasure to do business with you.'

She held out the bouquet, and Áróra took it, speechless with amazement. She had no idea why Agla was here, or what she meant by congratulating her, or where she should put the bunch of flowers. It was in a vase, but it was so big that the bedside tables were far too small for it and the table by the wall that she had been using as a desk was full. Flustered, she placed it on the floor by the window. None of this appeared to take Agla by surprise; she sat in one of the chairs, picked up a cup and poured herself coffee.

'Help yourself.'

'Just ten drops,' Agla said, filling her cup, reaching for a pastry and dunking it in her coffee so that it spilled onto the white cloth.

Áróra took a seat facing her and looked into her eyes.

'You're the German bank's representative?' she said, once she had marshalled her thoughts.

'Of course,' Agla laughed. 'Why did you think I was congratulating you? You did a fine job. Great to do business with you. I'm working for Hákon's largest creditors. It has been a long process – a few years, to tell you the truth. I had to invest in his hotels in order to get into the books and figure out where he keeps all the money he's pumping into the company. But he's cautious when it comes to me and my people, so we had to find another way to find the pot of cash.'

Áróra sighed. So that was the situation, she thought to herself. Of all the possible scenarios she could have imagined concerning Agla's involvement with Hákon's business affairs, this one hadn't even occurred to her.

'So you turning up was manna from heaven,' Agla said. 'The right person, in the right place and at the right time. Now everyone will get what's theirs. The bank gets a decent chunk of what's owed, and the taxman will take some as well. His accounts are being frozen right now.'

'Not forgetting me,' Áróra said, glancing at the briefcase, and Agla handed it to her.

'Richly deserved,' she said. 'Can I ask what your background is?'

'Didn't you say that you know who I am?' Áróra asked.

'I did some research about you when you first appeared on the scene. I found out that you're a skilled bloodhound when it comes to money, but I don't know how you got into this business, and I'm curious about your background.'

'That's simple,' Áróra replied. 'I don't have any training. I worked for an accountancy firm for a few years as a secretary, punching in numbers, and wanted to train as an accountant. But I gave up on the course when I found out how boring it was. Then I wanted to go into the theatre but found that I'm too big to be an actress. By coincidence, I was helping a friend who was going through a difficult divorce. Her husband took all their savings and hid the lot, and I managed to find it. That's how it started.'

'That's fantastic,' Agla said. 'There's plenty of work for you in Iceland. Nobody here knows who you are, and you don't have any baggage, so it would be easier for you to get close to people.'

'I'm not planning on staying,' Áróra said. 'I have a personal errand to finish, and when that's done I'll be going home.'

She felt her throat tighten as she said the words. There seemed to be no immediate likelihood that Ísafold would show up, so there was no telling how long she would be in Iceland.

'Let me know,' Agla said, getting to her feet. She slid a hand into her jacket, took out a business card and placed it on the trolley. 'Get in touch if you're looking for work.'

She vanished through the door, and for a moment Áróra sat numbly staring at the space in front of her. Then she jumped to her feet and leapt out of the door, just as the lift hissed open in front of Agla.

'What's in it for you?' she called after her. 'What do you get out of it? I reckon I must have just taken your fee for finding the money.'

'I own a majority share in the largest hotel in Akureyri, and I can sell it,' Agla said. 'At a sizeable profit, as far as I can see. Hákon has done a fine job making the accounts look so fantastic that its value must have gone through the roof.'

93

'Use this. Cut your hair using the shortest setting,' Grímur told the Arab boy, handing him his beard trimmer. 'Then you need to shave as close as you can. And put these clothes on. Pack only what you absolutely need into one small case and come back downstairs to my place as quickly as you can.'

He pushed the bundle of clothes he had pulled at random from Björn's wardrobes into Omar's hands, along with a blazer and a mustard-yellow scarf. They were top-quality clothes, expensive designer stuff, and much smarter than anything Omar could have ever been used to wearing. The boy left, clearly upset, and the look on his face brought both exhilaration and fear. Grímur waited until the door had closed behind him, snatched up the keys, hurried up the stairs and pulled on a pair of rubber gloves before he went into Björn's flat. He tiptoed through the living room, picked up the laptop from the coffee table and made his way quickly back to the door, where he hesitated. He turned back and went into the bathroom, where he picked up a jar of make-up from the little cosmetics bag that lay on the half-empty shelf. He left, silently closing the door behind him, and lost no time going back down the stairs. He didn't dare stay too long in the apartment, as someone might come.

In his own flat, Grímur opened the laptop, and to his delight found there was no password. This was amazing, considering Björn used this computer to co-ordinate his dealing activities. It was one more example of the man's arrogance: how secure and untouchable he considered himself to be. Grímur opened Björn's wallet and took out his credit card. He checked that the computer was still connected to the router in Björn's apartment before he tapped in the web address. He booked a return flight to Canada in Björn's name, checked him in online and added all the required information.

None of this had been thought out, but Omar, Olga's Arab boy, fitted in perfectly. He was stuck here in Iceland without a residence permit, and Olga seemed to be worrying endlessly about him being sent back to Syria. Nobody but he and Olga knew he was here, so nobody would miss him, and Olga wouldn't go to the police.

He was just finished on the computer when the boy returned, his hair cropped close to his scalp, clean-shaven and wearing Björn's clothes. Grímur told him to sit still and then opened the jar of make-up. He wondered what he could use to apply the cream to his face, and reflected that there was probably some tool in the make-up bag designed for just that, but to save time, he used his fingers. He hooked a blob onto one finger and put some on each cheek and in the centre of his forehead. Then he rubbed it in and stood back to check out the results. At a distance, it was convincing. The boy's skin looked considerably lighter, and he was satisfied with this crop-haired, paler-skinned version.

94

Olga started to get worried when she had been home from work for a while and there was still no sign of Omar. He had gone out after their conversation yesterday morning, saying that he was going to the gym, and after that she'd not seen him all day. She was sure that she had heard the door open and close again during the night, but as she had taken a sleeping pill, her head was heavy and her thoughts came slowly, so she couldn't be sure if it had been a memory or a dream. In the morning the door to his room had been shut, so she assumed he was asleep and quietly went out without waking him. But now she thought about it, he should have been awake before her, as usual, preparing their morning coffee. If everything had been as usual.

But it wasn't. It was more than likely that yesterday's conversation had changed things. She felt that it had gone well; she had seen the sincerity in his eyes and had believed him. He seemed to have accepted the situation and hugged her before going out. Thinking back, maybe something had upset the balance of the relationship they had shared before she had known who he really was. Not that she had the slightest idea now, but at least she knew who he wasn't. She could be sure that his name wasn't Omar, anyway. Perhaps she had pushed him too hard by asking about the murdered man in Istanbul? He could have some history that he preferred her not to know about. Maybe, in spite of everything, and in contrast to what her instincts told her, he really did have something to hide.

She picked up the toaster and put it on the kitchen table, plugging it into the socket that was normally used for the little kitchen radio. She put two slices of bread in it and reached for butter, cheese and jam from the fridge. As the two slices popped up, she immediately put two more in. It was a long time since she had done this. When she was younger, and Jonni was trying her patience, this was how she had sought solace, with endless rounds of toast. Sometimes she had lost count, only noticing when half a loaf had disappeared. She buttered the slices generously and added cheese right away so that it would soften and start to melt on the hot toast, and then she would take a bite, leaning forward so that the liquid butter would drip onto the plate in front of her and not down the front of her sweater.

She mulled over the possibilities while she chewed. She couldn't call the police to ask about Omar – whether he had been arrested – as that would reveal that he hadn't left the country. Calling the movement wasn't an option, as that would tell them that she had broken the rules and allowed Omar to stay with her for far too long. And the news that he had travelled to Iceland on a murdered man's papers would definitely exclude him from any future assistance from them. The only structure NDM seemed to have was that it chose carefully who would be helped and who wouldn't. Apart from that, it didn't seem to concern itself with how people passed from one household to the next. Omar had just been given a list of people on a sheet of paper of people willing to offer shelter to refugees, and after that it was up to them to look after themselves, so that nobody higher up in the movement would be in the position of having to lie to the police. It also stated on the piece of paper that people were recommended to stay no longer than two to three weeks in one place; and, as a further security measure, that refugees shouldn't say where they would be going next. Olga had feared this day would come, that one day Omar would pack up and leave, and that she would have no idea what had become of him. But that couldn't be what he'd done; she'd looked in his room, and as far as she could see, all his stuff was still there. Surely he hadn't left her, taking with him nothing but the clothes he wore?

She took the next two slices from the toaster and looked at them on the plate before her. She had only eaten one, and had another buttered and ready. She knew that these two freshly toasted slices wouldn't be enough to put her mind at ease over Omar, so she took two more and dropped them into the toaster. She would eat until she felt calm again.

95

In the hallway Grímur kneaded a thin layer of make-up onto the backs of Omar's hands and onto his neck, telling him to take care not to scratch his face and scrape a hole in the new pale skin that would open the gateway to the promised land.

'Icelandic passport holders with a valid ETA – that's an electronic travel authorisation – are exempt from giving biometrics when entering Canada, so you won't be photographed or have your fingerprints taken. So when you arrive there, if you avoid the automatic gates and go for a border control desk with an actual officer, it will all depend on whether he or she thinks you look like Björn.' He opened Björn's passport and compared his photo to Omar. 'And you kind of do look like him, now you've got rid of the hair.'

He handed him Björn's passport, his wallet and printouts of his travel documents: the bus ticket to the airport, tickets for the flight to Canada and a completed ETA travel pass, all of them in Björn's name.

'Use the time on the plane to memorise Björn's full name and date of birth. If border control asks you what you are doing in Canada, you are a tourist on holiday. If they do realise you're not Björn, you tell them loud and clear that you are asking for asylum in Canada. Then they will put you in the refugee system there.'

'Do you think this will work?' Omar's voice was low, almost a whisper.

'I think you have a fifty-fifty chance,' Grímur said. It was the honest answer. 'In any case you will be in Canada. And the biggest hurdle refugees face when trying to get to Canada through Iceland is actually getting out of Iceland. The outer borders of the Schengen area are very hard to cross, but you, my boy, you have an Icelandic passport this time, so that makes life easy.'

He inspected Omar one more time, and opened the hall cupboard, where he rummaged until he found a cap that he placed on his head. It didn't do any harm to cast a little shadow over his face. He wasn't convinced by his own efforts as a make-up artist.

'I'll drive you to the bus station,' he said, and when he saw the boy hesitate, he repeated the speech he had given him that morning. 'Olga must still be at work, so send her a message when you get to Canada. It's better for her if she doesn't know about this, because if you're caught, she'll be guilty as well. You don't want her to be guilty, do you? After everything she's done for you?'

Omar shook his head and looked downcast, like a scolded child.

He followed Grímur out to the car, walking stiffly, and Grímur told him to put his case in the boot. There was a towel over the back seat, which was still wet from being cleaned. He had finally gone to a car wash and used a high-pressure washer on the seat after he had soaked it with detergent. The bloodstain was no longer visible, but it would take a long time to dry out. On the way to the bus station, he lectured Omar on how he should behave in Canada.

'Only use the credit and debit cards to buy stuff for small amounts, less than five thousand Icelandic krónur, so you don't need to use a PIN. It's enough to just put the card quickly into the reader, like I showed you. Buy as much as you can of food and necessities over the first couple of days, and then get rid of the cards and the passport. You can give the cards to someone who's homeless. That'll lay a false trail for the police when they come looking for you. And take the SIM card out of your phone now and throw it away. Buy yourself a new one in Canada.

'OK,' Omar said, fussing with his phone as he opened it, while his knee pumped frantically up and down, as if he was struggling to maintain control over his body and needed to release some inner tension.

'And remember when you go to the departure gate, make sure you go to the one where there are manual checks. The automatic gates take a picture, and I don't know if these are checked against passport photos. In any case, it's easier to fool a person than to deceive a computer. And remember to breathe normally and walk tall, be confident. You have an Icelandic passport, so nobody should pay you too much attention.'

'I'll do that,' Omar said, his leg still pumping.

'Deep breaths,' Grímur said.

They were at the entrance to the bus station when Grímur handed him Björn's phone.

'Take this with you and drop it in a bin somewhere as soon as you get to Canada. I don't have the PIN to open it, so you can't use it. But it'll help if it can be traced out of the country.'

Omar took the phone and dropped it in his pocket.

'Björn will go crazy if he figures out that I'm pretending to be him and I've taken his stuff to Canada,' Omar sighed, then laughed nervously. Grímur gave him an encouraging smile and patted his shoulder.

'It serves the bastard right,' he said, and this time Omar laughed louder.

'That's right,' he said. 'He deserves it. He was bad to Ísafold, and Ísafold is my friend.'

'Mine too,' Grímur said. For a moment their eyes met and they understood each other.

'Did she come and say goodbye to you before she left?' Omar asked, and Grímur was sure that his eyes filled with tears.

'No,' he said. 'She left without a word.'

Omar sniffed and a few tears spilled down his cheek.

'Careful,' Grímur warned, rummaging in the glove compartment for a tissue, dabbing cautiously at Omar's cheek. 'Deep breaths, remember?'

'You're a good man, helping me like this. Thank you.'

Omar stretched out a hand, and Grímur took it lightly, taking care not to spoil the make-up he had applied to the backs of Omar's hands.

'Good luck,' Grímur said, and watched the boy disappear into the bus station, hoping fervently that everything would work out for him. This hadn't been part of the plan. The idea had come to him that morning when he found Björn's passport in the desk drawer. If everything were to work out, it would be perfect – and it needed to work; Omar had to make his escape to Canada. Because if he were caught, then they would probably both be in deep trouble.

96

The cash is in neat bundles in the briefcase. I pick up a wad of ten-thousand-krónur notes, weighing it in my hands. The notes are beautiful, blue, with a plover and its chicks on the back, as if the role of these birds was to be the harbingers of an endless springtime for the economy. But they don't spark any desire.

Normally I would have pulled the stack of notes apart, spread them out on the clean, white hotel bed and rolled around naked in them.

Usually I would have revelled in this, throwing banknotes in the air and letting them rain down on me, laughed out loud, cracked open a bottle of champagne. I'd have felt the power of money seeping into my body, quivering with anticipation as it took root in my heart.

But as I hold the cash in my hands, there's no feeling. All I can feel is a gnawing fear about what may have happened to my sister.

I put the wad of banknotes back in the briefcase and close it.

TUESDAY

97

The commissioner's office still felt oddly empty, even though it was now five years since she'd been appointed. The floor was bare, with no mats or carpets, and the walls were just as blank. The place gave the impression that the furniture had been delivered and put down anywhere, placed at random rather than with any kind of order in mind. When she'd started in the post, the commissioner had moved her office down a couple of floors at the station, and Daníel felt that this move, closer to the lower-ranking police officers, symbolised her approach, although the office still looked as if she had moved in yesterday. There were a few small red armchairs here and there, and when a meeting was called, these were arranged around a modest coffee table, as was the case now. The commissioner's desk and computer were in the corner by the window, almost like an afterthought – facilities necessary for the job, not status symbols.

'It sounds like grounds for suspicion of illegal activity,' the commissioner said when she had taken a seat, Ísafold's case files in her hands. 'We all know what domestic violence means.'

The two Jóns – CID superintendent Jón and deputy police commissioner Jón – both nodded in agreement. They waited in silence while she leafed again through the pages of the dossier Daníel had prepared for her so that she could evaluate the circumstances as quickly as possible.

'Daníel can decide how big a team he needs, and he'll consult with you, Jón,' she said, handing the dossier to the deputy police commissioner. 'As usual, the deputy national commissioner can handle the media, so everything needs to go through him,' she added. 'If there are any problems, I'll be answerable,' she concluded.

She always said that, and was as good as her word. On the occasions when the police had been criticised, she had stood up and responded to the media. She had apologised for errors, explained the facts and provided cover for those who were doing their jobs. As a result, she had little by little earned respect within the force. Even those who had been most suspicious of a young blonde woman from out of town being appointed commissioner had been forced to admit that she did a good job.

They stood up, and for a moment, just a second or two, they looked each other in the eye, the glances heavy with meaning and a tension in the air. Then the commissioner nodded and left her own office ahead of them, and Daníel took a deep breath. His first task would be to talk to family members, and that meant Violet and Áróra.

98

Olga hadn't even dressed when she decided to knock at the doors of the two neighbours she knew were aware Omar was staying with her. Maybe they had noticed something. Perhaps they had seen the police arrive and take Omar away to be deported. Or they could have seen him leave and might have asked where he was going, had a chat with him on the stairs. She knew she was clutching at straws, but she could no longer wait for a sign of life from Omar himself.

She quickly ran a brush through her hair. It wasn't much of an improvement; she had spent much of the night awake and restless, and now her hair was plastered down at the sides. She rubbed in some face cream, applied deodorant to her armpits and dabbed a drop of the aromatic oil Omar had given her behind each ear. This gave her a scent of incense, not dissimilar to the smell that had always been in Jonni's room when he tried to disguise the grass he smoked. She had thought the smell was harmless and so hadn't worried about it. She shook off these thoughts, went into the bedroom, pulled on a pair of tracksuit bottoms and an outsized T-shirt, and it was hardly over her head before she was out on the stairs, heading down a floor to talk to Grímur, the weird bald guy.

Grímur answered the door after she had knocked twice. She knew he would be in, because he always was. At some time or other he had mentioned to her that he was on disability benefits, and that hadn't come as a surprise. His manner was so odd, it was clear there was something not quite right about him. But she was grateful to him for not reporting that Omar had been staying with her, even though it was obvious that he knew everything about his situation. She had even heard him once on the stairs, warning Omar that he shouldn't spend so much time outside and that someone might report him, so Grímur had to be a decent person.

'Good morning,' she said, and he mumbled something in reply. 'I was wondering if you had seen Omar at all? I haven't seen him since the day before yesterday and I'm getting worried.'

Grímur had already begun to shake his head before she had finished her sentence.

'No, I haven't seen anything of him,' he said, and made to shut the door, but Olga put her hand on the door frame.

'You haven't seen the police, have you?' she whispered. 'I'm terrified they've arrested him and are going to send him back.'

'No, I haven't seen the cops,' Grímur said.

'Do you remember when you last saw him?' she asked, and he again shook his head. 'Could you try and remember?' she said. 'If you'd be so kind,' she added, realising how pushy she sounded.

Grímur looked down at the floor, and his forehead furrowed. He looked so odd, completely hairless; it had to be some kind of skin disease, maybe even cancer.

'No,' Grímur said at last. 'I don't remember when I saw him last.'

Olga sighed. This wasn't helping. Grímur closed his door and she went back up the stairs to knock at Björn's and Ísafold's door. She was surprised when a young woman opened it, and at first thought she had to be Ísafold, but quickly saw her mistake. This one was a very different type.

'Yes?' the woman said, and seemed to notice Olga hesitate. 'I'm Kristín, Björn's girlfriend. Well ... we're dating.'

Olga couldn't hide her surprise. 'Björn and Ísafold have split up?' she asked.

'Yes, quite a while ago. I gather she packed her stuff and just left. Back home to Britain.'

'Well,' Olga said. 'You know her family have been looking for her, and the police are involved? She hasn't turned up in England.'

Now it was the young woman's turn to be surprised. 'What?' she said. 'Björn hasn't said anything about this.'

Olga nodded and said nothing. It wasn't for her to tell the new girlfriend that what Björn called 'quite a while' was hardly even a month. It was certainly less than a month ago that she had seen Ísafold on her way up the stairs with a bag of shopping.

'It was Björn I wanted to speak to,' Olga said. 'I was going to ask if he had seen anything of Omar, a young foreigner who has been staying with me for the last few months. I didn't see him yesterday and I'm getting a little—'

She didn't manage to finish her sentence before the young woman let out a wail of surprise.

'You're joking,' she burst out. 'Björn has disappeared as well. I can't find him anywhere, and he isn't answering his phone or anything. I decided to call in on the way home from work to check up on him, but he isn't here.'

'Well,' Olga said, not knowing what else she could say. 'What on Earth is going on in this place?'

99

Grímur hadn't been awake long when Olga from upstairs knocked on his door. He couldn't have slept any longer, yet he was exhausted, and every atom of his body ached. He had spent the previous evening thoroughly cleaning the car again, and had taken pictures so that he could put it up for sale online. He no longer needed it; the car had done its work. He'd price it attractively for a quick sale, and he would fill in the paperwork himself and send it off. The fewer people who had anything to do with it, the better.

The bathroom was more of a problem. He would have to start by cleaning it exceptionally well, then the cash from the sale of the car could go into a complete makeover. The tiles would have to go, the washing machine would have to be removed, the walls and ceiling would need painting and tiling all over again, and he'd need a new washer and dryer.

There had been much more blood than he had anticipated. He had expected this to be a bloodless killing, for it to be neat, if that was the right way to describe it. But murder was never neat, of course; it had been harder than he had imagined. Björn had been agitated and hadn't wanted the beer Grímur had offered when he had seen him on the stairs. But when he said he had a few things to tell Björn about his girlfriend, he took the bait, followed him in, and accepted the beer. He had been flushed, his eyes flashing back and forth around the flat, and couldn't be persuaded to sit down. It was clear that the incident with the ring in the restaurant had upset him deeply.

'What have you got to tell me?' he demanded, pushing the can of beer aside.

Grímur mumbled something about knowing a thing or two about Kristín's past, but was then unable to think of anything that might get Björn to sit down and drink his beer – the beer Grímur had laced with the ketamine he had bought from Björn himself.

Björn had turned, snorting with disgust as he headed for the door, making it plain he had no interest in Grímur or anything he might have to say. So Grímur had no choice but to knock him out with the statuette of Venus de Milo. It was a decision taken on the spur of the moment; the statuette was close at hand, and heavy enough for a decent knockout blow.

But when he had pulled the plastic bag over Björn's head, he came to and fought back, turning out to be as strong as he looked. He pushed Grímur off, ripped the plastic bag from his head and hauled himself onto all fours, but Grímur hit him again with Venus de Milo. It was a poor blow, glancing off Björn's head. It was enough to lay him out, but not to knock him unconscious. So Grímur dodged into the bathroom and snatched up his old razor. Björn followed, furious and certain of his own superior strength. Arrogant arsehole.

Grímur slashed his throat with a single, determined movement that was so smooth and quick he might have been practising it for years. The hand holding the razor swished through the air, and Grímur was surprised at his own adroitness, as if thought had given way to some hidden ancient power that steered his hand. Then he stood gasping as Björn's life ebbed away, and he felt his heart fill with sympathy.

To begin with Björn had tried to clasp his hands over the gaping wound in his throat, which pumped an unstoppable flow of blood out between his fingers. This reaction – to cover the wound – was pointless and stupid, and at the same time so human. It was completely natural to fight for your life, an instinctive response. Grímur's sympathy was not because he thought Björn deserved a less brutal end – he had shown Ísafold no mercy, after all – but was a simple sympathy for a living thing, an animal of his own species that it went against his nature to harm. But he had to do it. Because murder was only sixteen years, out after ten.

Björn deserved a much, much harsher punishment for what he had done to Ísafold – for beating her to death, stuffing her body into a suitcase and then driving out to Reykjanes and dumping her in a crack in the lava, like someone would an old sofa.

For doing that he deserved to suffer the same fate himself.

100

Daníel was irritated with himself for having given in on Friday to Violet's insistence that they speak to Björn. Their visit had undoubtedly frightened him, to the extent that he had now fled the country.

Daníel stood with a cup of coffee in his hand by a window in the Hverfisgata police station's canteen, gazing out as he waited for the two of them to arrive. He had told Violet that it would be better for them to come to the station; it felt uncomfortable to give them the news at his place – that would give the impression that he was somehow on both sides of the table concerning this case. He had to remind himself to maintain his professionalism, particularly when he thought about the effect that Áróra had on him. Around her he seemed to lose his senses. He was still smarting with shame over his own reaction on Friday evening. He should have smiled and greeted her like a civilised gentleman. But it was too late to worry about that now. He just hoped that Áróra wasn't annoyed with him. He needed to give her bad news, and that would just add an extra layer of complexity.

'They're here,' his colleague Helena said, and he finished his coffee, took the cup to the sink, rinsed it and placed it in the dishwasher. He and Helena walked side by side along the corridor to the interview room on the fifth floor. Before going in they stopped by the door, each catching the other's eye, as if giving mutual encouragement. Interviews with a victim's relatives were always difficult.

Mother and daughter sat together at the table, and now he regretted not having taken them to the canteen instead. It was a warmer place, painted in dark colours, and with a carpet that lapped against the walls. In contrast, the interview room was empty and impersonal, and not the ideal place for breaking bad news.

'We are gradually piecing together a timeline of events concerning Ísafold's disappearance,' Helena said when greetings had been exchanged and they had taken their seats opposite Violet and Áróra. She had the folder in her hands containing printouts of documents relating to Ísafold. Daníel glanced at it and suddenly regretted how slim it was, how little information they had on this case.

'It appears,' he began, and cleared his throat, 'that Björn has absconded, to Canada.'

Helena opened the folder and continued, reading the information from the first sheet of paper.

'He caught a flight yesterday afternoon, was registered on arrival in Canada the same evening, and was seen on CCTV leaving the terminal building in Toronto, after which sight of him was lost. He's not answering his phone and hasn't made any appearance on social media. He has a return flight booked in two days, but we're fairly sure he won't be on it.'

Daníel watched Violet's and Áróra's reactions as Helena spoke; it was clear from the expression on Áróra's face that she understood all the implications. She blinked rapidly and nodded. However, some kind of hope appeared to have awoken in Violet's eyes.

'Could Ísafold have disappeared like that as well?' she asked. 'Could they have decided to disappear together? To run away from debts or to get away from people Björn was in trouble with over this pill business?'

Her eyes went from Daníel to Helena and back, desperately seeking confirmation that this might be a possibility. Daníel wished that he could, with a clear conscience, allow her to hang on to the idea that her daughter was safe and well in Canada, but Helena quickly extinguished this tiny spark of hope in Violet's eyes.

'There's no evidence that she has left the country. She does not appear to have bought a flight, or a ticket for the ferry from Seyðisfjörður. We have an active alert request that should flag her up if she's registered entering another country, but we aren't confident of getting a positive response.' Helena allowed this information to sink in before she continued. 'But it goes without saying that we will keep trying to find out as much as we can, and we'll carry on searching for her...' she said, and fell silent, leaving the final word to Daníel – the final word that would bring Violet's hopes to an end.

'The police are working on the assumption that Björn has fled justice,' he said, keeping his voice as mild as he could, in the hope that this might soften the blow. 'Because we believe he has harmed Ísafold.'

101

Áróra had expected Daníel to be the bearer of bad news, but all the same, she was shattered by the meeting at the police station. She and her mother had asked question after question, as if every moment they could prolong the meeting might extend Ísafold's life in their minds. But as they left the interview room and walked along the police-station corridor, they knew they would have to accept the reality that Ísafold had vanished for good.

Daníel and the female officer who worked with him patiently answered all their questions, explaining the process ahead. Björn would be listed on Interpol as a person of interest, they said. There would be an application for a warrant to search his flat. A court would be asked to grant permission for Ísafold's and Björn's banking details to be examined and card use to be checked. They would seek information on the use of their phones to try to find out where Björn had been around the time of Ísafold's disappearance, and so on and so on. They didn't say it directly, but the more they explained, the clearer it became to Áróra that Ísafold's disappearance was being investigated as a murder.

At the end, Daníel had taken her hand and held it tight, then put an arm around her shoulder and squeezed. Now she wished that he had hugged her properly, as he had her mother: firmly and with affection, so that she could breathe in the aroma of his after-shave and forget herself for a moment.

Now that she had taken her mother back to Daníel's place, given her something to calm her nerves and put her to bed in the guest room so she could cry herself to sleep, she longed for the same treatment herself. She was going to roll herself up in a duvet and lose herself in her own tears.

When she held the hotel room key up to the lock and the door opened with a click, however, she realised that she wouldn't be getting much rest. Hákon was waiting for her in the room.

'Something terrible has happened,' he said. 'I've lost everything.'

His face wasn't just pale; it had turned a shade of grey, and Áróra wondered if he was about to faint.

'What happened?' she asked, pretending to know nothing, even though she was fully aware that his accounts had been frozen the day before.

'As if you don't know,' he said. 'I found a camera in my room. And you're the only one who could have put it there.'

Áróra wanted to correct him, point out that the cleaning staff also had access to his room, but that wasn't her style. She didn't make a habit of blaming others for things that were her own responsibility. So she said nothing.

'My world has crashed around me,' Hákon said. 'Now, for the first time, I have literally lost everything I had.'

His voice rose in pitch as he spoke, as if he had lost control of it, like a teenager whose voice was in the process of breaking. Áróra wanted to point out to him that in reality the money had never been his, that he had borrowed it and then hidden it away. But she said nothing about that either.

Hákon repeatedly ran a hand over his face, as if trying to wipe away the bad luck that had dogged his steps, and his lips trembled.

'I'll have to sell the hotels to pay the tax bill, and if the worst comes to the worst, I could be back in prison.'

Áróra stayed silent; if she spoke, there would simply be too much to say. She would tell him that his desperation over the lost money was no genuine sorrow. That was a feeling that grabbed you by the throat when a policeman told you your sister was probably dead. You could always earn more money.

'There's one light at the end of the tunnel,' he said, mopping away the tears that flowed down his cheeks. 'My wife and I talked yesterday, after all this happened. We're going to try again. If she's talking to me when I've lost everything, then she must really love me.'

'Then what the hell are you whining about?' Áróra said. The words burst out of their own volition, and for a second she wasn't sure if she had said them out loud or if she had hissed them to herself. But Hákon's punch to her face removed all doubt. She had said it out loud and he had replied. He had given her an answer for the camera, the spying and the betrayal.

Áróra sank to the floor as the door closed behind Hákon. The main advantage of her work was being able to administer her own form of justice, but sometimes justice had a bitter taste. The eye the fist had landed on saw nothing but blackness, and behind it, inside her head, a rapid pounding had begun. She needed to cool it, to put a cold flannel against her eye, and then fetch ice from the machine along the corridor to cool it further. But first, before standing up to do all this, she was going to sit here for a moment and think of Ísafold, who had so often experienced exactly this; the bizarre feeling of having been struck by a hand that had previously been so gentle.

102

It was a relief for Olga to be back at work, even though the owner of the factory had told her that she would be welcome to stay at home if she was ill or had slept badly. A man of her own age, he understood perfectly how a night's sleep can be wrecked by the pain of arthritis, and she had worked there for so long with hardly a day's illness, clocking in late after a bad night wasn't a problem.

During the coffee break her colleagues were attentive and gentle. They patted her arm and asked if this was her sorrow for Jonni finally coming to the surface. She had nodded and gone along with it, because that could well have been the case. She had stood straight-backed the whole time after his death, boldly facing everyone and everything. She had turned up for work as usual, baked everything for the wake herself and hadn't let anyone see her shed a tear. But now it felt as if Omar's sudden disappearance had turned her world upside-down. Maybe she had become too fond of the boy, allowed him to get too close, let him too far into her heart.

She was at the traffic lights opposite Skeifan on her way back home, when she heard her phone ping. She reached across to her handbag on the floor on the passenger side, but then the car behind blew its horn, as the lights had changed to green, so she drove around the roundabout, past Skeifan, over the bridge and onto Miklabraut, but by then she couldn't wait any longer to check her phone. The message might be from Omar.

She knew it wasn't allowed, but she swerved off the road and into a lay-by next to a bus shelter, deciding to pretend the car had broken down. She switched on the hazard lights and reached for her bag.

Her fingers shook as she fumbled for her phone. How on Earth had all that junk collected in her bag? There were sweet wrappers, pens, receipts, sunglasses, a purse, a book of crosswords, house keys, hair spray ... But where was the damned phone? It pinged a second time just as she placed a hand on it, and the vibration sent a shiver of fear and hope through her.

The message was from a long unknown number, clearly foreign. She opened it and felt her heart sink into some indescribable emptiness, such was her relief.

I'm in Canada! the message read. *Staying with friend who will help find work. You will come and visit, Mamma? Yes?*

Olga laughed out loud as she wiped the tears from her eyes. She put the car in gear and headed back out onto Miklabraut, at the same time indicating to take the next exit. She was going home, to sit by the kitchen table with coffee and a couple of biscuits before answering the message.

This had always been in the air. He had always planned to go to Canada if Iceland didn't work out. Naturally, she had always expected that the day would come when he would no longer be there with her. But she had expected that to be a sad day, a day of sorrow and misery. So the happiness that surged through her came as a surprise. Most of all she longed to sing out loud. Omar seemed to have found a safe haven, somewhere he would be able to build himself a future.

Now her only regret was that she had never asked his real name. She would like to know what he had been called when he had been a little boy. But maybe he had become an anonymous nobody after leaving his home country, his people and his old life. Maybe people acquired their characteristics from the surroundings they were in now, as much as from where they were born. So maybe he was precisely the person she had seen and she knew. Her Omar.

Maybe she would use some of her savings for a trip to Canada so she could ask him in person what his original name was. She could extend a hand, and say, 'My name's Olga, what's yours?'

He would tell her his name, and then they would go shopping

to buy Canadian food, and he would cook for her. She didn't know anything about Canadian food, whether or not it was different to European food. But it would be interesting to find out. She had always wanted to travel more.

103

Daníel was the first one on the scene at the block of flats on Engihjalli. As he waited for the rest of the police and forensics teams to arrive, he thought of everything that would have to be done before he could so much as set foot in the apartment, and sighed. He went through the list of tasks to be carried out, relieved that it was a flat not a whole house with a garden that would have to be meticulously searched. Every crime scene was different, so the list generally had to be assessed against the specifics of each location. The aim here was to look for indications of where Björn might be now, and any signs of Ísafold and what might have become of her.

He looked around and noticed with satisfaction that no weeds grew along the walls, in spite of the long gap between the wall and the pavement. He was clearly not the only one who was serious about removing unwanted weeds early in the summer. Lady Gúgúlú and the hidden people she obviously believed lived in the rocks wouldn't be so impressed, he thought, smiling to himself. He shook off these thoughts as three patrol cars drove into the neatly swept yard. The first out was Helena, ready to get to work, with a folder of paperwork in one hand, containing all the forms they would need.

'Well,' she said, handing him a sheet of paper from the folder. 'There's a long day ahead of us.'

'True,' he said, stifling a yawn. There was always an inner exhaustion that took hold of him whenever he was presented with a potential crime scene. He looked down at the form. It was the registration document for Björn's car, a blue Subaru Outback. He glanced around and saw the car parked in the space marked with the number of Björn's flat. He compared the registration number on the form with the car's number plate, and when he was satisfied that they tallied, he handed the paperwork to one of the uniformed officers.

'We'll need to take the car as well.'

'I'll request transport for it,' Helena said, her phone at her ear. It was good to work with Helena. She was brisk, the type who made things happen right away, instead of collecting a list of jobs to be dealt with when there was time, as some people did. 'I wonder why he didn't use his own car to go to the airport?' she said as she waited for her call to go through, then walked away a few steps when it was answered, without waiting for Daníel's reply.

Daníel thought it over, and decided that the most probable reason was that Björn hadn't wanted it to be obvious that he had left the country. It was noticeable that he had avoided using any automatic gates at the airport terminal, so that no clear image of his face had been recorded, and in the images of him that customs had been able to extract he had always been looking downward. This could also have been a strategy to keep his face hidden.

The forensics team were now at the scene and began pulling on white overalls the moment they were out of their van. Daníel went over to them and pointed out the car that needed to be photographed before it could be moved to the workshop and pulled apart, and told them that they, along with himself and Helena, would be the first ones inside the apartment once the locksmith had opened the door. He expected they wouldn't take long to check the place out. They would go over the usual stuff, searching for any of Ísafold's belongings that might be there, to determine whether she had packed as if she were leaving for good, or as if she expected to be away only for a few days. Did it look as if Björn had packed his own things for a short trip or a long one? He had no expectation that there would be visible signs of a struggle in the flat, but the forensics team would use all their skills to detect any invisible signs.

He and Helena watched the locksmith open Björn's flat. He quickly dealt with the lock and gently took hold of the handle so that the door opened a crack, then nodded and stood back to make way for Daníel. He pulled on gloves and cautiously pushed the door open. Stepping inside, he could feel it.

The pulsing in his head flashed so fast that it almost interrupted his vision. He gasped, breathed it in, and it buzzed in his ears so that every hair on his body stood upright and every cell in his body could sense it. Someone had died in here.

104

Grímur left the door to the stairwell half open, and sat on the floor as he listened to what was taking place on the stairs and on the floor above – in their flat. A police officer had knocked and apologised for the disturbance, saying that a crime-scene investigation was being conducted in one of the flats in the block, but he wasn't able to provide any more information. Although Grímur feigned surprise, he knew exactly what it was about. The next police officer to come along was young and nervous, and wanted to ask questions about the neighbours. Grímur told him the truth, that Björn had beaten Ísafold, that he had injured her several times and that the man was a merciless thug.

It was when the police officer asked when he had last seen Björn that Grímur lied, saying that it had been the previous day, in the afternoon, on the stairs. He said he had asked Björn if he was travelling, as he had his passport in one hand and a bag over his shoulder. But he hadn't heard Björn's reply. The police officer wrote everything down and thanked Grímur for his help. Grímur asked if he wanted to come inside for coffee. He did this purely to pretend to be the inquisitive neighbour with his nose in everyone else's business. He was well aware that the policeman wouldn't come in alone, and on top of that he was too young to be tempted by coffee. Youngsters got their caffeine kick from energy drinks. The policeman shook his head, flushed, and said that he didn't drink coffee.

Now Grímur sat behind the door and listened to the sounds of the forensics team at work. There seemed to be people carrying boxes and cases up and down the stairs. It was clear that there was a whole load of equipment they needed to use.

'The luminol's lighting up half the kitchen,' a deep voice in the corridor said. 'Someone's lost a lot of blood in there.'

'Unless someone spilled bleach,' another voice, much clearer, replied, and Grímur couldn't be sure if it belonged to a man or a woman. 'Bleach returns the same results as blood.'

'And horseradish,' a third voice added. 'That's always likely in a kitchen. If a glass bottle breaks then the sauce goes everywhere.'

'Isn't that just a myth?' asked the first deep voice.

'What?'

'All that about horseradish and luminol. Isn't that just a myth?'

'No, I don't think so. Luminol detects all sorts of things, not just blood.'

'Isn't it coffee-break time yet?'

'Yep.'

Grímur heard the clear voice yell 'coffee' into the flat, followed by the sound of footsteps.

'She doesn't want coffee. She's on her knees in the bathroom scraping something up with tweezers and a cotton bud,' the deep voice said.

'Science is a tough taskmaster,' the third voice said and others joined in with the laughter.

Grímur stood up as the group trooped past, and opened his door wide. Two police officers in uniform and one in plain clothes with a police ID on a lanyard around his neck went past.

'How's it going?' Grímur asked, his eyes wide open with curiosity. He was determined to be seen as the nosy neighbour, the annoying, inquisitive, interfering one.

'It's going,' said one of the uniformed men, clearly the owner of the deep voice. 'We won't be much longer.'

Grímur watched them and could almost see them rolling their eyes at the unpleasant guy who always appeared on the stairs with something to say.

The annoying neighbour with his nose in police business wasn't suspicious. Quite the opposite, he was the personification of innocence.

105

When Áróra woke up on Daníel's sofa, it took her a while to figure out where she was. It was with surprise that she realised she must have fallen asleep moments after he had told her to lie down, spreading a thick woollen blanket over her. He had wanted to know how she had come by a black eye, but she had just shaken her head.

'You should see the other guy,' she had muttered.

The last thing she remembered was stretching out, tense with nerves, on the sofa, sweating but also shivering with cold, her eye aching, the coarseness of the blanket prickling, and still with the pounding heartbeat that had hammered in her chest since she and her mother had watched the flat on Engihjalli from the car as the police and forensics officers had gone about their work.

People had come and gone, got into cars and drove away, came back and got out again, went back into the block, occasionally stood for a while and chatted, drank coffee, ate snacks from paper bags. Her mother had sat with her knitting, taking the odd break to look up at what was going on outside the building.

'What do you think's happening?' she would ask, probably thinking out loud rather than directing her question at Áróra, and clearly not expecting any reply.

Áróra felt the tension mounting, and when the team in white overalls took their third coffee break, she longed to jump out of the car, march over there and yell at them to get back to work, to get on with finding something inside that could tell them what had happened to Ísafold.

She was close to bursting with impatience, when Daníel seemed to sense it, crossed the street and got into the back of the car.

'Let's go home and get ourselves some coffee,' he said in his mild tone of voice. 'This is going to take a long time, and there's nothing new so far.'

At Daníel's place, her mother had gone to the guest room to lie down, and Áróra wondered how many times a day she needed to take the weight off her feet, while Daníel told her to close her eyes on the sofa while he made coffee. He spread the blanket over her, and she fell asleep so soundly that when she woke up, it took her a while to get her bearings.

Now the daylight had gone from yellow to blue, so maybe it was evening. She sat up and rubbed her eyes. Her mother had to be asleep still, as gentle snores could be heard from the guest room, and Daníel was nowhere to be seen. Maybe he had gone back up to Engihjalli. She picked up her phone and was about to call him when she saw through the living-room window that he was in the garden. He was barefoot, his trouser legs rolled up to mid-calf, and appeared to be talking to himself. He had one hand on an outcrop of rock at the far end of the garden, and gestured with the other as he spoke, as if he was in the middle of a real conversation and not just muttering to himself.

Áróra opened the door and went out onto the decking. Daníel turned.

'Are you talking to yourself?' she asked, and he smiled apologetically.

'I was,' he said. 'I do that sometimes. I was trying to figure out how to get across what I need to tell you.'

Áróra felt herself go weak at the knees, as if all the strength had been drained from her legs.

'What?' she asked, and knew the answer before he said anything. She could see in his face that Ísafold was dead.

'I had a call from the forensics team just now. Initial findings – and I have to emphasise that these are preliminary conclusions – indicate that someone either lost their life or was seriously injured in the flat. It seems that a large amount of blood had been cleaned off the bathroom door, and also from the kitchen units.'

Áróra nodded to show that she had heard and understood,

because she couldn't speak. Her throat had constricted so much that she could barely breathe.

'But he beat her and injured her several times, so could this be old blood?' she gasped at last, and saw the sadness in Daníel's face at having to extinguish her last spark of hope.

'We use something called luminol,' he said quietly. 'That gives us preliminary results, and it showed a strong response in Björn's car. There was a whole pool there that we thought at first was a residue from blood, but it turned out to be urine, in the boot of the car.'

106

When the noise in the middle of the night had woken him, Grímur had peered out of the window and known instantly that Ísafold was in the case that Björn dragged behind him out to the car. He saw as Björn struggled to lift it into the boot that the case was heavier than a normal suitcase was supposed to be.

The whole time he had driven along Reykjanesbraut, following at a careful distance, and then, at an even more cautious distance and without lights, along the unmade road, he had known that Ísafold was in the case and that she was dead. His heart bled with the pain of this certainty.

He had loved Ísafold dearly. He had loved her enough to lie down and shed tears into the moss that grew on the rocks, after he had parked out of sight behind a heap of gravel and run through the jagged lava, following Björn as his car crept along in first gear. At intervals Björn got out to search for a suitable place to get rid of the case.

Once he had departed and the sound of his car had died away in the stillness, Grímur clambered down into the fissure in the rocks, where he pulled the zipper back a little and a pale hand fell out. This was a hand he recognised even though it appeared translucent in the blue midnight sunlight, and he kissed it, whispering 'I love you' into the quiet spring night in the hope that her soul hadn't yet slipped away from her body and might be hovering somewhere above the lava, hearing him speak the words he would never have dared say to her in life.

That moment in the lava field had been a turning point. The sorrow gnawed at him, and he felt a resolve, as hard as sharpened steel. Either he had discovered something inside him, there among the sharp rocks, or else the hour he sat there had changed him – because by the time he got to his feet, he knew that he could kill.

He could kill Björn, the man who had tormented Ísafold, the man who had no understanding of her love and patience, the man who could not appreciate how precious the love of a woman like her could be.

At that moment Grímur decided that sixteen years would not be sufficient. Sixteen years and out in ten was not a high enough price to pay for all those black eyes, for the wails and the tears and the desperation that seeped down to him through the floor. It wasn't enough for beating her to death, crushing the battered body into a suitcase and dumping it like garbage out in the lava field.

That was why Grímur hadn't called the police that night to tell them what Björn had done, but instead had decided that he would seek vengeance for Ísafold himself.

NOW

107

I'm floating a foot or so above the ground, and it's unpleasant. I'm struggling to stay upright and I feel faint.

Ísafold is in all likelihood dead, Daníel says. All the indications point that way.

There's nothing to say that she's on a sunny beach in Italy, sipping a cocktail and dancing, wearing a colourful summer dress.

There's nothing to say she's in Canada, starting a new life with Björn, free of debt and trouble.

There's also nothing to say that she's in someone's spare cosy bedroom, watching TV and waiting for the right moment to make an appearance.

There's nothing that suggests she's alive anywhere.

Blood on the door and piss in the back of the car tell us that she's dead. My little big sister, the one I was supposed to look after, is dead.

I'm feeling even more faint, feet off the ground, no balance. I feel like I'm falling.